THE [] AND [] DEAD

FIAT JUSTITIA

ERIC THOMSON

The Dirty and the Dead
Copyright 2022 Eric Thomson
First paperback printing February 2022

Published in Canada
By Sanddiver Books Inc.
ISBN: 978-1-989314-54-8

Sanddiver
Books Inc

— One —

After years of working solely in plainclothes, I still wasn't quite used to laying charges and making arrests in uniform. But such was Commissioner Sorjonen's directive. Investigations could be carried out wearing proper business attire at the senior officer's discretion, but come the moment of truth, he thought nothing was better than a senior government official getting cuffed by someone of much lower standing. I could see the merit of his logic when considering the role of the Commonwealth Constabulary's powerful and much-feared anti-corruption unit.

Compared with the professional malfeasance cases Chief Inspector Arno Galdi, Warrant Officer Destine Bonta, and I once handled out in the Rim Sector, our anti-corruption investigations belonged to the major leagues. It had been both somewhat intimidating at first yet also exhilarating. Who else can simply walk into the office of a federal star system chief judge and end her career — Justice Marian Achebe being a case in point and our current target.

The story of her downfall was depressingly familiar, even to the three of us who were more conversant with the small venalities of a supply clerk selling government inventory and pocketing the money or a patrol sergeant taking backhanders from the local mob to look the other way. Our current anti-corruption cases weren't much different, although the scale certainly was.

Justice Achebe didn't sell herself cheaply. On the contrary. By the time we wrapped up our six-week investigation, it became clear she'd been taking bribes not only from organized crime groups but every stratum of Arcadia's wealthiest elements, high-level star system officials included. The sums she'd stashed away in numbered accounts across the Commonwealth through layers of shell corporations were simply breathtaking.

Then, Achebe stumbled in much the same way as the supply clerk and patrol sergeant. She thought herself fireproof by dint of her office, so she began upping her demands and eventually priced herself out of the market. However, it's not a forgiving one, and we received an anonymous tipoff, complete with verifiable evidence in due course. Some corrupt officials were too much even for the mob.

I studied my service uniform in my bedroom's floor-length mirror to ensure every detail was perfect and realized I still wasn't fully accustomed to the assistant commissioner's three diamonds and oak leaf wreaths in silver on each shoulder. For the longest time, I thought I would stay a chief superintendent running the Rim Sector's Professional Compliance Bureau detachment until retirement.

That is, until Commissioner Sorjonen, the formidable commander of the Political Anti-Corruption Unit, recruited me after I solved a colonial murder with the sort of brio he admired.

A knock on the door cut short my uncharacteristic burst of self-admiration.

"Come in."

It opened, and Arno's bearded, grandfatherly face appeared. "Ready, sir?"

When he noticed me standing in front of the mirror, Arno chuckled. "You look sharp as ever."

I quickly ran my eyes over his uniform tunic, now with the three diamonds of his new rank on each shoulder. "As do you."

"Nothing but the best for bent star system chief judges. Destine is getting the car, and I just checked — Achebe is in her chambers taking coffee with the Arcadian attorney general."

"One of the few senior officials who hasn't been paying her off."

Arno let out a soft grunt. "Not that we could determine, but it wouldn't surprise me if Achebe was scratching his back to help her friends in low places. There's not a squeaky clean cabinet member in the Arcadian government."

"Comes from having the same party in power for so long they think themselves above the law, just like Justice Achebe." I put my beret on and made sure it was perfectly set, with the Constabulary's scales of justice badge over my left eye. "Not that there's any effective political opposition around here."

I patted the needler in the shoulder holster beneath my tunic, more out of habit than to check that it was still there. Arno was carrying his as well, but our uniforms were tailored so the bulge wouldn't show.

"Shall we?"

Luggage in hand, Arno and I took the suite's private lift directly to the ground floor — one of the many perks working for anti-corruption, not because of the comfort or even the convenience, but to stay out of sight while we put together an airtight case. Not even the local Constabulary group commander knew we were here, let alone Arcadian officials whose honesty and integrity was suspect.

The hotel lobby surveillance system would note our sudden transformation from business travelers sharing a three-bedroom suite on the top floor to Constabulary officers, but whether it would alert the duty manager was debatable.

We were unlikely to be the first Constabulary members using the NovoArcadia, seeing as it was on the list of approved hotels. We crossed the lobby and left through the front door without encountering another human. The reception's holographic AI didn't even appear since I'd already paid for our suite rental in full using the unit account.

As soon as she saw us, Warrant Officer Bonta popped the unprepossessing rental's passenger doors, and we climbed in. Silver and sleek, like so many cars in Tripoli, Arcadia's capital, with the polarized windows politicians and senior officials preferred so they couldn't be seen, it had served us well over the previous weeks. At this time of the morning, traffic was light, and we made good time across the city to the federal courthouse, where Achebe ruled with an iron, albeit corrupt, fist.

The courthouse, one of Tripoli's oldest buildings dating back to the late twenty-third century, reminded me of nothing so much as a tiered bluish glass and steel cake or a rather squat ziggurat. For something well over three hundred years old, it did look rather sprightly, however, a testament to its designer and builders.

Bonta pulled into a parking slot marked official business and stuck a Constabulary identification disk to the front window on the driver's side. A passing security guard made as if to come over and shoo us away, but then we climbed out, and he turned on his heels with alacrity. I couldn't tell if it was because of the silver-trimmed gray uniforms or because I outranked the commanding officer of the Arcadia Constabulary Group, making me the most senior federal cop in the star system.

We sailed through security on the strength of our credentials, took a lift to the top floor where the chief justice held court and barged into her office antechamber. The astonished clerk, a painfully thin, balding, middle-aged man, half stood.

"What—"

Arno pointed at him and then his chair. "Sit. Don't move, and don't call anyone. Don't speak."

At that moment, he seemed the furthest thing from grandfatherly, and the clerk obeyed in silence. I crossed over to the inner door, a magnificently polished example of the carpenter's art, all honey and swirls, and pushed it open.

A stout, gray-haired woman in her sixties with a fleshy face and small, mean eyes, Achebe sat in a luxurious executive chair behind a desk big enough to host gravball tournaments. Sitting across from her, the Arcadian attorney general seemed cut from the same cloth, although he sported a more luxuriously sculpted head of hair.

"Justice Marian Achebe, I am Assistant Commissioner Caelin Morrow of the

Commonwealth Constabulary's Political Anti-Corruption Unit."

Achebe reacted like most of them do. She scowled. "How dare you enter my office without permission?" Her voice, surprisingly high-pitched, held an irritatingly querulous edge. Listening to her expound at length on a legal point from the bench must not be a soothing experience.

"These are Chief Inspector Arno Galdi and Warrant Officer Destine Bonta." The attorney general gaped at me in astonishment, and I turned to him. "I think it would be best if you left now. We are here on a federal matter that doesn't concern your government."

He glanced at Achebe and stood. As his eyes met mine, I could tell he'd deduced our purpose, suggesting he was just as corrupt but better at keeping it hidden. Then he left without another word.

"Justice Achebe, I am charging you with eighty-two counts of corrupt practices and one hundred and six counts of perverting the course of justice. The Wyvern Sector chief justice who has ordered your removal from office pending trial countersigned these charges."

Achebe paled and slumped into her chair. Good. They usually try to bluster their way out, and I long ago lost patience with those who should know better when they grasp at straws instead of accepting it was over.

"Considering the severity of the charges and your status as a federal star system chief judge, I am detaining you for transport to Wyvern. There, you will face a judicial review before the sector chief justice, who will decide whether you should face trial. In the meantime, you do not have to say anything. But it may harm your defense if you do not mention when questioned something which you later rely on in court. Anything you do say may be given in evidence." I paused. "Do you understand?"

Achebe didn't immediately respond but licked her lips nervously. After a moment, she nodded. "Yes."

"We will go to your home where you will pack enough clothing, toiletries, and other personal effects for a lengthy trip. Then, you will come with us aboard the Constabulary cutter *Benton Fraser*, currently waiting at the Tripoli spaceport, and travel to Wyvern."

"My spouse... What..." Achebe stood on wobbly legs.

"We will inform him you've been detained on the sector chief justice's orders. Now we can do this in two ways. Either you obey my every direction and cooperate to the fullest, or we will shackle you."

Another nod. "I'll cooperate."

We'd set up the entire plan ahead of time, and while Achebe gathered her things, Warrant Officer Bonta sat at her desk, logged into the courthouse system using our override, and locked everyone out of Achebe's account. Only another anti-corruption unit member could access it from now on. Of course, we had already taken a copy of everything.

The drive to Achebe's palatial residence on the outskirts of Tripoli, in an area teeming with mansions, took somewhat longer, but the cutter wouldn't leave without us, so there was no hurry. Her husband wasn't at home when we arrived, which suited me. Spouses invariably made a distasteful scene. Some even ended up being arrested on assault charges, and we didn't have the appetite for drama.

While Warrant Officer Bonta stayed with the car, monitoring our surroundings, Arno and I followed Achebe around the mansion to make sure she packed nothing that might cause us grief.

"Why is it no one noticed before that a place like this just isn't possible on a chief judge's salary?" He asked in a low voice as we watched Achebe rummage through one of her many closets. "Her husband isn't exactly rolling in funds."

"People won't see what they don't want to see. A chief justice taking bribes? Heavens forbid."

Arno let out a snort. "Most of her neighbors were probably involved in helping pay for it."

"Most of her neighbors are just as corrupt, which, around here, is situation normal."

Would that I'd kept my words in mind as we walked out through the front door, Achebe between us carrying her suitcase.

One moment, she was alive; the next, she had a perfectly round hole in her forehead. As she fell forward, I could see that most of the back of her skull was missing.

The three of us instinctively fell into a crouch, looking for both the shooter and cover as we pulled out our sidearms. But no second shot followed the first.

"Railgun," Arno finally said. "Someone was making sure Achebe would respect omertà."

I stood and slid my weapon back in its holster.

"And I'm sure the Arcadian attorney general is somehow involved. He knew why we were there — I could see it in his eyes. He probably roused the entire circle of corrupt officials and organized criminals when he left her office. That was a professional long-range shot, so I'll wager the latter did it."

"No doubt." Arno pulled out his communicator. "How about we hand this over to the 11th Constabulary Group and lift off Arcadia while the going is good?"

— TWO —

Commissioner Taneli Sorjonen's office door was wide open when I entered the anti-corruption unit's executive corridor. It was on the tenth floor of the Commonwealth Constabulary Headquarters' Building D, part of a complex just beyond the city limits of Draconis, the Wyvern star system capital.

I came straight from the Joint Services Base Sinach spaceport upon landing, considering how the Achebe case ended, so I could confess my sins and see if the Grand Inquisitor would grant me absolution for letting an assassin take my prisoner's life. Even though I joined his command some time ago and carried out several successful investigations, I still hadn't developed a sense of how he saw success and failure, and my latest case qualified as both. One thing I knew from Arno's experience serving under Sorjonen, a clean breast without qualifications was the best approach.

He enjoyed a reputation for detesting prevaricators. Not that I could be one even if I tried. Professional Compliance Bureau officers were nothing if not honest with themselves. Otherwise, they couldn't, in good conscience, prosecute those who didn't show absolute integrity and uphold the rule of law.

Sorjonen spotted me before I could knock on the doorjamb and wordlessly waved me in. As I crossed the office, he watched me with his intense blue eyes set in a bony face topped with short silver hair. I stopped a regulation three paces in front of his desk and saluted.

"Assistant Commissioner Caelin Morrow reporting to—" At the last moment, I noticed the second star on his collar. "The assistant chief constable."

Sorjonen, who was bareheaded, gave me a grave nod in return and gestured at the chair in front of his desk.

"Please sit, Caelin. Your return trip was pleasant?"

"Yes, sir."

"A shame about the late Justice Achebe's messy end. To no one's surprise, the commanding officer of the Constabulary group on Arcadia has been protesting to the sector deputy chief constable about you leaving him with a high-profile murder investigation and absconding."

I grimaced. "We gave our statements, not that they'll do any good. It wasn't so much a murder as an execution by a professional who fired from a considerable distance. I didn't want my team to be next on the hit list in case someone figured we might know who paid for it. Sadly, we'll most probably never find the doer or sponsor, though I included my suspicions in my statement."

"The Arcadian attorney general." Sorjonen held my eyes with his emotionless gaze.

"Yes, sir." I hesitated for a moment. "I could have handled things better in Achebe's office, sir, and not give him the impression the game was up. Worse yet, as he glanced at me before leaving, I knew he knew and should have protected Achebe better."

Sorjonen nodded slowly. "True. Although I dare say, you won't let it happen again. Besides, you couldn't know how pervasive the rot on Arcadia was."

"But I'd developed a good idea, although I was probably being naïve in thinking the attorney general remained relatively clean until that moment in Achebe's office. In retrospect, he might simply be better at covering his tracks than most."

Another sage nod. "Indeed. Besides, the sector chief justice is rather relieved that he won't be presiding over Achebe's trial where the depth of her corruption would have been exposed for everyone to see. It's not quite like leaving a disgraced officer in a locked room with a gun and a single round, hoping he or she would do the honorable thing. But the results are the same. That being said, well done. Achebe was a festering wound in the judicial body. Now, you're no doubt curious about the second star on my collar."

"Yes, sir. And congratulations on the promotion."

"Thank you. While you were gone, we've officially been renamed the Anti-Corruption Division and embarked on both a reorganization and the expansion we discussed in the last few months. I decided it would be in our best interests if I realigned the units by specializing them in certain areas. Not that said specialization means they can't investigate cases in other areas."

As he spoke, I realized what would come next and found myself with mixed feelings.

"You will head Anti-Corruption Unit Twelve and focus on cases involving military forces. Need I explain why?"

I shook my head. "No, sir. But may I point out that my friendship with Rear Admiral Talyn and Colonel Decker, not to mention my gratitude for a SOCOM unit saving my life on Mission Colony, may place me in a conflict of interest? Then there's my tour as Constabulary liaison with SOCOM in my youth."

A faint smile tugged at his lips.

"I read the declaration you made upon joining anti-corruption, Caelin, and am well aware of the possibility." His tone, though gentle, was more that of a patient master reminding his pupil about something she should have already considered. "However, you are not only more familiar with the darker side of military matters than your fellow unit chiefs but being able to call on help from someone like Admiral Talyn can spell the difference between success and failure. If, and I consider it highly unlikely, you were faced with a situation where one of your acquaintances in the Fleet comes under suspicion, I would assign the case to another unit. In other words, the advantages of your contacts and knowledge far outweigh the risk you might face finding yourself in a conflict of interest. Besides, I trust you to tell me at once should you even so much as suspect there was a problem."

"Yes, sir. Understood."

"Right now, AC12 is you, Chief Inspector Galdi, and Warrant Officer Bonta, but that will change in the coming weeks. My intent is four teams under your command, each led by a chief superintendent or superintendent capable of conducting independent investigations. But that doesn't mean you'll be relegated to desk duty. On the contrary. And your first job as head of AC12 is already at hand."

"Sir?"

"I'm sorry to send you back out there when you've only just returned, but something blew up after your ship went FTL on the way back from Arcadia." He paused for a fraction of a second, gauging my reaction. "You surely caught the sensationalist newsnet story last week about a Marine Pathfinder squadron belonging to the 21st Regiment whose members allegedly committed war crimes in the Protectorate Zone."

"It received wide play on Arcadia, yes. But I paid little attention, seeing as how we were wrapping up the case against Achebe."

"You've heard of Senator Fedor Olrik, the senior representative from Novaya Sibir?"

I rummaged through my mental files. "Vaguely. Isn't he a bit of an anomaly, a centralist elected on a world that is more in sympathy with the sovereign star systems movement?"

Sorjonen nodded. "The very man. He pushed a vote through the Senate to demand an investigation into the claims of war crimes, the first such alleged since the Second Migration War. But his intent was for a full-blown, politically motivated commission of inquiry, or at least, so the Chief Constable, Deputy Chief Constable Hammett, and I believe. As does Grand Admiral Larsson. Olrik is no friend of the Fleet or happy with Larsson's growing disdain of all things political. But in a move that cut Olrik off at the knees, Larsson formally requested the matter be investigated by the Professional Compliance Bureau. DCC Hammett, in turn, made it a matter for the Anti-Corruption Division."

I gave him a wry smile. "And now it's mine. What about the commission of inquiry?"

"On hold, pending the results of your investigation. The optics of Olrik going on a witch hunt while the PCB ferrets out the truth are bad enough he wouldn't get the necessary votes in the Senate." Sorjonen studied me again, but I was getting used to his mannerisms by now. "*Benton Fraser* will take you and your team to Novaya Sibir the moment you're ready. You may draft whoever you wish from the Divisional Support Unit. I'll make sure the local Constabulary group commander readies facilities, quarters, and anything else you might need."

"Thank you, sir. I think."

"This will be a high visibility case, Caelin, with plenty of political and media attention, unlike the vast majority you've handled. Just ignore them and do what's necessary in keeping with our best practices."

"Yes, sir." As the implications of this case sunk in, I felt my enthusiasm wane. But I'd accepted a promotion and a posting to Sorjonen's department, knowing my responsibilities would broaden, and my cases become more complex and demanding.

"Here are the details." Sorjonen reached out and placed a data chip in front of me. "Go and uncover the truth, no matter who it annoys. What happens once you're done will be decided by others."

I picked up the chip and tucked it in a tunic pocket, stood, and saluted. "With your permission?"

"Dismissed."

When I reached our office suite two floors down, the first thing I noticed was a new door sign which read AC12. Upon entering, I saw the walls had been rearranged to give us more space, though my office remained as it was, with floor-length windows overlooking the Constabulary Headquarters' parade ground.

Arno Galdi and Destine Bonta were waiting for me in the bullpen, coffee mugs in hand, looking like two lost souls among a surfeit of vacant desks. When I gestured at my office door, Bonta stood and disappeared around a corner for a moment. When she came back with another of the white mugs, this one filled with black coffee, Arno climbed to his feet, and both joined me, taking seats in front of my desk.

"Big changes, I hear, Chief," Arno said after settling in. He'd spent weeks looking for a new nickname after my promotion, but none of the alternatives suited both of us. As a result, he stuck with my old one, although it no longer referred to my former rank of chief superintendent but my current appointment as the unit head. "Looks like we'll be getting more people, too."

I quickly described the new structure and our role. When I was done, Arno shrugged. "So long as we keep working as your investigators, I'm a happy man."

"Ditto." Destine Bonta nodded.

"Then you won't mind us not bothering to unpack. Or rather, pack a fresh set of uniforms. We're back aboard *Benton Fraser* as soon as we're ready, outbound for Novaya Sibir and our first case as AC12."

Arno's eyes lit up. "Don't tell me we're investigating the allegations against the 212th Pathfinder Squadron. I was wondering whether that journalistic hatchet job would trigger a political uproar."

Trust him to figure things out quickly. "We are. Grand Admiral Larsson pre-empted the establishment of a senatorial commission of inquiry by formally asking the PCB to take on the case. And for our sins, we got the assignment."

"Because of or despite your relationship with Admiral Talyn?" Destine asked.

"The former, I suspect. But there's also the tribal factor." I tapped the jump wings on my left breast. "The Marines of the 212th won't be able to snow Destine and me under quite so easily, considering we both served as Constabulary liaison noncoms with the 1st Special Forces Regiment."

Arno gave me a sharp glance. "And you think they might?"

"Something tells me there is more behind this allegation of war crimes pushed by an avowed centralist senator who dislikes the Fleet than a simple desire to see justice done. You know it's never straightforward when a case involves the Corps' sharp end."

Arno's beard bobbed as he nodded. "Oh, without a doubt. If the pricking in my thumbs means anything, we'll be neck-deep in red herrings within a day of arriving on Novaya Sibir. They may have dropped the word political from our division's name, but politics will always permeate our cases."

I fished out the data chip and placed it on my desk. "Let's see what they gave us."

It wasn't much. We watched a recording of the newsnet reportage based on the testimony of the primary witness, a merchant captain by the name of Toshiro Rahal. We also read a statement by Fleet Public Affairs denying everything and another statement, this one not for public consumption, from the Chief of Naval Operations to Deputy Chief Constable Hammett, our supremo. The latter said the captain of the patrol frigate *Chinggis*, which carried the 212th Pathfinder Squadron, and the officer commanding that squadron would place their personnel, logs, and war diaries at the disposal of the senior investigating officer. Both would arrive in the Novaya Sibir system as soon as possible.

Arno scratched his beard, lost in thought. "So, all we have are eyewitnesses and records. People lie, and data can be falsified, although I must admit the visuals of the alleged crime in that newsnet piece are both vivid and damning. But do they represent the full truth or only one aspect? I don't suppose a visit to Torga is in the cards."

"No. Inspecting the scene of the alleged crime in person wouldn't help in any case. There's nothing left of the alleged crime scene. But I'll put out a summons for Toshiro Rahal to present himself at the Novaya Sibir Constabulary Group as soon as possible."

Destine raised a hand. "We should bring one or more forensics data analysts with us, sir, specialists who can find out whether someone tampered with the records."

"See what the Divisional Support Group can offer. Let's try for two, so we can be really thorough."

"Will do."

— Three —

I'd taken a one-bedroom apartment in the commissioned officers' residence complex when I arrived rather than paying a premium for one in Draconis when I wouldn't use it much. My two colleagues had done likewise. But when I let myself in that evening, it felt little different from the hotel suites we'd been using during our investigations. And I noticed, not for the first time, that I owned little to make my home seem like one. Nomadic investigators, that's what we were. Everything we owned could fit in two duffel bags. But by the time I retired, I'd have racked up an impressive amount of light-years traveled, and human worlds visited.

At that moment, as happened several times since arriving on Wyvern, I experienced a pang of regret at leaving the Rim Sector Detachment and

Cimmeria behind. Oh, I would cross paths with my former team again one day, but it would never be the same. I knew eventually, the regrets would turn into nostalgia until I moved on again, except I suspected Wyvern would be my homeworld from now until I took off the uniform for the last time. There weren't many Professional Compliance Bureau assistant commissioners out in the sector detachments.

And speaking of uniforms, this investigation would be done openly and not *sub-rosa* like the one into the late Justice Achebe's wrongdoings. It meant bringing several uniforms, both working and service dress, rather than primarily plainclothes, along with warm overcoats, boots, and the regulation fur hat. We'd checked the weather on Novaya Sibir, and it was early winter in the habitable zone, which meant bone-chilling cold, blizzards, and snow, lots and lots of snow. Marvelous. I grimaced when I pulled my black fur hat with the Constabulary badge on the front flap from its storage box. Winters weren't my favorite season and what cold weather Howard's Landing on Cimmeria experienced was mild. Hence I couldn't remember the last time I wore it.

I donned the hat at a slight angle and studied myself in the mirror. Very Siberiak. I'd fit right in with the locals. Or would if it weren't for the fact I'd be the most senior Constabulary officer in the star system since the commanding officer of the 47th Constabulary Group was a chief superintendent.

Novaya Sibir fielded its own National Police Service, which left only liaison and federal cases for the 47th, rather than the sort of street-level policing carried out by the 24th Constabulary Regiment on Mission Colony, which I'd briefly commanded.

As I laid out my issue garb, I realized that years of working plainclothes left me with few spares. A glance at the time confirmed a visit to the clothing stores was no longer possible. But I could probably get a few extra uniforms fabricated on Novaya Sibir if necessary. The 47th undoubtedly contracted clothing supplies with a local provider.

Once my bags were packed, I spent a few hours reading before I settled in for what became a restless night, filled with strange dreams. They mostly drew on old memories of a time when I worked undercover and would have died if not for a Marine Pathfinder squadron rescuing me at the last moment. It left me with a great deal of long-lasting gratitude and led to my volunteering as a Constabulary liaison officer.

Clearly, somewhere deep inside, I was conflicted at investigating allegations of war crimes against a Pathfinder unit. As I climbed out of bed at dawn, tired and irritable, I wondered whether it wouldn't be best if I tried convincing Sorjonen to send another officer. Yet I knew it would not just be futile but annoy my redoubtable boss. Instead, I pulled a ready-made breakfast from the pantry and shoved it into the autochef, then brewed a cup of coffee. A large cup.

By the time I was dressed in my comfortable work uniform and pulled on my soft, black, calf-length service boots, I felt someone less anxious about the case, even though the embroidered jump wings on my waist-length tunic's left breast stared back at me from the mirror.

An AI-piloted staff car took me from the residential complex to the naval spaceport at Joint Services Base Sinach a dozen kilometers from the star system capital's outskirts, where *Benton Fraser* landed the day before and was waiting for us. The installation, shared by the Navy, Marine Corps, Army, and Constabulary, was home to the various headquarters in charge of the Wyvern Sector and saw plenty of high-level traffic — admirals, generals, and deputy chief constables coming and going.

Small starships and shuttles were lifting off and landing at all hours. Another Constabulary cutter headed out with a small investigative team would pass practically unnoticed. Or might if it weren't for the newsnets' breathless updates on the crime of the century.

As I passed through security, it became clear everyone in the spaceport terminal knew where *Benton Fraser* was headed and why. The new Professional Compliance Bureau shield on my right breast, above my name tag, told the rest of the story. A stylized black owl with outstretched wings perched atop the scales of justice, it symbolized both the PCB's watchfulness and its officers' skill at hunting down malfeasance. DCC Hammett had introduced the new command badge at, if rumors were true, ACC Sorjonen's urging a few weeks ago while we were on Arcadia, and this was the first time I wore it.

When I entered the departure hall on the second story, I could sense several dozen pairs of eyes watching me head for where my team waited, well away from other travelers. As soon as Arno spotted me, he stiffened to attention, imitated by Destine and our two forensic data analysts, Master Sergeant Teseo Cincunegui and Sergeant First Class Alina Esadze from the Anti-Corruption Division Support Unit. The former was a squat, broad-shouldered, black-haired man in his mid-forties with olive skin, a pencil mustache, and watchful brown eyes. Esadze, by contrast, was in her late thirties, tall, slender, pale, with chestnut hair and dark eyes.

I'd met both the previous afternoon when they reported to my office, coming highly recommended by their commanding officer. Not that he'd send us anyone but the best for this case, lest he disappoint Assistant Chief Constable Sorjonen. And nobody in his right mind wanted that.

"Good morning, sir. And how are you?" Arno sounded disgustingly cheerful, no doubt because he noticed I wore a slight frown.

"Wondering whether I should hold a press conference before boarding."

"Ah, yes. We are attracting more attention than usual, and it's not just because of our snazzy new branch insignia."

"Word travels fast around here these days." I turned to Cincunegui and Esadze. "And how are you?"

"Excellent, sir," the former replied in a deep baritone voice. "Chief Inspector Galdi has been regaling us with stories of your cases in the Rim Sector. Neither of us ever worked there."

"Don't believe everything he says, even if Warrant Officer Bonta offers corroboration. The more light-years we travel, the taller his tales become."

A knowing grin split Cincunegui's face. "Understood, sir. I gather you three worked together for a long time."

I smiled back at him. "Longer than any of us would care to remember."

Before Arno could offer a rebuttal, I spotted a petty officer first class headed in our direction. "I think that could be us."

And it was. The petty officer led us to *Benton Fraser*'s docking tube, where a bosun's mate waited. The latter stiffened and saluted.

"Welcome back, sir. You have the same cabin assignments as before, and Sergeants Cincunegui and Esadze's quarters are on the same deck, a few doors down. If you'll follow me."

We lifted off less than ten minutes later on what was probably a priority departure vector, considering the usual amount of traffic around oh-nine-hundred on a Wednesday at Joint Services Base Sinach. It spoke to the sense of urgency in getting my investigation up and running before Senator Olrik found a way of supplanting it with his commission of inquiry. They might nickname us the Firing Squad, but at least our inquiries were utterly devoid of political considerations. The Senate's, not so much.

Like all Constabulary cutters, *Benton Fraser* was built for speed, not comfort. Though they couldn't hit the highest hyperspace bands like Navy avisos, the cutters came close when their captains poured on the acceleration. But our private cabins, though small, were cozy and the passenger saloon comfortable with as many amenities as the shipwrights could jam in. One worry nagged at me as I lay on my bunk during liftoff, however, and I wondered whether I should speak with the captain about his planned FTL speed. On our trip to and from Arcadia, we'd sailed at a reasonable speed, but considering the presumed urgency of this case, he might consider pushing his drives.

A few people, such as I, were affected by traveling in the highest hyperspace bands, where time, space, and reality became fluid and experienced what the Navy called aviso dreams. They could be disturbing enough to leave me disconcerted for several days afterward, and considering my dreams of the previous night, it didn't bode well. The almost total recall of the worst day of my life while I slept as we traveled between Cimmeria and Mission Colony still remained fresh in my memory.

When an anonymous voice over the public address system gave his permission to secure from liftoff stations, I sat up, swung my legs over the side of my bunk, and debated whether I should stay here and read or settle into my usual chair in the saloon and read. Before I could decide, I heard a gentle knock on the cabin door.

"Come." As it opened, I stood.

"Welcome back, sir." Captain Julio Ryker, master and commander of the Commonwealth cutter *Benton Fraser* stuck out his hand.

"Thank you."

Like his crew and those of the other cutters, Ryker was a civilian member of the Constabulary instead of a sworn member, such as I. He and his people wore Constabulary gray but with merchant marine rank insignia patterned on that of the Commonwealth Fleet Auxiliary, the Armed Forces' very own interstellar shipping branch.

"My orders tell me time is of the essence — that I must land you on Novaya Sibir as soon as possible."

"True." I hesitated. "But not to the point of pushing the upper hyperspace bands. An extra day won't harm anything."

He studied me in silence for a bit. "Aviso dreams, sir?"

I nodded. "Unfortunately. I suffered a bad hit when you ran us from Cimmeria to Mission Colony before they posted me to Wyvern and would rather not repeat the experience. Don't worry. I'll take responsibility if anyone asks why you didn't redline the hyperdrives."

"Understood. I'll go easy on the throttles. As before, yours is the privilege of the bridge."

"Thank you again."

"I'll leave you to it then." He saluted and turned on his heels.

Now that I was standing, I grabbed my reader and ventured into the corridor servicing the passenger cabins.

When I entered the saloon, Cincunegui and Esadze were ensconced at a table along the port bulkhead, heads bent over a holographic chess set that seemed almost lifelike. I quietly crossed over to the far corner and my favorite chair.

It wasn't long before Arno and Destine joined us with their own readers. We spent a few companionable hours in silence, our forensics analysts playing game after game until the galley rang the mealtime bell shortly after we went faster than light at Wyvern's hyperlimit. Passengers and crew, regardless of rank, ate in the same mess aboard cutters, but as before, *Benton Fraser*'s people left us to our own table.

As he ate, Cincunegui made appreciative noises, and when he pushed his empty plate away, he smiled.

"Good food, as always, sir."

"Traveled in cutters often?" Arno asked.

Cincunegui nodded. "Alina and I are part of what you might call the fire brigade. Whenever anti-corruption, or the other PCB branches for that matter, need forensic data analysts on-site, we're it. Truth be told, I'd rather travel in a cutter than ride commercial. It's faster, and no civilians to pester you with questions about how they can fix a parking ticket. Mind you, when we tell them we're anti-corruption, they quickly find other amusements."

I had no aviso dreams that first night — starships can only reach a few low hyperspace bands within a star's heliosphere. Dropping out of FTL past the heliopause and jumping into interstellar space woke me from a sound sleep, but Ryker kept his promise, and I slept peacefully afterward.

The second night, however, wasn't quite as restful.

— Four —

Almost three decades ago, the Constabulary revived an ancient practice that consisted of recruiting fresh graduates from basic training for undercover work under the logic that their faces and identities would not have propagated through the various data networks used by criminals. With their personal records sealed away and no trace of them ever walking a beat or wearing the uniform of a trained constable, they were as anonymous as can be. And I became one of them.

Oh, I can't quite remember why I volunteered. Perhaps only to give back in gratitude for the Constabulary saving me from the Pacifican secret police. Remembering my motivations as a twenty-year-old from the heights of my assistant commissioner's perch a lifetime later wasn't easy.

Perhaps I felt invulnerable after escaping the planet of my birth when its government made my entire family vanish for crimes against a corrupt and illegitimate regime, leaving me the last of the Morrows.

Of course, I now realize those who ran undercover operations against criminal organizations and would-be rebels were more cynical than any PCB officer I'd ever met. To them, we volunteers were tools, not fellow sworn Constabulary members. It was no wonder the program folded a few years after I almost died because of it. I never tried to find out, but I'm sure the casualty rate during its existence would make the Fleet's Special Operations Command blanch.

Back then, Pacifica was exporting involuntary colonists, political deportees really, to Santa Theresa, its wholly-owned colony. This was well before the star system won independence. But those poldeps weren't just shipped out to rid Pacifica of irritating criminal elements, street gangs, dissenters, and the unwanted. They were also organized and well-funded — albeit without the poldeps knowledge — to disrupt any attempt by the colony of gaining independence from its colonial overlords. Not an uncommon thing in the age of increasingly militant independence movements, some of which were, as I found out much later, covertly supported by the Fleet. But the one they assigned me wasn't. On the contrary.

The undercover branch gave us six weeks of training, then they slipped me into a poldep shipment shortly after it landed on Santa Theresa. I went in under my real name — street cred since my father was a well-known dissident — with the cover story that the secret police had captured me after two years on the run. Considering the detainees were kept locked up individually during shipment, no one could say they did not load me aboard the transport on Pacifica, especially since the manifest was doctored. And once released on Santa Theresa, no one kept even the slightest measure of control over the poldeps.

Few of them were willing to work — they hadn't on Pacifica — and felt entitled to receive their 'bennies' as they termed the basic income payments that kept them fed and petty crime more or less under control. However, Pacifica wasn't paying anymore and the hard-working colonists, able to give everyone a job and still be short of labor, weren't about to subsidize lazy layabouts.

But they weren't given a say in the matter. The result was pretty much what anyone would expect.

And I found myself in the middle of it, charged with identifying the leaders, uncovering their plans, and sniffing out any agents provocateurs planted by the Pacifican secret police.

The first few months in Rosalito, the colonial capital, were a nightmare of being chased from squat to squat, clashing with the police, fighting off predators, and avoiding illicit drugs without arousing suspicion while most around me spent half their lives high. I cried myself to sleep many nights, wondering why I thought I was tough enough for undercover work, especially among the semi-feral whom I knew from living in Pacifican slums after they denied my father a livelihood for being a dissenter.

But I soldiered on, slipping information to the local Constabulary group via dead drops, even though I often thought about triggering the rescue beacon embedded in the cheap and tacky-looking armlet I wore hidden under my shirtsleeve.

Soon, a movement coalesced under a Pacifican street gang leader in her early forties by the name of Wella. Violent, unpredictable, and utterly devoid of a soul, she brought together those who wanted to take what they believed their due from the colonists. I never found out whether she was in the secret police's pay, or was being goaded by one of their hirelings, but the results would have been the same.

Soon, off-world weapon shipments began appearing as Wella's followers set up training camps in the wilderness. Within weeks, she'd created a brutal guerrilla force salivating at the thought of massacring the hard-working farmers around Rosalito. They were most vocal about denying the lazy layabouts their bennies.

I volunteered as a runner and supply carrier, which allowed me to move between the main camp and the city and inform my colleagues of developments. But the colonial police weren't completely useless, and I escaped a few close scrapes when they began scrutinizing the poldeps' newfound enthusiasm for camping and other nature activities. Unbeknown to me, the Constabulary was sharing the information I collected with Fleet intelligence, which sent its own operatives to prepare a strike against Wella's would-be insurgents.

The day it happened remains in my nightmares and will stay there until I die. And that particular one surfaced during my second night in *Benton Fraser* when we were interstellar and running up the hyperspace bands. Either I was overly sensitive, or Ryker's officer of the watch wasn't paying enough attention and let the cutter ride too high.

In any case, Wella, who proved less impulsive and more of a planner than I'd believed, announced late one afternoon that the first razzia on farming settlements would happen that night. As a result, no one would leave the camp until it was time. I felt a surge of despair at being unable to warn anyone and because of that, many people would die horribly. Wella had decreed the farmers would watch their children butchered in front of them before being burned to death when she torched their farms. Oh, yes. She was one of the worst psychopaths I met in my entire career, and that's saying something.

Wella probably sensed her trusted courier wasn't enthusiastic about the plan, especially when I searched for reasons to run messages that evening. She gave me a machete and assigned me to one of the assault groups under another former Pacifican street gang leader who enjoyed torturing the animals we caught for food and forcing himself on those at the bottom of the hierarchy. He'd tried me once and limped away moments later with hatred in his eyes after a knee in the groin. Like every bully, he didn't want to risk losing face again but nursed a festering grudge. My ending up in his group was like a dream come true for him, especially since he carried a blaster and I merely a large jungle knife.

As darkness fell, I risked it all and ran the moment I saw an opening, so I might warn the authorities. Naturally, taking part in their barbaric raid was out of the question. But since I sensed Wella was putting several of us through what amounted to a loyalty test, my time among her would-be revolutionaries was over. She would neither let me stay behind in the camp with her most trusted followers nor would I kill innocents.

My bully wasn't particularly intelligent, but he displayed the cunning of a verminous rodent who evolved to survive under any condition and noticed me getting twitchy. I knew from the sly looks and cruel smile. As the evening wore on and the people around me became increasingly excited by the upcoming massacres, I stepped into the shadows, pulled off the armlet containing the emergency beacon, activated it, and slipped it back on. Then I made my way along a path leading out of our hide. Without warning, something hard hit me on the back of the head, and I lost consciousness.

When I woke, they'd removed my clothes, tied me to a tree near the central firepit, and shoved a dirty rag into my mouth. It seemed as if everyone in camp stood around me, flames reflected in eyes eager to witness an act of savagery against a traitor.

Wella walked up and backhanded me across the face with such force it thought my neck would snap.

"So, what are you?" She asked in her accented drawl. "A cop? Military? Or just a stupid child who can't stomach grownup work?"

She produced my armlet. "And what is this? Costume jewelry?"

Unable to speak, I merely stared at her, knowing I faced a slow and agonizing death, just what her rabid followers needed to get their blood up before heading out for a night of rampage and murder.

Wella tossed the armlet into the fire. "Where you're going, you won't need that anymore, little rabbit."

She turned and faced the crowd. "What will we do with her?"

My bully stepped forward, knife in hand. "I lay first claim on the bitch for disrespecting me."

A man I couldn't see shouted, "Leave a bit for the rest of us."

Wella glanced at me over her shoulder. "I think there will be enough of her for everyone."

The terror that overcame me as I looked into a cruel face made hideous by shadows and dancing flames will stay forever engraved in my soul. I remember tugging at my restraints and gibbering wordlessly as he approached, and not much more. What followed happened so fast that I retained only a series of images as if a powerful strobe light was pulsing over the camp.

Plasma weapons coughed from among the trees, felling first Wella, then my bully. Within seconds, screams rang out as the poldeps tried to escape the onslaught of gunfire. Even those armed with power weapons ran instead of fighting the armored figures that emerged from the forest. I watched in disbelief and confusion as the Marines — because that's who they were — hunted every last one down until a figure wearing a major's oak leaf wreath and single diamond on the breastplate walked up to me.

"Constable Morrow, I presume." He reached out and pulled the rag from my mouth as another Marine cut my restraints.

I stammered a reply of sorts, one I cannot recall, then gratefully accepted my bundled clothes and put them on. The major flipped up his helmet's visor, and I will never forget the kind eyes in that square, craggy face contemplating me.

"What is the Constabulary thinking, sending youngsters like you to infiltrate these wastes of oxygen. Never mind. No need for a reply. If there's anything of sentimental value around here, grab it. We're taking you to our ship, and from there, you're headed home. Your mission is over."

Over the following days, the Marines of the 132nd Pathfinder Squadron and the crew of their ship treated me with such kindness that I swore I would never forget the debt of gratitude I owed them. Few people knew the story because it was classified top secret like every undercover operation. I received a commendation with no details about what I'd done and an early promotion to constable first class. Most of my colleagues couldn't understand when I volunteered for a Constabulary liaison job with Special Forces once I became a sergeant. I figured it was the least I could do to repay them for saving me from an agonizing death.

As the all too familiar nightmare of those terrifying events finally faded, and I woke up, I lay in my bunk, soaked in sweat, the sheets askew, and wondered whether I would sully the memory of that day with my investigation or reaffirm my oath.

— Five —

Fortunately, the dreams didn't return for the rest of the trip, and my mental equilibrium was back to normal by the time we entered Novaya Sibir's orbit. I felt a clear sense of purpose and knew I would do my duty no matter what transpired, even though I would always be a part of the broader family by dint of the jump wings on my breast.

Funnily enough, Destine Bonta and I never discussed our motivations for volunteering as non-commissioned liaison officers, nor did our paths cross in that environment. Her tour was several years after mine, at a time when I was a staff sergeant who'd been selected to attend the Constabulary Academy and become a commissioned officer.

After making sure I'd packed everything, I joined my team in the saloon for a last cup of coffee while

Brandon Fraser waited for landing clearance from the Yekaterinburg spaceport. We could have landed at the military strip at Joint Base Wolk on my sole authority as the senior Constabulary officer in the star system. But it was best if I didn't make too grand an entrance on the home turf of the unit I would investigate.

When I settled in my chair, Arno pointed at the primary display. "Looks as cold as the Infinite Void. I'm glad I packed my woolies. Shall we wear our fur hats when we disembark?"

"Sure. Why not. Our reception committee likely will be."

Novaya Sibir did indeed seem frigid from orbit. Everything other than the ocean that occupied over seventy percent of the surface was a brilliant white, from the extensive northern and southern icecaps across the planet's sole continent right to the equator. There most of the population lived in a narrow temperate band bordered by steep mountains, taiga, and tundra on each side. And though Yekaterinburg wasn't all that far from the equator, the planet's axial tilt and elliptical orbit ensured it and the other inhabited areas experienced harsh winters to compensate for sweltering summers.

It was early morning in the capital, shortly before eight, even though the ship's clock and our circadian rhythms told us the time was just after fifteen hundred hours. As often happened, the first day on the ground would be long.

"Do you think they're making us hang in orbit because they're miffed at our arrival?" Arno asked before taking a sip of coffee.

"Could be. Then again, low orbit and spaceport traffic will be heavier at this time of day." I took a sip as well. "I wonder if *Chinggis* has arrived yet."

After putting my cup down, I reached for one of the saloon communicators. "Bridge, this is Assistant Commissioner Morrow."

A few moments passed. "Bridge here. What can we do for you, Commissioner?"

"I wonder whether the patrol frigate *Chinggis* is docked at the starbase."

"Wait one, please." Several seconds later, "Yes, sir. She arrived ahead of us. Would you like me to feed a visual to the saloon?"

"Please do."

The bridge treated us to a flyby view of the sleek frigate hanging off a slender docking arm, but not for long. Starbase 25 was in a much higher orbit than *Benton Fraser* and vanished behind the planet's curvature as we sped ahead of it. Before we regained sight, the officer of the watch sent us to our bunks for landing stations. Soon, I could feel the sensation of descending as the cutter gradually cut over from artificial to natural gravity.

The bridge released us from landing stations once we'd come to a complete stop level with one of the terminal's gangway tubes. I stood, pulled on my issue parka, with rank insignia on a strap in the middle of the chest, and my fur hat, then grabbed my luggage and joined my team on the way to the main airlock.

Captain Ryker was already there, waiting to see us off.

"A pleasure once more, Commissioner. Chances are good I'll be taking you home once you're done here. Enjoy your stay."

"Thank you."

We shook hands. Then he stiffened to attention and saluted. I returned the compliment. "Fair winds, Captain."

I led my team into the gangway tube and what looked like a snowstorm beyond its windows. We couldn't see anything of the city nor much beyond the ship we had just left.

"Welcome to the deep freeze," Arno muttered. "Once, just once, I'd like to work a case in a tropical paradise."

"What was that, sir?" Destine asked in an amused tone.

"I was bemoaning fate, nothing more."

Two Constabulary members wearing the same outer clothing as us were waiting just inside the terminal. One wore a chief superintendent's twin diamonds and oak leaf wreath while the other, holding an antigrav luggage trolley, wore the blank strap of a basic constable. Judging by his youthful face, he was fresh from basic training.

Both came to attention as we neared, and the chief superintendent saluted. Since I carried a bag in each hand, I returned it with a formal nod.

"Welcome, Commissioner. I'm Ulf Skou, CO of the 47th Group."

"Caelin Morrow." I nodded toward my team. "Chief Inspector Arno Galdi, Warrant Officer Destine Bonta, Master Sergeant Teseo Cincunegui, and Sergeant First Class Alina Esadze."

Skou turned toward them and nodded politely. "Welcome to Novaya Sibir."

"Thank you, sir," Arno replied in a grave tone.

"Please put your luggage on Constable Renfield's cart. He'll see that it reaches your hotel suites." He gestured at the empty concourse. "If you'll follow me."

"It's good of you to greet us personally, Chief Superintendent." I gave him what I hoped was a winning smile. Even though the 47th wasn't in our crosshairs, Constabulary COs rarely enjoyed the idea of a PCB team working inside their unit lines.

"It's the least I could do, sir."

We probably landed at an isolated end of the terminal because we crossed a set of doors and found ourselves amid a stream of travelers, most of whom wore more stylish versions of our hats, minus the obligatory insignia.

"I see Novaya Sibir is welcoming us in style." When Skou gave me a questioning glance, I gestured at the windows. "A lovely snowstorm."

"Merely a squall, sir. It'll clear up momentarily. You can already see the sun burning its way through."

He took us through a door marked 'No Entry Except for Official Business' and into a more austere corridor, which ended at a lift. We took it down two levels and into a covered parking area reserved for spaceport vehicles as well as police and emergency ground cars. There, a large personnel transport with Constabulary markings on the side waited silently for us.

We climbed aboard while the young constable pushed his luggage cart into the aft cargo compartment and secured it. Within minutes, we emerged through the open door into brilliant sunshine on a road clear of ice and snow. I knew from my reading that the spaceport was twenty kilometers south of Yekaterinburg, separated from the capital by the Angara River, which ran west to east for over three thousand kilometers. Here, a mere fifty kilometers from the ocean, it was broad and bordered by marshes, although, at this time of year, ice-covered most of the river save for a small channel at the center. Six long, graceful bridges crossed the Angara near Yekaterinburg, and we took the middle one, which carried the main road into downtown.

As we crested the bridge, I caught sight of sharp-ridged mountains coated with snow reaching for the impossibly blue sky in the distance, while closer in, a cluster of high-rise structures marking the city center caught my eye.

"How's the mood around here these days?" I asked, settling back into my seat across from Skou after getting my fill of the scenery.

He grimaced. "Ugly. The Siberiaks, by and large, are proud of their regiments and don't believe the 212th Pathfinders did anything wrong. Many, especially those who distrust the Commonwealth government and Earth, see a conspiracy to undermine the Fleet and the sovereign star systems movement. There's growing talk about a petition to recall Senator Olrik, which surprises no one since his election was controversial in the first place."

"Do you think there were irregularities?"

Skou shrugged. "I couldn't tell you, but there were enough red flags, in my opinion. However, the Electoral Commission declined the request for an audit, and as it is independent of the Novaya Sibir government, that was that."

"Electoral commissioners in many parts of the Commonwealth are routinely corrupted or subjected to undue pressure," Arno remarked.

Skou glanced at him. "I suppose you'd know."

Arno smiled and tapped the side of his nose with an outstretched index finger.

"Do you have any sense of the feelings at Joint Services Base Wolk?" I asked.

"Not particularly. What brief contact I've had since this blew up revealed little, but I suppose it would only be natural if the 21st Marines were angry with the way the newsnets are characterizing their comrades in the 212th."

As we entered the city proper and drove along its broad avenues, I noticed a lack of people and ground cars and remarked on it.

Skou smiled.

"Half of downtown Yekaterinburg is underground, Commissioner. It allows the place to keep functioning even during the worst blizzards. And what's aboveground is connected by enclosed skyways." He pointed out the window. "Anyone living in and around the city center can literally spend the entire winter working, shopping, visiting bars, restaurants, and other entertainment venues, and never step outside. There are pedestrian streets and tramways beneath our feet, connecting the buried parts of every building. Those who live beyond the network can take municipal transit to one of the underground gateways, or if they drive, they can park their cars in municipal lots next to said gateways. Every other city on Novaya Sibir is built more or less the same."

"Interesting lifestyle."

"Believe me, when the temperature is forty centigrade below zero, and the wind is blowing snow across the landscape, it's an essential lifestyle, as you might well experience during your time here."

Arno rolled his eyes. "Oh, joy."

"Not a cold weather aficionado, are you, Chief Inspector?"

"Heavens, no."

Our vehicle slowed as it turned off the boulevard and onto a narrower avenue, and Skou pointed out the window again, this time at a tall structure that seemed to occupy an entire block.

"That's the federal building. We occupy from the third to the fifteenth floor. The usual assortment of Commonwealth government offices uses the bottom two. The federal courthouse is next door. And across the street is the Yekaterinburg Excelsior, where you'll be staying. The hotel offers short-term apartments on the upper levels, and we use them for off-world visitors. They're mainly studio and one-bedroom, but with kitchens, so you can self-cater. You're free to use the Excelsior's pool, gym, and recreational facilities, or use our gym as you wish. The restaurant is one of the finest in town, and the bar is a great place to unwind in a subdued atmosphere."

The driver slowed to a crawl, made a hard left turn, and aimed us at a sloping ramp that vanished beneath the federal building. A door opened at our approach, and we entered a realm of surprisingly clean, well-lit, smooth concrete filled with ground cars, many marked, the rest privately owned. We halted in front of double glass doors opening on a lobby with lifts and another set of double doors to one side.

As we climbed out, Skou pointed at the latter. "They lead to the underground network via an automated security station. We'll register your credentials after I show you the offices we set aside as your incident room, and that'll allow access to the building day or night. The hotel entrance is right across the tramway. And as I said, Constable Renfield will see that your luggage reaches your suites."

"Your courtesy does you honor, Chief Superintendent."

A faint smile tugged at Skou's thin lips. "One should always stay on your good side, no?"

I grinned back at him. "It's much appreciated, but we don't bite, so thank you."

— Six —

I couldn't fault the setup Skou arranged for us. He'd turned a top floor conference room into a bullpen and the adjoining room into my office. Both were accessible only by my team members once we'd registered our credentials, and they gave us a separate, secure network with a classified node so that no one else could access our data. I didn't tell Skou, but Destine would run her own checks before entering anything, and she could detect security vulnerabilities like no one's business.

After we viewed the incident room, Skou showed us his office and introduced us to the 47th Constabulary Group's operations officer, who would look after us during our stay. Then, he excused himself and left us to begin our work. When we were back in the incident room, Arno studied his surroundings again while Destine scanned it for listening devices. After she gave us a thumbs up, he let out a soft snort.

"If I were a cynical man, I'd wonder whether Skou's solicitude stems from a desire to avoid our scrutiny. But my instincts tell me he's just being professional."

"Of course he is." I gave Arno a sharp look. "You know what happens with PCB investigators who suspect everyone, right?"

He grinned at me through his magnificent beard. "They're promoted?"

"I think the term you're looking for is encouraged to take early retirement." I clapped my hands. "Okay. Let's settle in. I need to make a few calls, beginning with the captain of the patrol frigate *Chinggis.*"

"You'll discuss obtaining a copy of their log, sir?" Sergeant Teseo Cincunegui asked.

"Among other things, yes."

"If I may, sir, courts will not accept copies of ship logs that weren't extracted by Constabulary forensics. Anything that passes through crew members' hands, or even just the captain, is deemed tainted. Yes, technically, a log should be impervious to falsification or manipulation, but the burden of proof is on the forensics team, not the captain. By connecting directly to their core, we can extract the data without intermediaries."

"In other words, you and Sergeant Esadze should go aboard *Chinggis* and pull a copy of the log yourselves."

Cincunegui nodded. "Yes, sir. The number of otherwise law-abiding entities who try to falsify records because of venial sins we don't bother investigating would surprise you. Not that the captain of *Chinggis* would do so in this case, I'm sure, but compromising the chain of evidence by omission or neglect is so easy."

Destine, knowing I'd rather not throw my weight around and demand an unscheduled ride just for my team, raised a hand.

"I'll see about arranging their passage on the regular shuttle between Yekaterinburg and Starbase 25. Though they'll pass through Joint Services Base Wolk rather than the civilian port."

"Please do so, and thank you. If you could connect me with *Chinggis* for now?"

"On the way, sir. I'll route it to your office."

While waiting, I called up the basic data on the frigate and its embarked Pathfinder squadron again, looking for anything that might hint at differences from what I remembered. The patrol frigates with embarked Marines were an old idea, dating back to the years after the Shrehari War when small, dirty fights erupted among human worlds along the frontier. If I recalled correctly, Grand Admiral Kowalski came up with the proposal, and Admiral Dunmoore was the first to implement it. The

Pathfinder squadron's role was acting as an immediate response unit that could slice through nascent unrest before it became a significant bonfire requiring entire Marine regiments. The concept proved its worth, which was why they still existed well over half a century later and why I was still alive.

Destine's voice pulled me from what might become another stroll down memory lane. "Sir, I have Commander Laila Sonier, *Chinggis'* captain, for you."

"Excellent. Make sure you and Arno listen in." I touched my desk's control pad, and the office display lit up with the narrow, serious-looking face of a woman in her late thirties. Brown eyes on either side of an aquiline nose beneath a mop of black hair met mine. "Thank you for accepting my call, Captain."

"I was told to expect you, Commissioner," she replied in a husky voice. Her expression, tone, and choice of words made it clear she wasn't happy being forced to speak with a Professional Compliance Bureau officer. "And I'd like one thing clear between us before we begin. Those accusations dug out from under a manure pile by the newsnets, and Senator Olrik are not just false, they're libelous."

Definitely not a happy starship captain.

"Before we begin, I'd like something clear between us, Commander. My job is to gather and analyze the available evidence and present my superiors with facts that establish the truth beyond a reasonable doubt. I'm not here to find fault, make accusations or lay charges. Someone else, likely Grand Admiral Larsson, will decide what happens once my superiors send him my findings, and he will deal with the newsnets and Senator Olrik in whatever fashion is appropriate."

She stared at me for a few seconds, then nodded once. "Understood."

"Right now, I need a copy of your classified after-action report about the Torga raid, a copy of *Chinggis'* log covering the entirety of your last cruise. And if you keep a captain's log, I'll need a copy of that as well and of any other record germane to the matter."

Sonier's face tightened, but she nodded again. "I'll see they're transmitted as soon as possible."

"I'm afraid I'll be sending my analysts aboard your ship to download everything directly from your data banks. It's a question of chain of evidence."

Her eyes lit up with anger. "You don't trust us? I must protest at the implied insult to my integrity and that of my crew."

I raised a restraining hand. "At ease, Commander. As I said, it's a chain of evidence issue, not one of trust. The more evidence is handled during an investigation, the more it will be scrutinized for discrepancies introduced by accident or design between the point of origin and the casefile. Having my analysts extract the records directly means only one intermediate step between your computer node and mine. And since my analysts are not only sworn Constabulary members but accredited experts in their field, the chances someone will challenge any of the evidence they recover will be minimized."

Sonier didn't immediately reply, and I could tell she was parsing her words carefully.

"You'll need permission from my flag officer commanding, Rear Admiral Jasmine Meir. I am not authorized to give anyone who isn't either in my crew or my chain of command direct access to our records."

I didn't know whether it was true, and I suspected Sonier would call Meir the moment we were done, but I inclined my head.

"Fair enough. I'll do so."

"Was that it, Commissioner?"

"For now. Once we've examined the records, I'll be interviewing you. Thanks, and until later." I cut the link and sat back.

Though hostile reactions on first contact were part and parcel of the job, I wasn't expecting Sonier would behave so aggressively. If nothing else, she was a Navy officer accustomed to obeying orders. In my experience, that sort of reaction often, but not always, stemmed from a guilty conscience based on the notion that a good offense is the best defense. It made me wonder how the CO of the 212th would react when I contacted him.

Both Arno and Destine poked their heads into my office moments later. The former winced theatrically.

"Wow. Not intimidated by our reputation as the Firing Squad, is she?"

I cocked an eyebrow at him. "Guilty conscience or just feeling undue pressure and, therefore, touchy?"

"Or she simply doesn't like a senior internal affairs cop questioning her. Few people do in my experience, despite your natural charm. Then there's the difference in uniform color, marking us as members of another clan. You think we'll experience problems with Admiral Meir?"

"I hope not. She's no doubt received orders from her four-star, and they'll be presented as coming from the man who wears five. Destine, please contact Admiral Meir's office and see when she's free for a brief conversation, no more than five minutes."

"Will do, sir." She vanished into the bullpen.

"You know what strikes me?" Arno asked as he put on a philosophical air.

"No, but I'm sure you'll explain momentarily."

"Grand Admiral Larsson didn't want a politicized commission of inquiry looking into the war crimes accusations, but the way we're setting ourselves up, we'll not differ much from a board of inquiry instead of looking like a proper investigation."

I gave him a shrug. "Semantics. Besides, our crime scene is out of reach, and everything will be based on reconstructing events from existing records and eyewitness accounts."

"True, but I've gone back and studied the last few war crimes investigations, and they worked with plenty of physical evidence. You know, the sort we cops enjoy collecting because there's no arguing about a dead body or a murder weapon or unexplained funds in a federal judge's numbered bank account. They simply are."

"What triggered this train of thought?"

"Inactivity, I suppose. We're here, in a winter wonderland, light-years from home, and I'm inside a cop shop, idle. I don't enjoy being idle."

"We've barely been here an hour. What's really up?"

Arno sighed and dropped into a chair across from me. "Now that we're here, I'm not overjoyed at investigating this case. Accusing a Special Forces unit of war crimes committed in the Protectorate Zone, whose very creation *is* a crime stemming from war, strikes me as patently absurd. We might as well be handing out speeding tickets at the Wyvern Invitational Starship Race."

"We don't hand out speeding tickets at that or any race."

He nodded. "Right. And we shouldn't accuse a Marine unit of committing war crimes when what they do in the Zone is eliminate those who prey on innocents. If that's not doing the Almighty's work, then I don't know what is."

I couldn't restrain a chuckle. "You are out of sorts, aren't you? Anything we should discuss?"

He stood, shaking his head. "No. Other than the fact I'd rather investigate Senator Olrik. But he's the only one in this matter who's immune to anything other than Senate censure — unless he's seen shooting his opponents with a blaster at high noon on the shores of Lake Geneva, that is."

Destine appeared in the doorway at that moment. "I've linked you to Admiral Meir's office. As soon as you're on, her flag lieutenant will put you through."

"All right." I waited until Arno followed Destine back into the bullpen and shut the door behind him before touching my controls. Moments later, the image of a young naval officer with intricately braided gold cords over his left shoulder appeared. "Assistant Commissioner Caelin Morrow for Rear Admiral Jasmine Meir."

"Yes, sir. One moment, please."

His face vanished, replaced by the insignia of the 25th Battle Group, and almost thirty seconds passed before it too faded away, and I found myself looking at Rear Admiral Meir. She struck me as an older version of Commander Sonier — the same narrow face dominated by a patrician nose and intense eyes. But Meir's cap of iron-gray hair signaled more experience and cunning than Sonier's unrelieved black.

"Admiral, I'm Assistant Commissioner Caelin Morrow of the Constabulary's Professional Compliance Bureau. Thank you for accepting my call."

"I'm aware of who you are and why you're here, Commissioner Morrow. I understand you already spoke with Commander Sonier."

— Seven —

Her tone and choice of words weren't much different from those of *Chinggis*'s captain, and I wondered what I'd done in a previous life to deserve this sort of reception from senior naval officers. Usually, I got along rather well with my Armed Forces counterparts.

"I did, sir."

"If you'd called me first, we might have avoided any misunderstandings. I'm not sure if you're familiar with military protocol, but going through the chain of command is considered proper, although I'm aware you PCB people can do whatever you want, wherever you want, whenever you want. However, you may be wise to reconsider your methods. Fleet personnel respond better when outsiders observe protocol."

Her rebuke took me aback, especially the hint of contempt in her tone when she characterized PCB officers. Arno often accused me of annoying people faster than most, and not always in jest, but this probably counted as a record. She was certainly trying to put me in my place.

"And in that vein," she continued, "I strongly suggest you contact the 21st Regiment's commanding officer before speaking with Major Morozov, who, as I understand, has landed at Joint Services Base Wolk with his unit."

"Noted, sir." I sat back, and Meir saw more than just my face for the first time.

She suddenly frowned. "Are those Marine Corps Pathfinder wings on your uniform?"

"Yes, sir. I spent two years as Constabulary liaison with the 1st Special Forces Regiment when I was in my late twenties."

"Then you're well aware of protocol, Commissioner, but chose not to follow it. As you said, noted. Now, let's discuss your analysts tapping directly into *Chinggis'* databanks. You realize that's a highly unusual, if not completely irregular, request."

"As I told Commander Sonier, my analysts copying the relevant data directly from the source ensures the chain of evidence is as unimpeachable as possible, and that would be to everyone's advantage."

She gave me a pitying look. "Are you aware a starship's logs cannot be tampered with?"

"In my experience, anything stored electronically can be manipulated, Admiral. For example, judicial records were, for the longest time, said to be inviolable, yet over the years, I've arrested many hackers who broke in and messed with them."

Meir inhaled deeply and exhaled, then said, "Fine. I'll tell Commander Sonier she can let your analysts tap into the ship's computer core and make a copy themselves — but under supervision."

I inclined my head. "Thank you, Admiral."

"Try not to step on any more toes. Everyone around here is angry and dismayed at these baseless, politically motivated accusations and considers your presence a slap in the face."

"Then the chain of command should remind everyone I'm here at Grand Admiral Larsson's behest and not because I decided it would be jolly good fun investigating alleged war crimes. My primary duties are uncovering and investigating official corruption."

At least she had the grace to look vaguely uncomfortable. "Then why are *you* here, Commissioner, and not someone more appropriate."

I tapped my jump wings. "Because of my experience, and not just as Constabulary liaison. I've worked a fair bit with the Fleet on various matters."

A frown briefly creased her forehead. "Very well. Was that everything?"

"It was. I assume we can work out the arrangements with Commander Sonier?"

"Yes. I'll inform her I approved your request." And with that, she cut the link.

Arno, who'd listened quietly from across my desk, chuckled. "We've been on Novaya Sibir for what? Less than two hours? And you've already annoyed a starship captain and a two-star admiral. Whatever will you do for an encore?"

I smirked at him. "Add a Marine Corps colonel and a Pathfinder squadron commander to the list?"

Destine reappeared at that moment and asked, "Shall I call Colonel Freijs's office and ask if he's free?"

"Sure. Let's see if I can make it four out of four by lunchtime." I glanced at Arno. "Want to bet Meir is speaking with Freijs right now, warning him about the deranged anti-corruption cop who has the gall to wear Pathfinder wings?"

"No bet."

When Destine returned, she said, "Colonel Freijs is busy right now. His adjutant will call the moment he's free. And I received our room assignments. The young lad left us the access cards."

She gave Arno and me small plastic squares, which we tucked away in our tunics' inner breast pocket.

"I'm working on getting our own ground car. Meanwhile, Teseo is booking shuttle seats for himself and Alina to visit Starbase 25 and *Chinggis*. As soon as we have a day and time, I'll inform you so you can tell Commander Sonier."

I grinned at her. "The joys of serving with an efficient team. Thank you."

"De nada." A sound from her workstation attracted her attention, and she glanced at the display. "And that would be the 21st Marines' adjutant."

Arno let out an amused snort. "I guess his conversation with Admiral Meir is over."

A few moments later, my desk display lit up with the square, craggy face of Colonel Haakon Freijs. He seemed cut from the same granite as another Marine colonel of my acquaintance, only with silver hair and hazel eyes.

"Colonel Freijs, thank you for taking my call. I'm Assistant Commissioner Caelin Morrow, and I've been assigned to investigate the allegations of war crimes leveled against the patrol frigate *Chinggis* and the 212th Pathfinder Squadron."

"Utterly baseless calumnies. My Marines aren't murderers."

"As I told Admiral Meir—"

"The admiral relayed what you told her. She called me right after speaking with you. You'll have our full cooperation to clear the regiment's and the squadron's good names. This is a politically motivated hatchet job pushed by irresponsible newsnets and a senator looking to make a name for himself, nothing else. If you haven't yet met the Honorable Fedor Olrik, you can't appreciate what species of politician he is. Arrogant, self-important, and ready to stab anyone who disagrees with him in the back. And those are his good qualities." He gave me a humorless smile. "There. I got that out of my system, so now we can talk. But first, I'd like to ask a question."

Freijs tapped his jump wings. "When did you go through Fort Arnhem, and with what unit did you serve?"

I gave him the year and course number. "Then, I spent two years with C Squadron of the 1st Special Forces Regiment. I've logged half a dozen operational jumps during that time, but nothing since then."

"Interesting. We attended the Pathfinder School within a year of each other. Now then, I sense Jasmine Meir and Leila Sonier aren't fans of yours. Would that be a correct assessment?"

"Something of an understatement, in fact."

He nodded with understanding. "There's a lot of resentment at the allegations and the Constabulary's internal affairs branch getting involved. The atmosphere here at Wolk is rather somber — not just my regiment, but the Army and Navy units as well. Folks feel unjustly targeted."

"As I told Admiral Meir, Grand Admiral Larsson asked the Chief Constable to investigate, so I'm here because of your chain of command."

"I understand. I may not like it, but here we are. Still, whoever picked you for the task chose well. Those wings on your uniform will make you less of an outsider who can't be trusted. Perhaps not by much, but my Marines won't consider you someone who does not understand the Corps and the missions carried out by Pathfinders."

"My warrant officer wears them as well. She went through Fort Arnhem and the 1st a few years after me."

"Even better. So, what can the 21st do for you today?"

"For starters, I'd like to examine any logs or war diaries kept by the 212th, any recordings made before, during, and after the raid, as well as the Torga operation after-action report. All of it unredacted, of course. My entire team holds top secret special access clearances. Once we've digested that, we'll interview Major Morozov first, then the members of his squadron."

"All of them?"

I shook my head. "No. We'll decide who as we go along. After Morozov, we will want to speak with his battle captain, squadron sergeant major, and the troop leaders for the first round."

"I'll let them know." He studied me for a few moments. "I don't envy you, Commissioner. As crap jobs go, this investigation is right up there with the worst."

I allowed myself a faint smile. "Oh, we've seen some pretty bad ones over the years. At least we don't need to learn everything about the Marine Corps before we even begin investigating."

"Small mercies. Listen, I'll tell Dagon — Major Morozov — to pull everything he has and go through it with my operations officer to ensure nothing is missing. But you'll need to pick up the copies because I can't transmit them."

"Excellent. How long will it take?"

"If you send someone the day after tomorrow, or better yet, come yourself, and I'll buy you a coffee after giving you the grand tour, it'll be ready. The base isn't far from downtown Yekaterinburg. Half an hour tops. Less if the weather cooperates."

"I might take you up on that, Colonel. Thank you."

"If there's nothing else, I'll let you go."

"Goodbye."

Once Freijs's face faded away, I could finally look at Arno and grin. "Too bad you didn't take me up on that bet. I'd have won."

"That's why I never place wagers with you. He seems considerably more cooperative than the Navy, even though his Marines are the primary targets of the allegations."

Destine chuckled. "Never underestimate the power of belonging to the tribe that jumps from perfectly good shuttles in low orbit. I'm sure ACC

Sorjonen chose us because he understood the Marines would figure we'd give them a fair shake."

"Time to make our Destine an inspector. We're wasting her powers of deduction as a warrant officer."

"And go back to school? Perish the thought. Besides, a chief warrant officer first class earns as much as a chief superintendent, so why bother? But I have a question."

"Yes?"

"What about chain of evidence issues with the records from the 212th?"

"That ship has already sailed, so to speak. The data has been moved at least twice now, so there's a break. However, we should find copies of many, if not most, of the 212th's records in *Chinggis'* computer core, where they should be given the same protection as her log."

"Ah." Destine's face lit with understanding. "You're running an integrity check to determine if the 212th will give us manipulated data. Sneaky."

"Full disclosure — I confess to feeling a little guilty at doing so, but the opportunity is there, and I'd be remiss in passing it up. If what Colonel Freijs gives us matches what our analysts pull from *Chinggis*, then we can place a greater degree of confidence in the records."

"And if we find discrepancies?" Arno asked.

"Then we found a thread to pull on until the discrepancies unravel, and the devil takes the hindmost. We're dealing with highly intelligent people, those at the top of their profession. If there are irregularities, we won't find them easily, but even the best make mistakes. That's what we're looking for in the first instance. Irregularities between the ship's various logs and records and what the 21st Marines give us. And discrepancies between the official data and what the newsnets obtained from this free trader. We can assume that one side is lying, or at the very least, distorting the truth to advance a narrative."

"The Fleet doesn't do narratives," Destine said. "Or at least I hope not."

I gave her a sad smile. "The Fleet will push whatever is necessary to achieve the Grand Admiral's goals, and by this, I mean the collective goal advanced by Larsson and his predecessors. We're talking long-range here. Longer than Olrik or most politicians can grasp. It's been happening since Grand Admiral Kowalski's day. You've met Admiral Talyn and Colonel Decker and their Ghost Squadron operatives."

Both Arno and Destine nodded.

"Then you understand they're playing a longer game than the entire Commonwealth government put together, *Sécurité Spéciale* included, and we've just been dropped into that sweet spot where we can either stop or accelerate whatever's going on. Anything we do will have repercussions beyond the immediate reputation of the 212th Pathfinders and CSS *Chinggis*."

Arno made a face. "Here we go again."

At that moment, my display chimed as it projected a brief message. The head of the Novaya Sibir National Police Service wished to speak with me.

— Eight —

The face of a middle-aged woman wearing the National Police Service blue uniform with a captain's diamonds on her collar appeared when I accepted the call.

"Assistant Commissioner Caelin Morrow here. What can I do for you, Captain?"

"My name is Valliere, sir. I'm General Elin's aide. He would appreciate a few minutes of your time this afternoon. Are you free to join him in his office at fourteen hundred? We're two blocks from the federal building, a few minutes via the underground network."

"Certainly."

"I'll tell security to expect you shortly before fourteen hundred. Someone will escort you to the general's office."

"Thank you."

"Until then, sir. Goodbye."

I exchanged looks with Arno and Destine once the screen went blank. "When was the last time a star system police chief — other than one of our own — contacted me the day we showed up?"

"Never, as I recall," Arno replied. "In fact, they mostly try to ignore our existence for as long as possible."

"I can't really see how the National Police Service might be involved in an incident that happened well outside its jurisdiction."

We ate lunch as a team at a corner table in the federal building's basement cafeteria. The PCB branch insignia on our tunics attracted a fair bit of attention — it was a given the entire 47th Group knew who we were and why we were here, but none of the looks were hostile, as so often happened. The food was decent, not overly expensive, with many local dishes available.

Shortly after returning to our offices, a snow squall descended on downtown Yekaterinburg, hiding even the closest structures behind an icy white curtain. At that moment, I was glad about the city's underground network. I wouldn't have to brave the elements when I called on General Gregor Elin.

I oriented myself on a map projection, then took a lift for the basement level and walked through the doors Skou pointed out to us earlier. I'm not sure what I expected when I left the federal building.

Perhaps something grubby and industrial, but no. The underground was brightly lit, clean, and pleasantly decorated and reminded me more of a covered commercial district. AI-driven electric vehicles moved silently along a two-lane street bordered by broad sidewalks, where people, many in fur hats, were going about their business.

I turned left and looked for street signs to guide me, and after a five-minute walk at a sedate pace, I stood in front of doors marked National Police Service Headquarters. They opened when I touched them, and I entered a broad lobby with a security station at the far end. Before I even approached it, a young police sergeant in a blue uniform and black beret stepped forward and saluted crisply.

"Assistant Commissioner Morrow? I'm Sergeant Prokofieff, General Elin's driver and your guide."

I returned the compliment with equal gravity, then gestured at the inner doors. "Lead on, Sergeant."

He took me to a lift which opened at our approach as if it were waiting just for us. A short ride later, we emerged on what was clearly the executive level. The wide corridor exuded the same elegant solemnity as the one leading to the Chief Constable's office back on Wyvern. Portraits of past chiefs adorned one wall, while paintings depicting Police Service life hung on the other. The lighting was gentle on the eyes, as was the color palette.

When we entered the antechamber to Elin's office, Captain Valliere jumped to her feet. "Welcome, Assistant Commissioner. The general is waiting for you." She indicated the open inner door. "Please enter."

As a matter of protocol, I've always treated officers of other law enforcement agencies — and the military services — who hold a higher rank than me as if they wore Constabulary gray. Thus, I halted three paces in front of Elin's desk and saluted.

"Good afternoon, sir. I'm Caelin Morrow of the Professional Compliance Bureau's Anti-Corruption Division."

Elin, who'd climbed to his feet when I entered, nodded gravely.

"Welcome, Assistant Commissioner, and please stand easy."

He was a big man, tall, broad, almost ursine, with a thick gray beard, gray hair, and deep-set dark eyes that studied me intently as he came around his desk, hand outstretched. We shook. Then he pointed at a settee group around a coffee table to one side.

"Shall we take our ease?"

"Thank you, sir."

As we settled in, he nodded at my left side. "I see you're a jumper."

"Was, sir. Long ago. I haven't stepped off a perfectly good shuttle in almost two decades, and just between us, I don't miss it."

Elin's chuckle rumbled up his chest like a roll of thunder. "I never could see the attraction myself. But to each their own. Is that the PCB's new branch badge above your name tag?"

"Indeed. It was instituted a few weeks ago."

"A swooping owl over the scales of justice. Interesting allegory. Can I offer you tea, coffee, or another sort of refreshment?"

"Coffee would be nice, sir. Black."

Elin touched the chair's arm, and Sergeant Prokofieff poked his head through the office door.

"A coffee, black, for Assistant Commissioner Morrow, and my usual afternoon tea, please."

"Sir."

"You must wonder why I asked you over so soon after your arrival on Novaya Sibir."

"I rarely meet the heads of other law enforcement agencies unless they called the PCB in to help them with an internal matter they can't handle for a variety of reasons."

"Does that happen often?"

The door opened again, and Prokofieff entered, a cup in each hand. He placed them on the table before us. As he left, I picked mine up and took a sip.

"Very nice. Fortunately, it doesn't happen much. Generally, when an agency such as yours asks us for help, it means a senior officer, someone near the top, is suspected of wrongdoing, which can become awkward. For example, did you hear about the

Cimmerian Gendarmerie's General Goresson a while back?"

Elin nodded. "A real shock."

"I investigated and arrested her. This was before my promotion to assistant commissioner and transfer to the Anti-Corruption Division, when I was head of the Rim Sector PCB Detachment at the time. But I assume you didn't invite me here because you need outside help with an internal affairs problem."

"No. I was merely curious. One reads about your branch's work in the digests your Chief Constable sends to every star system law enforcement agency head, and I've always been curious about how you deal with cases other than those internal to the Constabulary."

"In pretty much the same fashion. There's no actual difference between a bent superintendent, a judge on the take, or a senior bureaucrat filching the taxpayer's money."

"And the Armed Forces? Did you investigate cases involving them?"

I nodded.

"Yes. But they tend to be rather unique. The Fleet takes care of its own the vast majority of the time. When they come to us, the situation is usually quite complex and messy, involving matters we don't see elsewhere in the federal government."

Such as the case that first brought me into contact with Hera Talyn, a mere commander at the time, on Aquilonia Station.

"How about war crimes?" He watched me over the rim of his cup as he took a sip.

"No one's investigated war crimes in living memory, sir. The closest we've come is multiple murders committed by Armed Forces members. And if you're wondering about my qualifications, I'm probably as experienced as any assistant commissioner in the PCB, perhaps more than most because I've worked with the Fleet before. And not just as Constabulary liaison, but on criminal matters. I don't want to sound rude, sir, but may I inquire as to your interest in this matter?"

Elin grimaced as he put his cup down on a side table. "A lot of people on Novaya Sibir are upset about these allegations and the fact that the Constabulary is investigating, President Antonovich and myself included."

"We're here at Grand Admiral Larsson's request, sir. If he hadn't asked my Chief Constable, I'd probably be digging through a federal judge's past indiscretions right now."

"Ah. We didn't know for sure about that. Larsson, your chief, and everyone other than Senator Olrik and his coterie is being uncharacteristically tight-lipped."

"For a good reason, sir. We PCB investigators must be seen as free of any outside influence, lest our conclusions are deemed not credible. Until I present my report, I will not discuss the investigation with my superiors, let alone the Grand Admiral and his staff. We picked up a few nicknames over the years—"

A grin split Elin's face. "Such as the Firing Squad."

"Yes. But we're also known as the Last of the Incorruptibles. And that's a title we cannot afford to lose, ever."

He nodded once.

"Understood. And my purpose is not to sound you out on the matter. My apologies if it came across that way. But the Siberiaks are angry, many that their native sons and daughters are being unjustly tarred by sensationalistic newsnets under Earth's thumb and others because those same sons and daughters might be guilty of such vile acts. More of the former than the latter, to be sure. Many more, and they cannot understand why Senator Olrik is pushing this. Surely he knows his chances of a second term are now nil."

I sipped at my coffee again as I studied him while deciding how candid I could afford to be.

"Senator Olrik wasn't getting a second term even before now, was he? I'm sure the voting irregularities that saw a centralist elected on a world more sympathetic to the sovereign star systems philosophy wouldn't have reoccurred."

A slow smile appeared on Elin's face. "No they wouldn't. President Antonovich would have made sure the Electoral Commission did its job properly. We also employ people who can ferret out the corrupt, Assistant Commissioner. And I daresay in our limited sphere, they're as good as you."

"Without a doubt, sir. But I think you might be wondering why Olrik is doing this and alienating his fellow Siberiaks in the process."

"Because people on Earth or from the centralist faction promised him lucrative rewards once his term ends. Clearly, this has to be a centralist move aimed at discrediting the Armed Forces."

"And we've just reached the point where I can no longer comment, sir. My people and I will investigate the allegations to the best of our abilities, no matter where the evidence takes us, and report our conclusions to my superiors."

He stared at me for a few moments. "Understood. This brings me to my next question. Would you be willing to meet with President Antonovich, so he is reassured that this will be investigated properly rather than become a politically motivated circus?"

"Certainly."

"Are you free right now?"

I cocked a surprised eyebrow at him. "That's rather sudden."

"But necessary. The President will clear his calendar the moment I call."

"Are you also trying to impress the gravity of this case, as seen by Novaya Sibir, on me? If so, there's no need. Every investigation is serious, and this one more so than any I've handled in my career. That being said, it would be an honor to meet President Antonovich. But please, none of the usual publicity."

Elin touched his chair's arm again, and this time, Captain Valliere appeared. "Sir?"

"Call the Palace and let them know Assistant Commissioner Morrow and I can see the President at his convenience."

"Shall I fetch my parka?"

Elin shook his head. "We'll take my staff car from the headquarters garage directly to the Palace's underground parking space. If ever there are problems along the way, we keep emergency overcoats in the vehicle."

— Nine —

Fifteen minutes later, I found myself sitting beside General Elin in a spacious, unmarked staff car driven by Sergeant Prokofieff at a sedate speed across Yekaterinburg toward the Presidential Palace. The streets were as white and empty of both cars and pedestrians as before, and it somehow made the city feel like a stage set. Considering the heritage of Novaya Sibir's first settlers, the term Potemkin village came to mind, even though I realized the underground network was teeming with activity.

The snow squall had passed, and a brilliant mid-afternoon sun made everything sparkle as if diamonds covered the planet. And that sun swam in a sky so heartbreakingly blue it seemed almost artificial to eyes that spent most of the last decade on often cloudy or hazy Cimmeria.

Our car turned onto a broad boulevard separated by a median covered with evergreen trees lined up like soldiers on parade. It ended at the fenced-in Presidential Palace on its western end and the Duma, Novaya Sibir's legislature, on the eastern end. Both were rather extensive and severe-looking stone structures built in what I recalled as the neoclassical style.

As we approached the Palace, I realized it sat on a low rise and noticed underground parking garage entrances beneath a formal, flag-lined driveway that curved from one gate to the other, passing in front of the main hall at its apex.

We stopped at a security arch just short of the right-hand gate and waited while the AI scanned us, our vehicle, and our credentials. Satisfied, it admitted us onto the Palace grounds, and Prokofieff aimed the car at the underground garage entrance, where another security station briefly held us while it confirmed nothing changed since the outer AI granted us admittance.

The garage itself was huge, with clean, shiny floors and embedded lights guiding our driver to the car's assigned parking spot. The support columns matched those on the Palace's facade while walls covered in murals shone under gentle light globes hovering at precise intervals.

When we came to a halt, a serious-looking young man in a high-collared, dark business suit materialized out of nowhere and waited patiently until Elin and I disembarked. Once both of us straightened our tunics, he bowed his head formally.

"General Elin, Assistant Commissioner Morrow, I am Artur Ketola, one of President Antonovich's aides. The President is waiting for you in the formal office. If you would please follow me."

Ketola turned on his heels and headed for a set of glass doors etched with the presidential seal. Elin and I fell into step and followed wordlessly. After a brief lift ride, we found ourselves in a formal hallway, which nonetheless seemed in sync with the Palace's exterior, both refined and severe. None of the paintings, side tables, sculptures, and curios seemed out of place, though the whole felt sterile as if staged for a quick sale, and the Potemkin imagery resurfaced for a moment. I told myself I was being unfair to the Siberiaks and wondered whether my unease with the entire situation was more significant than I was willing to admit.

We cops don't enjoy politically charged situations, even those of us in anti-corruption who deal with them more often than most. But this one was quickly becoming something else, and I questioned my judgment in accepting an invitation to the Presidential Palace less than half a day after landing on Novaya Sibir. But it was too late.

Artur Ketola opened an unmarked door and ushered us into President Antonovich's office, a space big enough to house half a Marine Corps air wing. An enormous desk with a stand of flags behind it sat by a bank of windows facing south, while a settee group big enough for two dozen people surrounded a low, elongated coffee table in the middle. Bookcases with what I figured were antique tomes covered one wall, while paintings of what were undoubtedly the founding settlers covered the other. The walls themselves were painted a pale salmon pink, and the carpet, primarily a pleasant light blue, featured Novaya Sibir's coat of arms in the space between the settees and the desk. The sofas and chairs, upholstered in white cloth with equally white embroidery, seemed refined and comfortable.

Antonovich himself was Elin's opposite — tall, slender, with receding black hair and a neatly trimmed black mustache. But his eyes held the same watchfulness as he came around his desk while we crossed the room. Elin and I halted together and saluted, a gesture Antonovich returned with a grave nod.

"Welcome, Assistant Commissioner Morrow." He held out his hand, and we shook. Then he gestured at a sofa. "Please, take your ease."

Antonovich had a pleasant baritone voice, a friendly smile, and a straightforward manner, assets for a politician who lived through the persona he projected in front of the electorate. As Elin and I settled in, Antonovich took the easy chair at the head of the coffee table and leaned forward.

"Thank you for accepting my invitation. I know someone in your position must tread carefully lest she is accused of showing bias. However, I wished to make your acquaintance and tell you about the mood of Novaya Sibir's citizens since our very own senior senator presented these allegations before his colleagues on Earth."

I met Antonovich's open gaze. "You and Senator Olrik don't see eye to eye, sir?"

He shook his head. "No. More's the pity. A sovereign star system's representative in the federal legislature should be in harmony with said star system's government. But Fedor and I disagree on so many fundamental issues, it's difficult for him to be Novaya Sibir's voice on Earth."

I knew he was being diplomatic and really meant Olrik was, in many ways, working against his home world's government by supporting policies Antonovich's administration opposed. And now, Antonovich thought he was using the pride of Novaya Sibir, the 21st Marine Regiment, to strike a direct blow at the integrity of the Commonwealth Marine Corps and, through it, the entire Armed Forces.

A sad smile tugged at his lips. "But that's not your worry."

"No, sir. My sole concern is following the evidence wherever it takes me without fear or favor."

"Of course. You're among the Last of the Incorruptibles, as I believe your branch is colloquially known. But I think you'll find the 212th Pathfinder Squadron innocent of these allegations. Certainly, most Siberiaks believe so, and many are quite angry that the Constabulary's fearsome anti-corruption unit is investigating what they see as trumped-up charges. As much as I wish it weren't so, I'm afraid you might encounter hostility, and for that, I apologize in advance. Our world is cold at this time of year, but our tempers, once roused, can be fiery. And right now, tempers are riding high, especially between those outraged at the allegations and those who aren't. For example, earlier today, the official opposition leader in the Duma notified the prime minister she would bring forth legislation to start the process of recalling Senator Olrik. And that will add to the acrimony. Recalls are never pleasant."

"Is it a quick process?"

Antonovich let out a humorless chuckle.

"Heavens, no. First, the legislation must pass in the Duma, after which Senator Olrik may contest its validity in front of the supreme court. And he'll use that right, believe me. If the court upholds the recall bill, the Electoral Commission must trigger a star system-wide recall vote by eligible citizens, giving them twenty-eight days' notice. Once the vote is held and the results go against Senator Olrik, he must step down, and a new election is called, one in which he can take part, let it be said." He shook his head. "At times like these, I envy star systems where the legislature selects senators. Such a process would spare us much of the current anguish since a man like Olrik would never be considered by any of the key parties in the Duma. They know him too well. But reopening our constitution at this time would only make matters worse. Earth takes a dim view of worlds that, in its eyes at least, would limit the citizens' right to choose their representatives directly."

"In other words, my investigation could be long over by the time Senator Olrik faces the electorate."

Antonovich nodded. "Indeed, and I let me say I fervently hope your inquiry won't drag on."

"As I said, I go where the evidence takes me at whatever pace is necessary."

"Well, I'm sure you're already quite busy, and I won't keep you any longer, Commissioner. Thank you for accepting my invitation, and good luck in bringing this investigation to a just and proper conclusion."

Knowing we were dismissed, Elin and I stood. "Thanks, Mister President, but luck is rarely a factor in solving a case. Hard work, on the other hand..."

Antonovich stood as well, but instead of holding out his hand, he considered me for a few seconds.

"I'm hosting the First Winter Levee of the season on the solstice, Commissioner. Perhaps you might like to join us and meet the star system's leading figures. General Elin, Rear Admiral Meir, and both regimental commanding officers will be in attendance."

"I appreciate the thought, Mister President, but I should avoid social events while I'm in the middle of an ongoing investigation."

"Ah, well. If you change your mind, let General Elin know, and he'll contact my social secretary."

We shook hands, saluted, and left.

During the short ride back to Police HQ, Elin and I spoke little, and I made my goodbyes in the garage so Sergeant Prokofieff could walk me directly to the underground street.

Once back in the incident room, I headed for my desk, Arno and Destine hard on my heels. As I expected, they wanted to hear about my meeting. Both forensic analysts were absent, however, and I figured Arno gave them the rest of the day off since there were, as yet, no records to analyze.

"So?"

"I met not only with Elin; I also spent a few minutes speaking with President Antonovich at the Palace. He invited me to an upcoming presidential levee if you'll believe it."

Arno's eyebrows shot up. "Really? Do tell, Chief."

I gave them an almost verbatim account of both discussions, the one with Elin and the other with the President.

"Skirting close to improper utterances, weren't they?" Arno asked when I fell silent. "At least

General Elin should know to say nothing that could be construed as exercising undue influence within hearing of an anti-corruption investigator."

"For what it's worth, I think they weren't playing games. The meetings were more about obtaining reassurances we wouldn't run roughshod over the 212th and inflame an already tense situation on Novaya Sibir. I don't know if I succeeded, but they understand we will go where the evidence takes us, nothing more." I glanced at the time. Still a tad early, but we'd put in six extra hours because of the time difference between Yekaterinburg's clocks and *Benton Fraser*'s universal time. "With that, sufficient unto the day is the evil thereof. Let's lock up, go across the street, and treat ourselves. I wouldn't mind a relaxing swim in the pool, followed by a drink, a meal, and an early bedtime."

— Ten —

I swam lazy lengths in the hotel pool, which was on the top floor under a transparent canopy, after a good workout session in the gym. As I propelled myself through the warm water, I watched the sun kiss the western horizon while swimming in one direction and the darkness creeping out of the east in the other. I hit the sauna afterward, and a fifteen-minute session left me feeling mellower than I had since ACC Sorjonen laid this investigation on us.

Though Destine was a fitness fanatic, I didn't spot her in the hotel's exercise facilities, nor Arno. Of our two sergeants, I saw nary a trace. We hadn't made definite plans to meet in the bar before supper, let alone eat together in the hotel restaurant. Over time, like every close professional family, we'd developed our own ways of taking a break from each other, especially after several days cooped up in a cutter, and I was fully prepared to spend the evening by myself.

I put on a subdued civilian suit, nothing fancy or formal, grabbed my reader, and headed for the wood-paneled bar on the next-to-last floor where a wall of windows looked south toward the Angara River and the distant Southern Mountain Range. Not that I could make out much by way of the landscape beyond the river, thanks to the thick carpet of snow. The evening sky was clear, and now that the last rays of Novaya Sibir's sun had vanished, I could admire the Milky Way's river of stars rising from the horizon, a sight that never failed to enchant me.

I took a small table in one corner and placed my reader in front of me. Within moments, a human waiter appeared and took my order for a gin and tonic, which I charged to my room. Once it arrived, I turned on my reader and took a sip as I called up one of the books on my to-read list, *Faster Than Hope*, a twenty-second century classic novel of betrayal and redemption. The title, of course, referred to despair, which spread more quickly and insidiously than its counterpart.

I hadn't taken more than a few sips of my drink before I saw a tall, elegant, dark-haired woman in her mid-forties make a beeline for my table. She wore an expensive business suit, and her hair, thickly braided, hung halfway down her back.

As she came within earshot, she gave me a smile that didn't quite reach her cold, watchful green eyes.

"Assistant Commissioner Caelin Morrow of the Commonwealth Constabulary's Professional Compliance Bureau?"

I nodded once, studying her. "Yes."

"My name is Carla Hautcoeur. I'm the Novaya Sibir correspondent for Galactic Newsnet."

"My apologies, Madame Hautcoeur, but I don't give interviews or discuss my cases."

"I am aware of that and not here to obtain information from you. On the contrary, I brought something *for* you." She gestured at the chair in front of me. "May I? It won't take long."

I kept my expression carefully neutral, remembering the ancient saying, beware Greeks bearing gifts, a reference to the Trojan Horse. Since Galactic Newsnet belonged, via the Interstellar Media Group, to the ComCorp zaibatsu, whose top executives were leading centralists, I would look upon anything she gave me with the proper degree of suspicion.

"Why not come see me at the office in the morning?" I took a sip of my drink, eyes never leaving hers. "Why here and now?"

"I figured you being seen speaking with me in an official capacity, other than because I'm a witness called to make a statement, might make people question your impartiality. There would be a record of my entering the federal building, the 47th

Constabulary Group's HQ, and what are no doubt your segregated offices. It wouldn't pass quite as easily with the ordinary people of Novaya Sibir as your visit to the Presidential Palace will once word gets out. This star system has its own newsnets, and they'll gleefully go after an unwanted federal official, never mind a senior anti-corruption officer from Wyvern."

"And how would you know about such a hypothetical visit?"

Her smile returned, this time more dazzling and with even less warmth than before. "I'm a reporter, and finding out about such matters is my stock in trade. Besides, you're a high-profile visitor to this world."

"Yet we're being seen talking right now."

Hautcoeur glanced around the room.

"By those who know better than telling tales out of school. The Yekaterinburg elite frequents this bar, people in government and the private sector who like conducting their business — legitimate, it goes without saying — in a place that offers discretion and a modicum of privacy. It's one reason the 47th and other federal agencies use this hotel to put up off-world visitors, besides the convenient location. And, if you'll pardon me for saying so, out of uniform, you're rather unremarkable. You could be anyone, as far as the patrons of this bar are concerned."

"We anti-corruption investigators do our best to seem innocuous when we're in civilian attire. Now, what did you bring for me?"

"My superiors in the highest home office," she gave me a significant glance as she spoke those words, which probably meant ComCorp HQ, "wish to give you a copy of the raw data and recordings we got on the matter you're investigating. Call it the zaibatsu's contribution, as a good Commonwealth corporate citizen, in aid of your efforts uncovering the truth."

I found her use of zaibatsu to indicate the Honorable Commonwealth Trading Corporation immensely curious. As far as I knew, the people who headed the conglomerate weren't big fans of the term, which carried negative connotations pointing at monopolistic and cartel-like behavior. That the major zaibatsus, by and large, heavily favored the centralists didn't help their reputation in the OutWorlds either, and they knew it.

Perhaps there was a message in her choice of words. But if so, I couldn't see it.

"Isn't a newsnet handing over raw data voluntarily rather than demanding law enforcement present a duly signed warrant from a judge rather unusual?"

She showed me her unnaturally even and brilliantly white teeth again. "Yes, however, these are unique circumstances, and everyone is keen on ensuring that you uncover the truth."

I searched for potential traps in her offer but couldn't see anything that might trip me up. Of course, I'd make sure our forensic data analysts treated her information with the utmost care and a healthy dose of skepticism.

"Very well." I held out my hand to signal I would accept what I figured was a data wafer.

She reached into her tunic pocket, extracted a small case no bigger than the quarter lemon slice in my gin, and placed it on the table between us.

"It's yours. On behalf of my superiors, good luck with the investigation." Then she stood and walked away without a backward glance.

No sooner was she gone than Arno and Destine emerged from the shadows and made for my table. Like me, they wore elegant but straightforward civilian suits, and no one would make them for cops, let alone internal affairs officers.

As they joined me at my table, the waiter reappeared, and I ordered a second gin and tonic while Argo asked for a local stout he'd heard about and Destine a glass of white wine.

Once the drinks were served, Arno asked, "So what was that about? Who is she?"

"A ComCorp messenger." I recounted our conversation, and Arno gave the little plastic case, which I'd not yet touched, a stern look.

"What do we do with this, Chief?" He gestured at Hautcoeur's gift.

"We try to not make the same mistake as the Trojans."

"Agreed. What we need is an emissions-blocking secure storage box and a set of tongs." Arno glanced at Destine. "Can do?"

She nodded. "May I finish my glass first?"

"Carla Hautcoeur's gift isn't going anywhere for the next bit."

Destine finished her wine, but rather quickly, and I made a mental note to buy her another on my tab. She returned fifteen minutes later with a small box, no wider than her palm and half as high, along with tweezers.

"The duty officer was kind enough to let me rummage through their armory. This is actually a boom box on top of blocking emissions through the entire spectrum. It can absorb the explosion if that little thing there is designed to blow a hole in anyone who tucks it in her tunic pocket."

"Not that ComCorp would be stupid enough to try assassinating a senior Constabulary officer," Arno said. "The *Sécurité Spéciale,* maybe, and I suppose she could work for them. So better safe than sorry. Even the biggest zaibatsus have their share of utterly imbecilic executives."

We watched Destine open the box, pick up Hautcoeur's offering with the tweezers and deposit it inside. She gently closed the lid and locked it with what she said was her own biometric code.

"I'll put it in your office safe now, sir," she said, standing.

"Thank you. When you return, join us in the restaurant next door. I think we're done here."

"Yes, sir."

We finished the evening together, enjoying a fine meal on the other side of the hotel's penultimate floor. I was hoping for an aurora, but the conditions weren't right that evening, according to Arno.

By the time we headed for our separate suites, I felt the weight of a rich meal and several drinks on top of a long day drag me into the abyss. I crawled into bed, thankful for its cocoon-like embrace, and fell into a deep sleep unencumbered by dreams of any sort.

— Eleven —

I took a quick and solitary breakfast in the federal building cafeteria the next morning since I was running a few minutes behind. Knowing my colleagues, I assumed they were already in the office, waiting for their tardy but refreshed leader. I received sideways glances from a few uniformed Constabulary members, no doubt wondering why the most senior ranking officer in the star system and a visitor from HQ on Wyvern to boot, wasn't using the hotel restaurant.

After disposing of my tray, I took the lift to our floor and, as expected, found my four team members clustered around Master Sergeant Cincunegui's workstation. The moment Destine spied me from the corner of her eyes, she straightened.

"Good morning, Commissioner."

Arno, Cincunegui, and Sergeant First Class Esadze turned and stiffened to attention.

"Good morning, everyone. I trust you slept well in those magnificent beds the hotel offers?"

"Oh, aye," Arno replied in a rumbling tone. "And you seem more chipper than last night, Chief."

"I was blessed with the sleep that soothes away our worries." I gestured at Cincunegui. "What's up, Arno?"

"Teseo was demonstrating the art of forensic data analysis on the newsnet clip HQ gave us before we left Wyvern. The amount of manipulation he can detect is rather gratifying. Would you like a demonstration?"

"Yes, but how about we work our way through the data Carla Hautcoeur gave me yesterday?"

"If there's data on that chip and not something nasty."

Cincunegui raised a hand.

"If you'll let me, sir. Chief Inspector Galdi briefed us on last night's events. Part of our training involves detecting nasty surprises disguised as data storage, and we brought our tools of the trade."

Destine nodded toward my office. "Shall I get the storage container from your safe?"

"Please." I turned to Cincunegui again. "What did the newsnet piece reveal?"

He shrugged. "Not much, really. It was obviously edited — everything newsnets send out is. But the sequences showing people in what appears to be Fleet-issue armor shooting civilian men and women with what appears to be Fleet-issue weapons weren't. However, as the chief inspector noted, we can't see any faces, unit insignia, or even evidence those were Marines and not mercenaries who somehow got restricted gear and guns."

"And the sequences showing dead bodies lined up side-by-side?"

"Also not tampered with. Again, as the chief inspector said, it's impossible to say whether those were genuine civilians or irregular fighters wearing civilian clothes. But if they were feigning death, it was well choreographed. No twitching, no signs of breathing, genuine-looking wounds, the works."

Arno raised a finger. "Did anyone see children among the dead?"

Both sergeants shook their heads, and Destine called out 'no' from my office.

"There could have been children but placed to one side and that part of the sequence cut," Sergeant Esadze pointed out. "The newsnets wouldn't be showing rows of dead kids."

Arno nodded. "Alina has a point."

"And the bit showing a kinetic strike on what we will, for now, call the village?"

"Also genuine, sir," Cincunegui replied. "But it need not have been at that particular location or even on Torga. We saw nothing that placed it there or anywhere near the bodies. And it was only a few seconds, which doesn't give us much."

"Let's hope Carla Hautcoeur's so-called raw recordings are more useful."

"Yes, sir." Cincunegui nodded once. "Because the newsnet data stream strikes me as an assemblage of disparate pieces taken from various sources rather than a distillation of one single recording. But that's just a gut feeling at this point. Until we obtain corroborative evidence, it doesn't mean much." He shrugged.

Destine reappeared, carrying the box. She placed it on the conference table that occupied one end of the room and glanced at Cincunegui.

"All yours, Teseo."

"Thanks, Warrant." He stood, opened his personal kit pack, and withdrew a handheld sensor.

"This," he said, raising it up for us to see, "is a souped-up police version of the military's Mark Twelve. It's so secret I promised the classified stores custodian I would sacrifice the life of my firstborn if I ever let it fall into the wrong hands before he would allow me to take it off Wyvern." Cincunegui grinned. "But since I'm not blessed with children, it was an easy promise."

He walked over to the table and gently opened the box which Destine had already unlocked.

"It appears to be a standard data wafer case, the sort mass-produced for the civilian market." He aimed his sensor into the box. After a few moments, he said, "It is definitely what it seems, with a standard data wafer inside. I'm not picking up any substances that shouldn't be there."

Arno gave me an amused smile. "I guess the villains aren't trying to murder you by stealth, Chief."

"I never thought that was a possibility. Killing me wouldn't help Senator Olrik's cause, or rather, the goals of the people behind him."

"So, you think there is an agenda at work and not just law-abiding citizens raising the possibility a crime was committed." Arno's amused smile turned into a faint smirk.

"When it comes to centralists butting heads with the Fleet, there's always an agenda. But that doesn't mean they trumped up the allegations. Something happened on Torga, and our job is determining whether that something was legitimate military action against an actual threat."

Cincunegui pulled on a pair of gloves, lifted the case from the box, and walked it to his workstation. There, he placed it on an isolation mat he'd previously taken from his pack. Then, he opened the case, picked up tweezers, and retrieved the data chip, which he placed on the mat beside the case.

"Standard wafer. Billions of them are produced every year throughout the Commonwealth, and this one is a sixty-four-petabyte specimen manufactured by Cosidyne Memory Incorporated, part of the ComCorp zaibatsu."

Arno snorted. "Naturally."

"Not top of the line but not single-use throwaway trash either." Cincunegui moved his chair over to the next workstation. "This is a shielded stand-alone I requested yesterday and tested earlier this morning. Alina has one as well. If the wafer is more than just a data repository, it won't radiate emissions beyond the confines of the reader, nor can it attack any network."

He pulled a slim drawer out of the workstation's base, placed the data chip inside, and closed it again. "I'm now checking the shielding's integrity before activating the reader."

A few seconds passed, then he nodded. "We're good to go. There's nothing other than ones and zeros on that wafer, and they won't escape containment. Starting transfer."

Cincunegui swiveled his chair to face us. "There won't be much to see, for now, sir. We must scan every single byte for nasty surprises embedded in the code, and that'll take time."

"Right. How are you two set on visiting *Chinggis*?"

"We're making the round trip later this morning. Up to the station on the ten o'clock run and back on the sixteen hundred. They're expecting us, or rather, the ship's first officer is."

"You're flying from Base Wolk, I assume?"

Cincunegui nodded. "Unfortunately, that means we won't be analyzing this stuff until tomorrow."

"Understood."

I must have taken on a thoughtful expression because Arno eyed me with suspicion. "Are you thinking of adding yourself to the flight manifest at the last minute and paying Commander Sonier a surprise visit?"

"The thought is crossing my mind. We don't face any pressing engagements today."

Destine held up a hand as she stepped over to her workstation. "Let me check if there are seats left before debating the wisdom of the commissioner's impulse."

A few moments passed, then, "A half dozen seats are available to Commonwealth Armed Forces and Constabulary personnel."

She smiled at Arno and me. "I've always wanted to visit Starbase 25 and a patrol frigate like *Chinggis*. How about you, Chief Inspector?"

Arno shrugged. "Why not. Let's make it a team outing, but I suggest we wear berets, not fur hats."

Half an hour later, Sergeant First Class Alina Esadze, as the junior member of our team, was piloting our ground car out of the federal building's underground garage and gingerly finding her way to Yekaterinburg's northeastern outskirts. There, a highway connected it with Joint Services Base Wolk. The sprawling installation sat on the edge of the foothills that rose in ever-higher waves toward the cordillera separating Novaya Sibir's temperate belt from the northern subarctic taiga. She and Cincunegui sat in front while we officers, commissioned and warrant, sat in the spacious rear with our legs outstretched. As Arno suggested, we wore berets and lighter jackets over our working uniforms rather than parkas. In controlled environments such as the starbase and the frigate, winter gear would seem not only out of place but be uncomfortable.

Once beyond Yekaterinburg's city limits, we traversed broad, snow-covered agricultural expanses shimmering under a bright sun, many of them tucked into vast greenhouses capable of providing the capital and its environs with fresh vegetables and fruit year-round. We also saw several ranches in the distance, where herds of animals bred to develop thick coats in winter were variously thundering about, exercising, or clustered around water and feed stations, their exhalations steaming up the sub-zero air.

Further away, dark lines and patches of native evergreens marked the upper slopes, where the snow had not covered them. Reflecting on the scene, it struck me as strangely bucolic, in a frigid kind of way. But I couldn't see myself living on Novaya Sibir. I was a warm-weather sort who would be happier spending her retirement on Wyvern, perhaps in the hinterlands surrounding Draconis. Winter there was a quick afterthought, more of a temporary cooling in an area that never experienced scorching weather during its summers either.

A trio of black specks emerging from the white countryside in the distance in perfect triangle formation gave a clue to the existence of Joint Services Base Wolk beyond the first set of rolling hills marking the northern limit of the equatorial plains. They veered in a smooth arc toward the west and quickly vanished from view.

The road rose smoothly in front of us, and eventually, our car reached the crest of the hill, revealing a panorama of the base, which was spread out across countless square kilometers. As military installations went, it was huge, a forbidden city on Yekaterinburg's outskirts, home to almost ten thousand Navy, Marine, and Army personnel, along with at least as many family members, if not more.

I knew from my reading that the main base was divided into four quadrants, with the housing area on the western edge. The military spaceport occupied one quadrant while the 21st Marines and Novaya Sibir Regiment each had their own. The final quadrant belonged to the Novaya Sibir Naval Support Unit and the Headquarters, 25th Battle Group, where Rear Admiral Meir held court. I would visit her in due course as well. Perhaps the same day I saw Colonel Freijs.

We reached a series of side-by-side security arches, and Esadze pulled us into the one furthest to the left, beside a guardhouse where, presumably, a few humans monitored the AI running the arches. The five of us held up our credentials and allowed the AI to scan them, us, and our car.

But the energy barrier preventing our car from entering Wolk didn't vanish. Instead, an androgynous voice asked us to wait for a member of the security detail. Arno and I exchanged glances, but before we could speculate, a soldier in battledress uniform emerged from the guardhouse, approached our vehicle, and saluted.

"Assistant Commissioner Morrow, Rear Admiral Meir has asked that we direct you to her office the moment you arrived."

— Twelve —

My team members turned to stare at me, waiting for orders or a reaction, but I merely smiled at the soldier.

"Thank you. I'm sure we can find the 25ᵗʰ Battle Group's headquarters."

"Yes, sir." He stepped back and saluted again, then the barrier vanished.

"Drive on through, Sergeant, and head for Admiral Meir's HQ."

Arno squinted at me. "You're going to see her instead of visiting *Chinggis*? The unexpected summons is rather suspect, considering we didn't know you'd visit Wolk an hour ago."

"She obviously gave orders to warn her whenever my name cropped up, and it did, on the ten o'clock shuttle manifest."

"More the reason to ignore Meir, Chief. You don't dance to anyone's tune in this star system, especially not that of the 25th Battle Group's commander — she's in a conflict of interest, just for starters."

Arno sounded so annoyed by Meir's obvious ploy that I smiled, but he was right, of course. I answered to Assistant Chief Constable Sorjonen on Wyvern and no one else. Besides, even though I was a member of a uniformed Commonwealth Service, I didn't belong to the Armed Forces and could safely ignore any admiral in the line of duty if I felt it necessary. We came under different codes of service discipline. And heading an investigation into the alleged misconduct of a unit under Meir's command definitely qualified as necessary, should I consider it so.

But was now the time to prove my complete independence from, perhaps even indifference to, the niceties of protocol and possibly anger her? I could only do so with effect once in any given investigation and therefore must time it well.

Then, there was my experience humoring and even helping Deputy Chief Constable Maras, the Rim Sector Constabulary Group commander, when I headed the sector's Professional Compliance Bureau detachment. Both of us reported to different superiors on Wyvern. But I'd always treated her as I would my own commanding officer, and, among other benefits, it helped my investigations in no small way.

"I think I'll visit Rear Admiral Meir. There's no need for me aboard *Chinggis*. It was more a notion of mine, seeing if my surprise arrival might result in unguarded words. But if Meir knows about my intentions, then so does Commander Sonier. I'll save my ability to ignore senior officers for a more propitious moment when it can make a real difference. But you and Destine may go, Arno. Keep the car. I'm sure I can find a ride back into Yekaterinburg. My status as Chief Inquisitor should at least grant me that."

"May I assume you're hatching a fresh plan?"

"Always." And with that, I turned my attention to the base beyond our car's windows.

Joint Services Base Wolk resembled every major Armed Forces installation I'd seen over the last few decades, and for a good reason. They were built to the same general specifications. The main difference between Wolk and its counterpart just outside Draconis back on Wyvern — Joint Services Base Sinach — was a gleaming coat of snow and ice that hid what little vegetation might soften its utilitarian lines.

Plain, light gray three and four-story flat-roofed concrete buildings with large, dark, polarized windows lined perfectly straight and meticulously kept streets. Here and there, statues, stone murals, decommissioned fighting vehicles, and obsolete aircraft on tall pedestals provided relief from the sameness. Signs, variously hung above main entrances on set on the ground by the curb, announced the various buildings' functions. Unit headquarters were easily identifiable thanks to stands of flags fronting them — Commonwealth, Armed Forces, branch of service, and that of the unit itself. Here and there, men and women in uniform marched or jogged, either alone, in pairs, or in groups with the determined purpose only military discipline combined with icy weather could impart.

Esadze turned right at the main intersection where two avenues crossed, quartering Wolk into its separate areas. I was once again reminded how the Fleet had adopted the ancient Roman castra's basic design, even though the intersecting avenues weren't named Via Principalis and Via Praetoria anymore. Or at least I've not heard of a base using those names, but anything was possible.

After a few hundred meters, Esadze turned right again and entered Wolk's naval quarter. We found the standard flag-lined rectangular parade ground at its heart, with the 25th Battle Group's HQ on one of the long sides and the Novaya Sibir Naval Support Unit's HQ on the other. Most parade grounds served as a parking lot for personal vehicles on workdays, and this one was almost full.

Esadze halted our car in front of the battle group headquarters' main entrance, a pair of sliding transparent aluminum doors. They opened on a shallow, airlock-like space beyond which I could see a two-story-high lobby with double stairs winding their way upward at the far end, framing a sizeable naval crest affixed to the wall. A reception counter with security gates on either side slashed across the lobby from side to side.

After bidding my team a pleasant trip into orbit, I climbed out of the car and walked toward the outer doors. They parted at my approach and closed behind me while the inner doors opened. The two Navy ratings behind the counter, both leading spacers, watched me approach with curious eyes. I held up my credentials, knowing their security AI would register them without human intervention.

"Assistant Commissioner Caelin Morrow, Commonwealth Constabulary. I'm here at Rear Admiral Meir's invitation."

The older of the two spacers nodded once.

"Yes, sir. We were warned of your arrival. If you'll please follow my mate. He'll take you to the admiral's office."

The younger man stood and waved me through the nearest security gate, then led me across a polished granite floor toward the left-hand corridor. I briefly noted a few display cases with mementos lining the walls before entering what I supposed was the executive wing, where Admiral Meir and her senior staff held court. The meticulously clean blue wall-to-wall carpet, the proliferation of paintings displaying ancient scenes, both wet and space navy, and the almost reverent silence gave its function away. I'd seen the like too many times before to mistake it for anything else.

My conclusion was proved right moments later as we passed polished mahogany doors bearing brass signs identifying the occupants of the offices as the 25th's senior staff. It culminated with that of the Flag Captain — Meir's chief of staff — on one side of an open door with a plaque marked 'Flag Officer Commanding' above it and the one assigned to the Battle Group Coxswain, the formation's senior enlisted spacer on the other.

A youthful Navy lieutenant wearing a braided gold cord on his left shoulder stood as the leading spacer ushered me in before disappearing. Though functional rather than decorative, his desk nonetheless fit with the antechamber's rich mahogany wainscoting and naval-themed decorations — paintings, plaques, statuettes, and other knick-knacks. Comfortable chairs were arrayed around a low table near a window overlooking what I supposed was a patio during warmer weather, while a shiny silver coffee urn, along with cups and saucers, sat on a nearby sideboard.

"Commissioner Morrow, welcome. Admiral Meir is expecting you."

He walked to the inner door bearing a sign that said, 'Rear Admiral Jasmine Meir' and knocked once, then pushed it open without waiting for a response and announced, "Assistant Commissioner Caelin Morrow of the Commonwealth Constabulary."

I entered and walked up to Meir's desk, which was definitely more decorative and much larger than her aide's. It was backed by the usual stand of flags, including hers, a fringed blue rectangle with two gold stars. I glanced briefly at my surroundings as I crossed the carpeted floor and saw that her office occupied the entire width of the building. In addition to windows on three sides, it boasted a door leading out to what I could now see was definitely a patio. Nice.

A man wearing the stripes of a Navy captain on his collar sat in one of the chairs in front of her desk. Middle-aged, slightly on the heavier side with wavy dark hair, a thin mustache, and jowls, he and Meir watched me approach with emotionless eyes. Both remained seated, though she gave me a grave nod when I stopped and saluted.

"Admiral."

"Thank you for accepting my invitation, Commissioner." She gestured at the man. "This is my flag captain, Edwin Cotard."

Cotard nodded once, though he, just like Meir, didn't offer his hand. "Pleasure."

"Likewise."

Meir gestured at one of the empty chairs. "Please sit, Commissioner."

I did as she asked, wondering why her flag captain was in attendance, but carefully schooled myself to keep a neutral expression.

"To what do I owe this unexpected pleasure, Admiral? Other than my unplanned appearance at Wolk's main gate just now."

I kept my tone light, though respectful, but chose my words to convey that I knew damn well she'd summoned me so I would miss the ten o'clock shuttle run to the starbase.

"I thought a face-to-face meeting between us might be more useful to your investigation than spending half the day in orbit. Your officers are no doubt capable of handling the data transfer from *Chinggis* without direct supervision."

Meir's tone and calculated use of words mirrored mine so perfectly that my opinion of her rose by several notches.

"You obviously feel the same," she continued after a second or two. "Otherwise, you wouldn't be here. I know Professional Compliance Bureau officers are a law unto themselves and need not heed Navy flag officers if they don't feel so inclined, not even within the confines of Armed Forces installations said admirals command."

I allowed myself a faint smile of amusement.

"Being a law unto myself doesn't absolve me of using my judgment when it concerns an officer of more senior rank. Besides, I'm curious about why you invited me here this morning. I've only been on Novaya Sibir for little more than a day."

She held my eyes for a few moments before asking, "How much do you know about the alleged incident?"

"At this point? Probably less than you or Captain Cotard. I've seen the newsnet reports and read Senator Olrik's accusatory statement, and that's it."

"I understand you met with Carla Hautcoeur of Galactic Newsnet in the hotel bar last night."

So much for other guests being discreet about who is seen with whom in that place. "She approached me, yes."

"Why? Or should I not ask?"

I shrugged. "She supposedly gave me the raw data Galactic obtained on the alleged incident, on orders from head office. We didn't study it yet, seeing as how my forensic data analysts are headed upstairs in a few minutes, so I don't know whether that's true."

"You're aware Hautcoeur is more than just the local correspondent for Galactic, right?" Cotard asked.

"That's the impression I got, Captain. What is she? An agent of ComCorp's intelligence and security division or of the SecGen's own special security organization?"

He nodded. "The former is what we — the Fleet — figure. She's also on speaking terms with high-level members of the Novaya Sibir mafia."

I gave him a sardonic smile. "And we know ComCorp isn't above using organized crime to advance corporate priorities at a deniable remove."

"Indeed. Hautcoeur has been on Naval Intelligence's watch list for some time. I do hope you're taking precautions with her gift."

"You may rest easy. My forensic specialists subjected the data wafer to extensive analysis this morning and found no surprises, which is why they've not yet looked at the data. And when they do, it'll be using appropriate equipment that ensures nothing can escape to infect any networks." I turned my eyes back on Meir. "So, tell me, Admiral, why are you so concerned about my speaking with Commander Sonier alone aboard her ship? Because that's why I'm here, not because you're curious about how much we know so far, right?"

Cotard let out a humorless chuckle. "I told you she'd see right through us in no time, Admiral."

— Thirteen —

"Seeing through civilian and military officials is what I do for a living, Admiral. And I'm quite good at it, which is why I was appointed to lead Anti-Corruption Unit Twelve, whose focus is on investigating malfeasance at the senior levels in the Armed Forces. Now, why am I here?"

"This morning, the assistant judge advocate general assigned to the Novaya Sibir Support Unit contacted me to discuss the rights of the Armed Forces members under my and Colonel Freijs' command in light of your investigation, as was his duty to me. Had he not called first, I would have spoken with him about the matter, as is my duty to my subordinates."

Meir's glare challenged me to refute her, but I couldn't fault her or the local AJAG. In fact, I should have anticipated the situation, but this sort of inquiry was new to me, so I merely inclined my head.

"Fair enough. That is well within your rights and those of persons touched by my investigation. And what did the AJAG say?"

"That one of his people should be present during every interview you conduct, in the interests of the parties involved, including the Fleet as an institution."

"You might have told me so instead of carrying out this charade, Admiral."

At least she had the grace to seem slightly embarrassed.

"There wasn't time. When the spaceport warned me you were on the ten o'clock shuttle manifest — yes, I've ordered your name flagged, and you'd do the same in my position — I'd just finished speaking with the AJAG. At that point, I figured intercepting you for a face-to-face discussion was the best way. And here we are."

"What if I'd ignored your invitation and flown up?"

"Then I would have told Commander Sonier to make herself scarce." Her gaze hardened. "You will not interview any Armed Forces member in the Novaya Sibir system without legal representation being present."

"Far be it from me to infringe on anyone's rights." I could have sworn I heard a soft snort come from

Cotard but ignored it. "Very well. I hope the AJAG can assign someone for whatever time it takes because the Fleet cannot afford delays, especially when they might make it look like witnesses are dragging their feet via legal maneuvers."

"Justice must not only be done but seen as being done impartially," Cotard said in a soft voice.

I glanced at him and nodded. "Just so, Captain. And especially in this case, which has already garnered more publicity than any other I've investigated."

"Then we're in agreement," Meir said, giving me a sneaking suspicion I'd just been sandbagged. She confirmed it moments later by summoning her aide. When he poked his head into the office, she said, "Please ask Lieutenant Commander Racitina to join us."

"Yes, sir."

Moments later, a thirty-something, dark-complexioned woman of middling height with short black hair and dark eyes entered the office. She wore the Judge Advocate General's insignia on her beret and the two and a half stripes of a lieutenant commander on her tunic collar.

Racitina stopped a regulation three paces in front of Meir's desk and saluted. The paucity of qualification insignia and ribbons on her uniform made me think she hadn't been in the Navy for long. Racitina probably came in on a direct commission as a lieutenant after a few years in civilian practice and was promoted to lieutenant commander when she reached the minimum time in rank.

Meir returned the compliment with a nod, then turned toward me once more.

"Commissioner Morrow, this is Katy Racitina of the Novaya Sibir Assistant Judge Advocate General's office. She's been assigned as counsel to the Armed Forces members touched by Senator Olrik's allegations."

Unlike the greeting Meir and Cotard gave me, I stood and held out my hand.

"A pleasure to meet you, Commander."

Racitina studied me with perceptive, intelligent eyes as we shook, and I somehow knew there was more to her than I'd first thought. How I came to that conclusion in a split second eluded me, but my hunches about people were rarely wrong. We PCB investigators are among the best judges of character in human space.

"Likewise, sir."

"Please sit. Now that the introductions are over, why don't you tell Commissioner Morrow a bit about yourself, Commander."

"Certainly, Admiral." Racitina's voice was strangely melodious, and I wondered what effect it had in court, be it on the judge, the jury, or opposing counsel. "I'm a Siberiak, born and bred, and earned my law degree from the University of Yekaterinburg while serving in one of the Novaya

Sibir Regiment's reserve battalions as an aerospace defense specialist. Once I passed the bar, the Fleet offered me a commission and a transfer to the Navy JAG Corps as a reservist attached to the Novaya Sibir Naval Support Unit's AJAG office. When I'm not in uniform, I practice criminal law as a civilian defense attorney in Yekaterinburg."

Sandbagged indeed. "And you can work full time on this inquiry however long it takes once I interview witnesses?"

She gave me a faint smile that didn't quite reach her eyes. "My firm is very supportive of the Armed Forces and has graciously given me leave without pay to serve in my naval capacity for the duration."

"Glad to hear it." For a moment, the unaccustomed feeling I was losing a measure of control over the investigation crossed my mind. None of my targets had ever produced a defense attorney before I'd even begun in earnest, and it was a strange sensation. My instincts told me I needed to regain the upper hand as quickly as possible before someone else drove the agenda. "If Admiral Meir has no other matters she wishes to discuss, we should find a quiet spot and discuss ground rules, Commander."

"Ground rules?" Her eyebrows shot up, and an air of amusement crossed her face. "They're simple. I sit in on every interview you conduct and make sure the Constabulary doesn't infringe upon the rights of Armed Forces members."

"And that tells me you're unfamiliar with the Professional Compliance Bureau's powers and protocols because there's more to it than that." I turned to Meir. "If that was it, Admiral, I think Commander Racitina and I need to discuss the parameters of this investigation."

"You can do so right here and now."

"Sorry, Admiral. But no." I climbed to my feet, pleased by the astonished looks in all three pairs of eyes. "Thank you for a most illuminating discussion. You'll hear from me in due course. Commander Racitina, let's find a quiet spot."

She glanced at Meir, who gave her an almost imperceptible nod, then stood as well. We both saluted and turned on our heels.

Once we'd donned our overcoats and were out in the corridor, Racitina said, "Will my office do?"

"The one here or at your firm in town?"

She seemed taken aback by my dry tone as much as my words. "Why do I feel you don't like me, Commissioner?"

"Oh, I neither like nor dislike you. However, until further notice, I consider you a potential security risk, a possible impediment, and someone who might well become an obstacle to resolving this matter. That being said, your office here will be fine." We passed through the security station and stepped out into the crisp winter air.

She gestured at the Naval Support Unit HQ building across the wide-open space fronting Meir's headquarters. "My office is in there. We can cross the parade square. Why am I a potential security risk?"

I let out a humorless bark of laughter.

"The fact you even ask isn't helping ease my misgivings. Look, Commander, you're a reservist, so you hold dual allegiances at a minimum. You practice criminal law on the civilian side, which means you're in frequent contact with this planet's criminal elements. And before you raise the matter of client-solicitor privilege as a way of claiming every case you work on is hermetically sealed off from every other one, I've run across too many lawyers who'll breach privilege if it serves their purpose. Government lawyers, including members of the Fleet's Judge Advocate General Corps." When she made to speak, I raised my hand. "And then there's the security issue. Since this involved a Pathfinder squadron, it's a given the records on the operation are classified top secret, perhaps even top secret special access. Operations conducted inside the Protectorate Zone usually are."

"I hold a top secret clearance. Every JAG officer does."

"No doubt. But then you'll be aware anything with that classification is always need-to-know. And unless the competent authorities tell me differently, you do not need to know, which will exclude you from most interviews. This means I will need clearance from SOCOM and Naval Intelligence.

That, in turn, makes you an impediment at the moment and possibly an obstacle later. Why the local AJAG didn't assign a regular Armed Forces lawyer baffles me. It would make things much less messy."

We entered the Naval Support Unit building and took the stairs to the third-floor landing, where a sign pointed the way to the various sections which called it home. The AJAG offices were at the far end of the eastern wing, incongruously next door to the public affairs section.

Racitina's office, small and spare, overlooked the parade square, and once inside, we removed our overcoats and berets and hung them on the rack behind the door.

"Why did they assign you rather than a regular?" I asked, taking one of the chairs in front of her desk.

"The regular staff is the AJAG and two other officers. There's not much call for a large legal contingent when the permanent garrison is just under ten thousand people. I'm one of four reservists who come in to handle the overflow."

"Doesn't Admiral Meir have a legal adviser?"

Racitina shook her head. "No. That's one of the AJAG's secondary duties, along with being the legal adviser to the commanding officers of the Naval Support Unit, the 21st Marines, and the Novaya Sibir Regiment. Back to your question — the three regulars are carrying a full load right now, and it was more expedient that I be assigned to your investigation rather than re-assign a half dozen cases for who knows how long. I am the most experienced defense counsel among the reservists. Two of my part-time colleagues work for the Novaya Sibir Prosecution Service, while the third specializes in property law."

"I see."

"Let me ask you a question, Commissioner. You spoke of security classification and need to know. Won't your findings end up being declassified when they're presented to the Senate?"

"And that's a good segue into explaining how the Professional Compliance Bureau differs from every other law enforcement organization in this part of the galaxy."

— Fourteen —

"As a lawyer, you're no doubt familiar with ancient Latin terms, such as the famous question from Juvenal's Satires — quis custodiet ipsos custodes?"

I waited as she searched her memory, in vain as it turned out because she shook her head. "No. Sorry."

"It can be variously translated as who watches the watchers or who will guard the guards themselves. Keeping rulers and their enforcers reasonably honest is something that has preoccupied humanity since governments were first invented, with depressingly little long-term success. Every locus of authority eventually abuses it without an external countervailing force.

"In the twenty-sixth century, we — the Professional Compliance Bureau — are the current answer to that question, and we've been given the most wide-ranging powers in the history of internal affairs organizations. My division of the Bureau, Anti-Corruption, has the widest-ranging powers of all. Now, to your question of whether my investigation will be declassified. I don't make that decision. Most of my investigations stay top secret, and my reports never see the light of day, not even in court.

"Many, perhaps a majority of my targets, never even face a judge. They're simply removed from their positions and sent into early retirement for a variety of reasons which I cannot discuss with you. A few don't even survive long enough to face charges.

"Here's how this one will probably unfold. I will collect the available evidence, formulate conclusions, and present recommendations to my superiors on Wyvern, under the appropriate classification, either top secret or top secret special access. Once I've done so, my job is over, and I go home. Whatever happens next is up to the Chief Constable and the Grand Admiral. This way of doing things ensures my fellow officers and I don't bring our egos into play.

"As a fundamental principle, we're utterly uninterested by what happens once we've carried out our orders. In corruption cases, it's either when we clear the suspects or arrest them. Here, it'll be once I've collected all possible evidence to formulate a conclusion. That's it. Will they make any of my findings public? I don't know."

I paused and studied Racitina's face. But like any good trial lawyer, she was in full control of her expression.

"That being said, I wish Admiral Meir hadn't gone down this road without consulting her chain of command, despite the local AJAG's intervention. I'm sure my investigation has Grand Admiral Larsson's personal attention, and he might not be happy about the admiral assigning a reserve officer as counsel to the witnesses. She'll undoubtedly hear about it in due course because I will report this up my chain of command. There's no choice in the matter. But what do I do with you in the meantime? There is no absolute legal right for counsel when Armed Forces members offer witness statements to a duly appointed Constabulary investigator. But considering my investigation may result in serious charges against one or more of the people involved — may not will — then having counsel present during interviews can be useful. For example, it may forestall attempts by the defense at invalidating said statements now that Admiral Meir has opened the door. And yet, you're not cleared to sit in on our interviews."

"You're the senior investigating officer. You're able to clear me."

I shook my head. "Not in this case. Control over the information that will, without a doubt, be revealed is not mine. Fortunately, we'll be reviewing data dumps over the next few days, which will allow me to seek direction from Fleet HQ via my chain of command before we speak with those involved. In the meantime, you will not communicate in any fashion with the members of the 212th Pathfinder Squadron and the crew of CSS *Chinggis*, nor discuss the allegations against them with their superiors, since you aren't the legal adviser."

She sat up straighter and frowned. "You can't tell me that."

"I can. When the Grand Admiral calls on the PCB to investigate, we become the Fleet's internal affairs branch for the duration and carry the same authority as within the Constabulary. Check the relevant section in Volume Two of the Armed Forces Regulations and Orders." I thought of mentioning she should have done so before showing up in Meir's office, but I'm sure Racitina was smart enough to reproach herself later.

"If you disregard my orders, and they are entirely legitimate, I will charge you with perverting the course of justice. I'm sure you know what happens to your legal career if a court-martial finds you guilty." When she stared at me without uttering a word, a wintry smile played on my lips. "I told you there was more to this than you imagined. We are the Last of the Incorruptibles, and we investigate every case with impartiality and integrity and without fear of retribution. We cannot be pressured, blackmailed, or threatened into deviating from the path of duty. Anyone who maliciously interferes with us will be prosecuted. Those who accidentally interfere with us will remember to never do so for as long as they live. That is why when we prove innocence, no prosecutor in the Commonwealth will question us, and when we decide someone broke the law, no one questions our conclusions."

I saw disbelief mirrored in her face, and my smile grew.

"We in the PCB will do whatever is necessary to protect our reputation because it is the only thing that keeps us effective as the ultimate guardians of the law across human space. Thus, I will let no one, not you, Colonel Freijs, Admiral Meir, nor anyone else, dictate how I proceed because our investigation cannot be tainted by even the slightest whiff of interference, let alone impropriety. If that means telling Admiral Meir she should jump into the nearest black hole, politely and respectfully, of course, then I will do so, and she would have no recourse against me. I will accord senior officers the respect due to their rank, but I don't fear them or their power. Unless senior officers are in my chain of command, I can ignore them, their orders, wishes, and directives if those might impact my investigation." I paused for a moment to let her absorb my words. "Are we clear on where you and everyone else around here stand, Commander Racitina?"

A small nod. "I guess we have no standing whatsoever."

"Got it in one, Counselor. Do you also understand why we're not discussing this in the admiral's office?"

Another nod. "I think so. There's no point antagonizing Admiral Meir and her flag captain by pointing out that while she might outrank you, the balance of power is clearly in your favor."

Interesting choice of words. Perhaps Racitina was smarter than I first thought.

"Here's how this will unfold. I'll see what those who own the information surrounding *Chinggis'* and the 212ᵗʰ's foray into the Zone say about letting you hear witness statements. If they agree that the benefits of having counsel present outweigh the risks, I'll receive instructions reading you in. If and when that happens, any unauthorized release of data will not only end your naval and legal careers but see you spend quality time in a penal colony on Parth. If they disagree, you're out. Period. No questions, no discussions, no appeals."

"Understood, sir. May I ask what your preference is?"

She seemed genuinely curious, so I gave her a straight answer.

"You may ask, but I'll reserve my opinion until after we analyze the records of the operation, and I know what sort of witness statements we'll be collecting. Questions before I take my leave?"

Racitina shook her head. "No."

"Now, how do I make my way back to the federal building in Yekaterinburg? My team parked our assigned ground car at the spaceport, where it's waiting for their return from orbit."

She reached for her desktop communicator. "I'll ask one of the duty drivers to take you, sir."

"Thanks."

Five minutes later, I sat in the back of a black Navy ground car headed for the capital and arrived in time to eat lunch by myself in the federal building cafeteria. The young spacer at the controls was silent the entire time, which suited me as I was mentally composing a message for Commissioner Sorjonen and another for the one person who could cut through Fleet bureaucracy at hyperspeed and find out if Racitina was in or out.

Our office suite seemed strangely empty with my team gone, and I felt a touch lonely at my desk. But I wrote both messages and encrypted them, one with the PCB's proprietary algorithm and the other with the special code Rear Admiral Talyn gave me.

I hand-carried the data chip to the communications center and watched as they packaged the messages for subspace transmission, one over the Constabulary's frequency and the other on the Fleet's. That done, I set myself to researching Katy Racitina, Esquire, first in the 47th's database and then every open source I could think of.

The Constabulary didn't have much on her, only what we record about any other Armed Forces member, regular and reserve, which is basic information. She'd never interacted with the Constabulary in her civilian employment, meaning she never appeared as a defense attorney in federal cases.

The open-source references to Racitina, however, proved more interesting. Though she was only in her late thirties, Racitina came across as a high-profile criminal lawyer if the press releases, newsnet articles, law society papers, and court summaries were correct. She even lectured at the University of Yekaterinburg Law School and other institutes of higher learning occasionally, imparting her experience to budding lawyers.

It made her failure to read up on PCB powers over the Armed Forces even more puzzling. Of course, she wouldn't have enjoyed much prep time between the AJAG's brain spark and being introduced to the first and only PCB officer she'd ever met, so perhaps there were extenuating circumstances, but it seemed sloppy. And I distrusted sloppy where otherwise intelligent-seeming individuals were concerned.

Only one thing bothered me about this, and it was her firm representing alleged members of the Siberiak mafia. Wherever organized crime stuck its rotting nose, official corruption followed. I couldn't find any instances of Racitina defending suspected mobsters, but her partners did, and for what it was worth, they racked up a perfect record of getting their clients off. Did that mean they weren't guilty? Or was the Novaya Sibir prosecutor's office lackadaisical?

Maybe the National Police Service habitually tainted evidence either by accident or on purpose. Or perhaps organized crime had corrupted the Novaya Sibir judicial system in part or whole. It wouldn't be the only star system in that situation. My native world of Pacifica is only the best-known example. There, the eternal ruling party had always been the largest organized crime group, so corruption was baked into the system.

By the time sixteen hundred hours rolled around, I'd exhausted the available sources without being much wiser about Katy Racitina. She was well regarded in the legal community, did pro bono work besides pleading high-profile cases, sat on the boards of several charities, and found time to serve as part-time assistant judge advocate general officer in the Commonwealth Navy. It made her failure to research PCB powers before meeting me even more puzzling, although perhaps she simply didn't find the time between her being assigned the case and this morning's meeting in Meir's office. Or she suffered from a blind spot where the Constabulary was concerned. Or something else was going on.

Since my team was only now leaving the starbase, I figured I might as well pack it in for the day. After securing the office suite, I made my way down into the underground network and across to our hotel. I did so even though the outside air looked crystal clear as the late afternoon sun painted long, dark shadows across the city's clean and mostly empty streets. If the locals weren't wandering around outdoors, neither would I. And I found plenty of them below ground, making their way home after another long day toiling in downtown Yekaterinburg.

Once in my room, a driving need to sweat out the day's irritations overcame me, and I changed into gym clothes. The hotel's exercise room was empty, and I took a cardio machine in front of a northeast-facing window, wondering whether I might spot the shuttle on final approach to Wolk's spaceport. And I did.

By the time I deemed myself sufficiently exercised and returned to my room, Arno and the team would be back in Yekaterinburg, and knowing him, he'd have dismissed them after securing the data download. Therefore, I experienced no guilt at heading for the bar after a quick shower and change of clothes. The chances of Arno joining me there were almost one hundred percent, and I wanted to study the other patrons for a bit to see if I could spot someone who might be watching me on Meir's behalf.

— Fifteen —

I was halfway through my gin and tonic when Arno appeared in the doorway. He gave me a nod, then picked up a glass of ale at the bar before joining me at my corner table, the same as before from which I could see most of the bar. So far, I didn't notice anyone paying me more than a passing shred of interest, and no faces seemed familiar.

"Pleasant trip?" I asked once he sat across from me.

"It had its moments. And your call on Admiral Meir?"

"Strange, and then some. But you first. Oh, and are the others joining us?"

Arno shook his head.

"No. The sergeants found a place more to their liking next door, and Destine joined them, preferring to leave us ancient, commissioned officers by ourselves." He took a sip of what I learned was Russian Imperial Stout, or as Arno called it, a meal in a glass. "That's the good stuff. So, our visit to the Commonwealth frigate *Chinggis*. To say we weren't welcome aboard would be an understatement. The first officer met us at the gangway and made a pointed remark of only being warned about two Constabulary members, not four, with a chief inspector at the head of the delegation. I can only wonder about his reaction if you'd shown up with us."

I let out an indelicate snort. "He knew there would be four of you. Bet on it. Admiral Meir has her own little intelligence network going. For instance, she knew about Carla Hautcoeur approaching me right here last night and our being booked on this morning's shuttle."

Arno grimaced. "Nice. Do you think we're facing a case of the thin blue and black lines closing ranks against the inquisitors in gray?"

I took a sip of my drink, then shrugged. "Probably. Our Navy and Marine Corps comrades are no keener at seeing internal affairs dig through their underwear drawer than Constabulary members. But you were saying about *Chinggis*?"

"Yes. The first officer took us to the frigate's heart, where its computer core beats at speeds faster than any human brain could ever comprehend."

"Nicely lyrical." I waved my glass at him. "Sorry for the interruption."

"There, the ship's communications and information systems officer, a young lieutenant who evidently didn't know what he should think of four police officers entering the ship's holy of holies, waited for us. Teseo put him at ease rather quickly and deserves kudos for his people skills, not something forensic analysts usually possess in my experience. In no time flat, he'd plugged his retrieval unit into the core under the lieutenant's keen supervision. Then he and Alina worked their way through the relevant records, taking care to avoid those which were not germane.

"I quickly became bored with watching proceedings I didn't understand, so I asked the first officer if I could make my manners with Commander Sonier on your behalf. His reply, quite abrupt and dismissive, quashed that idea because of Sonier's unavailability, with no reasons given. I didn't press the issue. So, Destine and I spent a good hour in the ship's core watching Teseo and Alina work while the lieutenant and the first officer watched the four of us. It wasn't one of our more comfortable moments.

"Once Teseo pronounced himself satisfied, I signed the receipt — a standard retinal scan. Then, the first officer ushered us off the ship as if we were deadly plague vectors, even though by then it was lunchtime and a visit to the wardroom wouldn't have come amiss. But there wasn't a glimmer of hospitality for the police aboard *Chinggis*. We ended up taking our meal on the starbase, though word surely spread through the grapevine because no one would so much as look at us.

"Call it the usual persona non grata phenomenon when we show up in uniform, but with a kick of antimatter to make sure we felt the sting. We spent the rest of the afternoon in our very own corner of the shuttle terminal lounge, reading and drinking coffee before returning to the chilly embrace of Yekaterinburg. Teseo stored the data with the same care he showed the stuff graciously gifted by Carla Hautcoeur. Now, what was the admiral's summons about, Chief?"

I grimaced at him. "She decided, in a fit of executive leadership, to implement the local AJAG's recommendation that legal counsel should accompany everyone we interview and introduced me to said counsel."

A thunderous expression crossed his face. "She can't do that on her own initiative. The right to counsel only kicks in when and if we caution them."

"Oh, don't I know it. And I'm sure Katy Racitina, the part-time JAG officer appointed as counsel, is equally aware."

I recounted my conversations with both Meir and Racitina in fine detail. When I fell silent, he scratched his beard, eyes narrowed in thought.

"If I were a suspicious man, I'd think something untoward happened during the operation on Torga, and Meir is trying to stay ahead of us by injecting a high-powered criminal lawyer into our investigation. You told her where to go, right, Chief? This is clearly undue interference in an ongoing case by the chain of command."

I raised a restraining hand. "Oh, they can spin it in as many ways as possible, including the chain of command taking care of its people by ensuring a fair and transparent investigation. There are probably plenty in the Fleet who believe our job is finding guilt no matter what. We might consider our nickname amusing, but a firing squad is no joke to the military mind. So I kicked the problem of allowing Racitina to potentially hear top secret special access information up our chain of command and also dropped it on Admiral Talyn's desk. If something we're not aware of yet is at play here, she's the one most likely to know. And her people will surely find out more about Lieutenant Commander Racitina than we ever could."

"Am I to infer that if you receive the go-ahead, you'll allow this Racitina to sit in on our interviews?" Arno's frown deepened. "Why?"

"Because should the allegations bear some truth, no one will be able to cry foul about our interactions with the people involved — legal counsel was by their side."

"Ah." Arno's frown vanished. "Of course. I should have worked that out by myself. This is you being sneaky again."

I gave him an amused glance.

"Not so much sneaky as navigating through what could become rather choppy waters. We're never welcome anywhere at the best of times, but I sense that we're especially not wanted here. But I must admit, Meir knowing about Hautcoeur's approach last night bugs me the most at the moment."

He shrugged. "It could be perfectly innocent."

"Nothing involving the newsnets is innocent, especially when their correspondents are probably also operatives for their parent zaibatsu's security and intelligence division. And in this case, we're talking about ComCorp, the biggest and most corrupt of them."

"True." He took another sip. "In which case, Hautcoeur could have passed the word herself via mutual contacts out of sheer devilment. Or, since Racitina works for a high-profile law firm, perhaps someone connected to her saw you and Hautcoeur and told Racitina, who then told Meir. I'm sure your identity and purpose made the rounds of Yekaterinburg within hours of our arrival. It isn't every day a PCB assistant commissioner — one from the dreaded Anti-Corruption Division, no less — and her team land on a sleepy human world where nothing of note ever happens. And what with

Hautcoeur well-known among governing, legal, financial and other circles..."

"Whatever she's up to, it's really none of our business."

Arno gave me a knowing smile. "Yet. You know how our cases often expand to take in any other federal crimes within reach."

"I'd rather we don't collect more work this time." I downed the rest of my gin and tonic. "How about the evening meal?"

Arno sketched a sitting bow. "Lead on, fearless Assistant Chief Inquisitor."

We saw no persons of interest watching us in the restaurant and repaired to our respective rooms well before twenty-hundred hours. Considering we'd seen no sign of Destine and the sergeants, I felt every bit of my age as I settled in with a book, a cup of tea, and a view over the rooftops of downtown Yekaterinburg. The twinkling stars and the broad brush of light and dark that was the Milky Way filled my bedroom's single window with a tableau I'd rarely enjoyed. And after turning off the lights, I spent a long time studying the heavens, wondering about the suns I'd felt shining down on me as I traveled from world to world, doing the Constabulary's bidding throughout my entire adult life.

Sleep didn't come easily that night, and not just because I still hadn't adapted to the time shift between the cutter's coordinated universal time and

Yekaterinburg's clock. On the contrary. I should be even more tired. But it was well past midnight, at least according to the time display on my nightstand, before I finally found enough peace to drift away. And yet, I still woke before sunrise on another cold winter morning feeling, if not entirely refreshed, then eager to tackle the investigation rather than wallow in my bed's comforting cocoon until my team sent a search party for me.

When I entered the federal building cafeteria for breakfast, I wondered whether I should search for them, but in fairness, I was early — the cafeteria had just opened. They trickled in one by one as I was on my second cup of coffee, the remains of a healthy Siberiak morning meal in front of me. The novelty of our presence must be wearing off because no one paid my team or me any attention. We were just another handful of gray uniforms in a building where eighty percent of the occupants wore the same one, albeit without the swooping owl insignia.

"Slept well, Chief?" Arno settled across from me, his usual protein-heavy selection heaped high on the plate.

"Reasonably. You?"

"A bit of tossing and turning, but I eventually faded away." He tucked in with gusto and merely nodded when Destine, along with the sergeants, joined us.

After downing a healthy slug of his coffee, Sergeant Cincunegui looked at me and asked, "How would you like to proceed with the data, sir?"

"What do you suggest?"

"First, we go through the newsnet stuff and look for anything that might indicate issues — splices, data manipulation, that sort of stuff. If everything seems honest, we'll do the same to the frigate's data because I don't believe Navy starship logs are inviolate — all data repositories can be manipulated. If that seems honest as well, I suggest we use the newsies' records as a baseline and look for discrepancies between them and the frigate's."

I nodded. "Sounds like a plan. I should hear from the Marines today as well."

"Right. Let's make that the third run-through, under the same principles."

"How long?"

Cincunegui shrugged. "Can't say just yet, sir. It depends on how many anomalies we detect. Each one of them requires separate analysis to eliminate false positives. If Warrant Officer Bonta could help, it would speed up things."

I glanced at Destine, who immediately nodded. It wouldn't surprise me if they discussed this last night when they ditched us.

"I'll backstop Teseo and Alina, sir. They might come across artifacts that I can explain from having served as liaison."

"Good. That leaves Arno and me to visit Colonel Freijs, provided his data dump is ready for pickup."

And it was. Shortly after I sat behind my desk and opened my communications folder to check for messages from home or Fleet HQ, Freijs invited me to join him for coffee in his office at ten-thirty. I should bring a top secret rated data transfer case.

— Sixteen —

When we passed through the base's security checkpoint this time, no soldier stepped out with a message from Admiral Meir or anyone else. Arno, who was at the controls, found the 21st Marine Regiment's headquarters without hesitation. Save for the flags and signs, it was, in almost every respect, a duplicate of the 25th Battle Group's.

Someone from the gate must have called ahead, however. Shortly after we parked on the parade square, along with dozens of civilian and Marine Corps ground cars, a captain in black garrison uniform came through the HQ building's main doors and waited for us to walk across the street. As we approached, he came to attention and saluted.

"Commissioner Morrow, I'm Victor Garov, the regimental adjutant. Welcome to the 21st. If you'll follow me, I will take you to Colonel Freijs' office."

With that, he turned on his heels and led us through a lobby very much like the 25th's except more heavily decorated with various souvenirs from long ago campaigns on distant worlds both in display cabinets and hanging from the walls. Here too, a grand, sweeping staircase ran up to the second and third stories. But instead of a simple Navy crest on the wall, the regiment's colors, heavily embroidered with battle honors, were arrayed in a glass cabinet on the staircase's first landing, where everyone entering the building could see them.

I wasn't surprised when the adjutant led us down the first floor's left-hand corridor, but the decor was much less ostentatious and more functional. Yes, paintings and other memorabilia hung on the walls. Still, there was no carpet, the doors weren't of a mahogany-colored wood, and the office signs were simple white rectangles bordered in the regiment's colors — blue, gold, and silver — with the occupant's title in the center.

Freijs' office also sat at the end of the corridor but didn't occupy the entire width of the floor. Nor did it boast a large antechamber where visitors could kick their heels while sipping indifferent coffee and wondering why a military headquarters had a patio just outside the commander's office. The corridor ended at a window overlooking the building's side, with Freijs' office to the right and the adjutant's office next door, and both the regimental deputy commander and sergeant major's offices across from them. Evidently, a rear admiral was entitled to more grandiose surroundings than a mere colonel of Marines.

Garov ushered us through the open door and announced, "Assistant Commissioner Morrow and Chief Inspector Galdi, sir."

Freijs, who'd been sitting behind his desk, stood and came around it, smiling, hand outstretched. As we were both of the same equivalent rank and wore the same rank insignia, I could skip the niceties and greet him as an equal instead of making my manners as I did with Meir.

"Commissioner, welcome to the 21st Marines." We shook. Then he turned to Arno and offered his hand. "You as well, Chief Inspector Galdi."

"Sir."

The fact he treated my winger with respect raised my estimation of him by a few degrees. But then, Marine colonels didn't reach this point in their careers without learning that treating those more junior in rank with respect reflected on their own characters.

"Please," he gestured at the small conference table to one side of the room, "take off your coats and sit while I pour the coffee. What do you take in it, Commissioner?"

"Nothing. I like it black as my soul."

My quip earned me a brief chuckle from Freijs, who glanced at Arno. "And you?"

"Same as the Chief, sir."

Freijs walked over to a sideboard where a small silver urn sat silently and drew three cups, serving us first, then himself, before sitting at the head of the table.

"Thank you for coming." He seemed relaxed, friendly, a marked contrast to Admiral Meir. "I understand the Navy called in legal counsel."

I took a sip of what turned out to be a rich, flavorful brew, then nodded. "At the AJAG's suggestion, Admiral Meir wants a legal officer present during our interviews, and the one appointed by the AJAG is a Lieutenant Commander Katy Racitina."

A grimace briefly crossed Freijs' face. "That's what Meir told me. I know Katy. She's smart, capable, and has helped several of my Marines. But she's a reservist, and it's no secret her firm handles cases involving alleged underworld figures. The answers Dagon Morozov and his troopers will give in response to your questions are classified above top secret. As are the recordings I'll give you in a moment."

"And you're wondering how I'll handle this."

He nodded.

"Yes. I'm of two minds about the idea our people should have legal counsel during interviews. On the one hand, they did nothing wrong and need not fear you. Yet on the other, your lot has a reputation for being the Constabulary's fiercest inquisitors, and facing you doesn't sit well with many folks. They can't understand why this isn't being investigated by the military police."

Before I could open my mouth, he raised a hand. "I do understand you're our internal affairs division as designated by Grand Admiral Kowalski last century when she created the Constabulary, and many do so as well, Dagon included. But the fact remains you're not Fleet, let alone Marine Corps. We are tribal about our uniform colors. Black, blue, and green are three shades of the same clan. Gray belongs to a different one, even though we share a common tribal DNA."

"Ultimately, the decision doesn't rest with me because of the nature of what might transpire. I fired a message up my chain of command. They'll contact Fleet HQ so your superiors can rule on the matter. Until I receive a reply, Commander Racitina will not sit in on any interviews. I specifically barred her from speaking with anyone involved until this is sorted."

An eyebrow crept up Freijs' forehead. "Barred? You can do that?"

"Yes. And if she transgresses, I will charge her with perverting the course of justice, which could well end her legal career."

"You don't mess around, do you, Commissioner?"

"I prefer absolute clarity. It reduces the chance of errors that might derail an investigation. Our credibility depends entirely on achieving unimpeachable results that stand up to any level of scrutiny."

Freijs gave me a calculating look. "And do you always obtain those results?"

"No." I shook my head. "Not always, but mostly. By the time we're called in, the behavior has been going on for a while, leaving us with plenty of evidence. If that proves enough, we make the arrest. When we can't prove guilt beyond a doubt, we turn the matter over to the chain of command, and they decide on the course of action. Usually, when it involves a Constabulary member, and we know he or she is guilty but can't prove it to the satisfaction of a federal judge, the chain of command pressures said member to retire or resign."

"And in this case?" Freijs took another sip of coffee while watching me.

"I collect evidence, analyze it, present my conclusions to my superiors and go home. We won't be making arrests or laying charges here, Colonel. Nor will I be sharing my findings with you, Admiral Meir, or anyone else unless I'm entirely satisfied that my superiors won't challenge them."

To my surprise, he grinned at me.

"Pretty much what I expected. My colleague in Army green across the way is the only one enjoying life right now because he's not involved in any way or fashion. Makes me want to reconsider my career plans. There are worse options than transferring to the Army for a last tour of command on one's homeworld before hanging up the uniform." He let out a heartfelt sigh. "Not that I have the option. Okay, Commissioner. Message heard and understood. You're in charge. Admiral Meir notwithstanding, you'll do as you see fit, and that's that."

"Got it in one, Colonel. Now, about the data from Major Morozov and his squadron?"

"You've brought an appropriately rated container?"

Arno pulled ours from his tunic pocket and held it up. "This is a Constabulary issue top secret carrier, what we call a zap box, sir. If anyone attempts to open it without the correct code, the data wafer within will be carbonized instantly."

"Like ours, then." Freijs pulled a similar-sized case from his pocket and placed it on the table, then reached back in and produced a small pad. "I'll need your retinal print on the receipt for the data wafer, Commissioner. You know how it works. Once you take custody, you're responsible for its security and proper disposal."

Arno opened our case and turned it toward Freijs, who opened his and withdrew a chip the size of my thumbnail. The actual data storage element was a tiny speck within the metal and plastic envelope, but human fingers needed something they could handle. Freijs carefully placed the wafer into our container, then handed me the pad.

"If you would, Commissioner."

While Arno secured the case, I signed the receipt with a retinal scan, thereby taking full responsibility for what we'd been given. Then, after returning the pad, I emptied my cup.

"Thank you for your cooperation, Colonel, and for this excellent coffee."

"I'm eager to see these allegations disproved, and Senator Olrik's lies exposed. My Marines did nothing wrong. I can guarantee you they followed the applicable rules of engagement to the letter, which we've given you along with the records. The senator, on the other hand, I'm not so sure of, but I don't suppose you'd investigate him for corruption."

I shook my head. "Not without the Speaker of the Senate calling us in. Or Olrik would have to be caught red-handed committing a criminal act."

"Shame. He's an embarrassment to Novaya Sibir and now an enemy to the honorable men and women serving in the Armed Forces."

Practiced anti-corruption investigators that we were, Arno and I showed no reaction to Freijs' inflammatory comment. Instead, we stood by common accord, Arno pocketing the zap box.

"We'll no doubt speak again in the coming days, Colonel. Once we've digested the records, we'll be setting up an interview schedule. Thanks again for your cooperation and hospitality."

Freijs stood as well. "I'm merely doing my duty."

He extended his hand, and we shook. Then, we donned our overcoats and followed the adjutant back to the main entrance. Within minutes, we were past the base's security barriers and out in the snow-covered countryside surrounding Yekaterinburg.

"Our good colonel certain isn't shy with his opinions," Arno finally said, breaking the silence.

"No. And it makes me wonder why. Senior officers are usually rather circumspect around us. But he was more hospitable than Admiral Meir, for what it's worth."

"Probably not much."

I glanced at Arno and smiled. "Cynic."

"I prefer the term realist, Chief."

When we returned to the office, Destine and the two sergeants were staring at workstation displays in silence while a newly liberated coffee maker was humming away happily on a sideboard.

Arno immediately went to the safe in my office and secured the data case alongside Sergeant Cincunegui's container with the copies of *Chinggis'* logs.

Destine pushed away from her workstation and stretched. "How were the Marines, sir?"

"Friendly. From where did the coffee machine come?"

"The 47th's canteen, a spare we borrowed for the duration."

I gave her an amused look. "Really? When's the last time anyone trusted us with their gear?"

"Since we didn't come here to dig up their dirty laundry, they're rather friendlier than you might expect."

Arno, who'd re-entered the bullpen, let out a skeptical grunt. "Or they have a guilty conscience, and the good cheer is a way of hiding misdeeds."

Destine chuckled. "Ouch. Did you get up on the cynical side of the bed this morning, Chief Inspector?"

Before the two of them could enter into a verbal sparring match, I raised a hand. "Let's move on from the coffee maker. Did you make any discoveries in the newsnet's raw imaging so far?"

"Yes, sir," Cincunegui said without turning around. "One of the data points we look at is the spectral class of the sun illuminating scenes in visual recordings and compare it to the expected spectral class of the target planet's sun. A first-pass analysis shows a slight discrepancy when comparing the visuals to what I would see if they were lit by Torga's sun.

"Both are G-type main-sequence stars, but there are subtle differences which I cannot as yet explain. Mind you, our data on Torga could be lacking — after all, it's in the Zone — so it may be perfectly innocuous. Other than that, nothing yet. However,

I would like to compare these with the free trader's logs, even though they won't carry the same evidentiary weight as *Chinggis'* records, and the newsnet claims what they gave us are direct copies."

"He should land on Novaya Sibir any day unless he's on the run from someone or something more threatening than the Commonwealth Constabulary."

"Let's hope."

Destine raised a finger to attract my attention.

"Before I forget, you received an encrypted message from Fleet HQ. May I assume it's from Admiral Talyn? The message is in your private queue."

"You may because she's the only one on Caledonia with whom I'm corresponding these days."

And with that, I headed for my office, anxious to read what the redoubtable head of Naval Intelligence's Special Operations Division wanted to tell me.

— Seventeen —

I wasn't sure what I was hoping for as I closed my office door and sat behind the desk. A single touch pulled up my message queue, which contained precisely one item marked sent by Armed Forces Headquarters, Caledonia. It demanded my personal cipher and gave me three chances at decryption, after which it would self-destruct and place a tracer on this node.

I've always been good with codes, passwords, and other forms of decryption and entered the sequence Admiral Talyn gave me as my personal identifier. The words that filled my desk display vanished in a fraction of a second, replaced by a single sentence.

Read her in, signed HT.

No explanation, no hello, no acknowledgment of my mission. Nothing else. Yet the origin tag was undeniably Admiral Talyn's, as were the initials. Those three words 'read her in' were an order that transcended service and uniform color, one I couldn't disobey. We'd made a pact years ago, one which pledged close cooperation between Naval Intelligence's Special Operations Division and the Professional Compliance Bureau to help prevent a third migration war.

I couldn't say how much my boss, Assistant Chief Constable Sorjonen, knew about this pact. But I somehow figured he, and his superior, Deputy Chief Constable Hammett, the Conscience of the Constabulary, were part of the deal between the Fleet and the Constabulary to prevent a war that could destroy humanity across the stars.

Read her in. Did that mean I should allow Racitina to witness every interview? Or did Talyn expect me to share more, perhaps even everything, with her? I knew she didn't trust anyone entirely other than her long-time partner and now husband, Zack Decker. But those she trusted, at least in part, were either on the Fleet's side or working toward the same goals. So, where did Racitina fit in that narrow definition?

I would likely never find out short of asking Hera Talyn in person. And yes, I remembered she'd used me before. Spymasters did that, even if they were friends of sorts, or in our case, more like trusted allies who helped each other whenever possible.

Her sending a company from the 1st Special Forces Regiment to Mission Colony when I was in trouble ended up saving my life, which created an indelible debt of honor.

Arno must have seen my thoughtful expression through the open door because he stuck his head in and asked, "So what does the Ace of Spies say?"

"You mean the Spymaster General. She hasn't been acing it out in the field for a few years. Her answer was typically brief and came with no explanations. She said, and I quote, read her in. Which means Lieutenant Commander Racitina gets to sit beside witnesses during our interviews after I make sure she understands that talking out of school will result in a long, painful sojourn in a military prison colony on Parth."

Arno let out a thoughtful grunt as he frowned. "And no explanation why."

"No, but that's not unusual. Remember Curtis Delgado?"

"Sure. He's the officer commanding Ghost Squadron's Erinye Company, who we met on Mission Colony, right?"

"That's him. He told me they receive little by way of explanation when Naval Intelligence assigns a mission. Still, I'll wait until we receive official confirmation from Wyvern before speaking with Racitina."

"Good call, Chief."

The rest of the day went by slowly — for me. I was loath to hover around my team as they screened recordings while the forensic AI searched for even a single pixel out of place. Arno had joined Destine in researching every potential discrepancy Cincunegui and Esadze picked up. However, by the time sixteen hundred hours rolled around and I called it for the day, they were still working on what Carla Hautcoeur gave me.

The entire team, Arno included, hit the hotel fitness center before the evening meal, then enjoyed a drink at the bar as a team and a quiet meal in the restaurant. Even though my day wasn't particularly strenuous, I still turned out the lights before twenty-two hundred and fell into a dreamless sleep.

Shortly after I sat behind my desk the following day, wondering how I'd keep busy while the others waded through another day of data analysis, my communicator lit. It was the 47th Constabulary Group's operations officer, a sad-looking chief inspector in his fifties whom I'd met on the first day when I did my rounds to exchange a few words with anyone who I might call on for assistance.

"Morrow."

"Hesperel here, Commissioner. You asked to be notified when the free trader *Prospero* shows up."

"Indeed."

"She just entered orbit and is awaiting instructions from Novaya Sibir Traffic Control, who, in turn, are waiting for instructions from us since I let them know it was a ship of interest for the Constabulary. The crew manifest lists one name, Toshiro Rahal, as you expected. What should I tell them?"

"They should make sure *Prospero* lands at a secure docking station on the commercial end of Yekaterinburg spaceport. I don't want Captain Rahal to disembark or speak with anyone until my team and I get there. If he tries, we need to know right away. Rahal has evidence I want, and I can't afford to risk that it becomes even more contaminated, or worse, goes walkabout and ends up in the wrong hands."

"Will do. And I'll contact the Police Service, so they assign an officer to stand guard on *Prospero* until your arrival."

"Excellent, thank you, Chief Inspector."

He gave me a wan smile. "We aim to please all our visitors, sir. Is there anything else operations can do for you?"

Considering the emphasis Hesperel placed on the word 'all' while smiling, a sense of humor indeed hid beneath the usually mournful expression.

"No."

"I'll advise you when *Prospero* lands. Operations, out."

When I looked up, I saw Arno leaning against the door jamb. He'd obviously heard the entire conversation because he asked, "Am I right in assuming we'll pay Captain Rahal a visit as a group?"

"Might as well."

"I'll make sure our data sleuths can wrap current operations up or suspend them in the next hour and be ready."

In the end, it was almost two hours before the spaceport called operations to say *Prospero* was on the ground and had been for over forty-five minutes, but that Captain Rahal, in keeping with his instructions, remained aboard pending our arrival.

We piled into our car a few minutes later, with Sergeant Esadze at the controls, and headed south after navigating through downtown Yekaterinburg and over the same bridge we'd taken the day of our arrival. The cargo terminal sat at the western end of the tarmac, opposite the sprawling passenger facility, and seemed busy enough to our untrained eyes.

At the security gate, we presented our credentials, and, thanks to Chief Inspector Hesperel warning spaceport security, they passed us through with directions to *Prospero*'s berth. There, we found a Siberiak police officer standing guard outside the closed personnel entrance set into the much larger cargo doors.

Like every other berth in this part of the spaceport, *Prospero*'s was part dock, part hangar, and part warehouse. The structure could shelter small starships and shuttles of all sizes from Siberiak blizzards while keeping them isolated until the customs and excise agents cleared their cargoes. Anyone trying to evade the protocols would be spotted by the commercial apron control system and apprehended. This was the only way out. Or so the spaceport claimed.

Esadze pulled our car off the ring road and onto the berth's small plaza where, in normal times, ground trucks would pick up the containers disgorged by whatever brought them down from orbit. We climbed out, and when the police officer saw the rank insignia on my coat, he snapped to attention and saluted.

"*Ryadovoy* Petrov, Commissioner," he said in a stilted tone, identifying himself as a regular patrolman, the equivalent of a basic constable.

I returned the compliment. "At ease, *Ryadovoy*. Has anyone entered or left this berth since you arrived?"

"No, Commissioner."

"How long have you stood guard here?"

"Thirty minutes."

I repressed a grimace. We were warned about *Prospero*'s arrival forty-five minutes late, and it took us another twenty minutes to reach the spaceport. That meant the berth wasn't watched by anything other than the spaceport security AI for over half an hour, and artificial intelligences could be fooled, sometimes by even the least intelligent humans.

"No reports of unusual activities?"

"No, Commissioner."

I could see Petrov's vocabulary wasn't particularly extensive and wondered whether his field of vision, physical and moral, was equally limited. Call it professional deformation. After my long years in the PCB, evaluating a cop's honesty and integrity on first contact was reflexive. Unfair? Yes. But sometimes, first impressions were on target.

"Could you ask spaceport security to unlock the berth's entrance?"

He bowed his head stiffly. "At once, Commissioner."

After a quick exchange via radio, Petrov turned toward the personnel entrance and touched its control panel. The door slid aside with a tired groan.

"You and your party are free to enter, Commissioner. I will stay here as per my orders."

We stepped into a sizeable transfer warehouse which wasn't much warmer than the outside — our breaths still generated brief clouds — but it was brightly lit and empty. Another door, like the one we'd just passed through, led to the berth itself at the far end. As we crossed the fifty or so meters of concrete floor, the sound of our boot heels echoed off the slick walls.

The far door opened at Destine's touch, and we found ourselves in a half-covered enclosure filled by *Prospero*'s bulk. The sloop-sized starship sat on thick landing struts, like a giant, albeit quiescent, beetle, while a faint ozone tang from her thrusters still hung in the air even more than an hour after landing. Her hull bore evidence of long service and the wear and tear from multiple atmospheric re-entries.

Our limited vantage point at the foot of the open belly ramp didn't allow us to see much evidence of armament, but it was there, somewhere, beneath protective blisters. No starship ventured to the Rim Sector's outer edges, much less into the Protectorate Zone if it couldn't outgun what it couldn't outrun.

"Big bugger for a single-hander," Cincunegui remarked to no one in particular.

"Automation is cheaper than paying and feeding a crew, never mind running environmental systems for a bunch of smelly spacers," Arno replied. "If you don't mind solitude and can turn your hand at any job aboard, a single-hander is just the thing. What now, Chief? We simply go up the ramp and knock at the outer airlock?"

"Rahal is expecting us, so yes."

We trudged up the incline, but my repeated attempts at getting Rahal's attention via the call panel set into the airlock failed.

I felt my forehead knit into a frown. "Strange. If he left the ship, spaceport security would notice and warn the 47th's operations center or, at the very least, the officer standing guard outside, no?"

Arno gave me a strange look. "You'd think he would at least see that his ship's AI greets us if he's taking a nap or in the heads."

"Should I search for the emergency release, sir?" Destine asked.

"The what now, Warrant?" Cincunegui asked.

"Starship airlocks are equipped with mechanical releases hidden behind panels accessible to those who know how and where they should look, for cases like this when no one aboard is responding. They can be overridden, of course, and the Navy does it routinely, as do the bad guys, but *Prospero* is a simple trader, and with the ramp up, this airlock is inaccessible anyway."

"I see. But don't we need a warrant or probable cause to board without permission? Pardon the questions, but Alina and I aren't familiar with this sort of thing."

I nodded once.

"Yes, usually we do. But since we're expected, and yet, no one is responding, I'm making the decision to board because Captain Rahal is a major witness in a federal investigation. If he objects, he can lodge a complaint with the Novaya Sibir National Police Force, and we'll take it from there. Find the release, Destine."

She, like me, was trained to the basic Special Forces operator standard when we were assigned as Constabulary liaison, and boarding ships was part of the syllabus. It, therefore, didn't take her long to find the panel hiding the emergency release mechanism. Moments later, we heard an audible click, and Destine pulled the outer airlock door to one side. As I'd hoped, the inner door stood open, and we entered the ship, Destine in the lead, her parka zipped open so she could access her sidearm if needed.

"Captain Rahal? This is Assistant Commissioner Morrow of the Commonwealth Constabulary. I head the investigation into the allegations of war crimes on Torga. You're here at my behest."

My words echoed down the main corridor, but beyond the soft hum of the ship's environmental systems, we heard nary a sound.

"Let's see if we can find the bridge, Destine."

"Yes, sir. It should be pretty much dead center."

As we cautiously made our way forward, I had the eerie sensation this was a ghost ship, one devoid of life until we entered. I repeated my call twice more in case Rahal was hard of hearing or blind drunk but to no avail. We eventually passed a combination galley and saloon along with several cabins, one of which bore a sign marked Captain, proving *Prospero* could carry more crew or passengers. Beyond them was an open door through which I saw a helm console with a single chair facing a large, albeit currently black, primary display.

Destine took one step through, then came to a sudden halt. She cursed beneath her breath before saying, "I found Toshiro Rahal, sir, and it looks like he won't be testifying now or ever again."

— Eighteen —

Destine stepped aside to let me enter and pointed toward the port side. It was Toshiro Rahal, without a doubt. He looked precisely like the images we'd obtained, although not nearly as lively. He lay on his back, legs straight, arms by his side. His eyes were wide open, and I could immediately see there was no life in them. I'd come across enough dead bodies in my time to know Captain Rahal was sailing into the Infinite Void on a one-way trip.

"Who has a service issue sensor?"

My four team members responded at once, with Destine producing hers first. I pointed at Rahal. "Scan him to confirm."

"Sir." She stepped over to the body and stared intently at the sensor's screen. "Dead, but judging by the body's temperature, it hasn't been for long. No visible signs of what killed him."

I retrieved my communicator and asked for a link to the 47th Group's Operations Center. Within moments, the by now familiar voice of Chief Inspector Hesperel came through the speaker.

"What can I do for you, Commissioner?"

"We're aboard *Prospero* and found Captain Toshiro Rahal on the deck of his bridge with vital signs absent. No indications as to the cause. Since he's one of my witnesses and appears to have died shortly after landing, I want to treat his death as suspicious until proved otherwise. I don't know what the protocol is here on Novaya Sibir between the Constabulary and the National Police Service about overlapping areas of jurisdiction, but I am claiming a direct interest in any investigation on Rahal's demise because of his involvement in a major federal case."

"Understood, sir. Do you intend to investigate personally alongside the Police Service people?"

I thought about it for a moment. This wouldn't be the first time I took charge of a murder case — if Rahal didn't die of natural causes — during a professional compliance investigation, but there was no reason I should do so now. The Novaya Sibir National Police could deploy the necessary resources, as could the 47th.

"No. But I want it conducted jointly with Constabulary investigators. If I need to speak with

Chief Superintendent Skou on the matter, I can do that at once. A joint team must take this on from the outset, though I don't mind if the National Police handle forensics and the postmortem."

"Not a problem, Commissioner. There are protocols in place for joint operations. If you could secure the scene and wait for the investigators, things will be easier. I'll warn the super, set our murder squad into motion, and speak with the Yekaterinburg Police CID. Give it, say, forty-five to sixty minutes."

"Thank you, Chief Inspector. That was it."

"Operations, out."

Arno stepped onto the bridge and studied Rahal's body. "There goes the most important, perhaps the only, prosecution witness. I wonder if that's convenient for anyone. How about you, Chief?"

"The thought occurred to me."

"What next?"

"We treat this as a crime scene, meaning Destine scans the bridge for what it's worth, and we pull back to minimize contamination." I turned my eyes on Cincunegui. "Find the core, Sergeant, and see if you can drain *Prospero*'s data banks without us suffering from the forensic investigators' ire."

"And if I can't?"

"Then we wait. Rahal's death takes precedence over anything else."

In the end, the joint investigative team didn't show up until almost ninety minutes after my conversation with Chief Inspector Hesperel. But judging by the almost palpable tension between the Police Service *Kapitan* and the Constabulary Chief Inspector — who were of equivalent rank — I could well imagine the heated debate about who took the lead during their ride from Yekaterinburg.

After introducing themselves, *Kapitan* Taina Kutuzov for the National Police and Chief Inspector Yaromir Rolfsson for our lot, I gathered the three teams, mine and both of theirs, in the saloon while the crime scene investigators processed the body and the bridge compartment.

"I'm Assistant Commissioner Caelin Morrow, head of the Commonwealth Constabulary's Anti-Corruption Unit Twelve, and senior investigative officer into the war crimes allegations against the 212th Pathfinder Squadron and the Commonwealth Starship *Chinggis*. The decedent, next door on the ship's bridge, was a primary witness in my case, which makes his death suspicious until proved otherwise. I will not oversee the inquiry into his death because that isn't my brief. But you will report any and all developments, no matter how insignificant, to me at least once a day because they may well be connected with my primary investigation. Is that understood?"

I speared Kutuzov and Rolfsson with what I hoped was a suitably icy gaze and each, in turn, nodded, then I let my eyes meet those of their team members. Kutuzov was accompanied by a *starshina* and a *starshiy serzhant*, senior non-commissioned detectives, while Rolfsson's squad comprised two Constabulary sergeants first class, veteran detectives by their demeanor and bland expressions. They wore sober civilian attire, which wouldn't be out of place in the office towers of downtown Yekaterinburg's financial district.

"My people will shortly download a copy of this ship's entire computer core because it's evidence in my investigation. If you find any physical evidence when you search the ship, I want to know about it at once. Now I'm sure you'll need statements from my team and me, and we can do that while CSI clears the scene. I'll go first."

We made it back to the federal building in time for lunch, satisfied that the joint investigation would proceed as I wanted. Of course, the Constabulary half of it wouldn't dare disappoint a high-profile anti-corruption unit commander. And the Police Service half? Let's just say I figured my meeting with General Elin and President Antonovich made the rounds at the Yekaterinburg precinct.

As I expected, the calls from various interested parties came in one after the other in the following two hours. First was Chief Superintendent Skou, who wanted to assure me his detectives would do their utmost. The second call was, not surprisingly, from General Elin with the same assurances, though I could somehow tell he wanted to know how this would affect my investigation. Thankfully, he didn't ask. Admiral Meir, on the other hand, wasn't so circumspect.

"And what does losing your primary witness mean for the case, Commissioner?"

"Nothing at this point. Should the matter ever come before a court of law, then perhaps there could be issues. And that's everything I can say, Admiral."

"I understand you barred Commander Racitina from even speaking with the Fleet personnel touched by these allegations when I specifically told you she was to counsel witnesses. Why?"

"Neither you nor I possess the authority to allow an outsider during interviews that will necessarily deal with top secret operational data, and no, I can't read Commander Racitina in without orders from my chain of command, who will obtain it from yours. I've asked for a ruling but didn't hear back yet. Considering the sensitivity of the case, I'm sure you'll be notified by your chain of command as well. And as for overriding your orders, I am fully empowered to do so if I think they might interfere with my case. If you need confirmation, please ask Commander Racitina, who's likely read the relevant section in the Armed Forces Regulations and Orders by now. Was there anything else?"

Meir glowered at me for a few seconds. "No. But this discussion isn't over."

My office display went dark as she cut the link without a single word of goodbye. There was a prima donna in every investigation. This time that irritant wore two stars on her collar, which made things just a bit easier than if she were a senior civilian official or, worse yet, a zaibatsu executive with a sense of entitlement ten parsecs wide. Armed Forces officers could be controlled — with effort. Mercifully, Colonel Freijs didn't add his voice to the chorus.

I felt relief when my next caller turned out to be Chief Inspector Yaromir Rolfsson. At least he had the sense to keep the conversation within the limits I wanted.

"The Police Service prioritized Toshiro Rahal's postmortem, Commissioner. I just received the results. He died from cardiac arrest."

I felt my lips curl up in a faintly sardonic smile. "Like everyone does."

"True. But he was healthy for a man who spent his life in space, heart included. Fortunately, the medical examiner is nobody's fool. He's dealt with enough Siberiak mobster assassinations to look for signs a regular pathologist might miss."

"Perimortem puncture marks."

Rolfsson tapped the side of his nose with an extended index finger.

"Just so. The ME figures a fast-acting poison with an equally short half-life. No traces left by the time he autopsied, but one thing is certain. Rahal passed away soon after landing, say, forty-five minutes before you found him."

"And a quarter of an hour before the Police Service sentry showed up to guard the landing berth's door. Did spaceport security pick up any activity in the area?"

"That's what we're looking for right now. *Kapitan* Kutuzov is collecting the security surveillance records from the time *Prospero* touched down to the moment we showed up on the scene." Rolfsson hesitated for a moment. "Just between us, there's enough funny business at the spaceport that I wouldn't put my hopes in a straightforward answer."

"Corruption?"

He nodded. "Like everywhere else in the Commonwealth, if not a touch worse. Organized crime has many collaborators with security clearances who make sure certain shipments go through without question, and others are held up. Or certain individuals slip past security checks in both directions. But since it's not under federal jurisdiction, the only thing we can do is feed whatever intelligence we pick up to our counterparts in the Police Service."

"And how clean are they?"

Another moment of hesitation. "No better and no worse than any other star system law enforcement agency I've worked with. They could probably use a larger and more motivated internal affairs branch, but then, not counting the Constabulary, who couldn't?"

"Can I trust Kutuzov?"

Rolfsson nodded. "She's one of the good guys. So are her sergeants. Bent cops in the Police Service are concentrated in the usual branches — vice, narcotics, smuggling, human trafficking — where there's more money floating around than common sense."

I gave him a quick smile. "That's been my experience as well. But here's a question for you. Were the doer or doers hoping we'd think Rahal suffered from a natural cardiac event that killed him, or did they carry out the assassination knowing we'd figure out right away it was a hit?"

Rolfsson didn't even hesitate. "The latter. They either wanted us to know or didn't care."

"What does that tell you?"

He shrugged. "Professionals. Either the Siberiak mafia or considering your investigation…"

Rolfsson left the thought hanging between us, but I knew precisely what he meant, and it was a possibility that already occurred to me, even though I wouldn't voice it until more evidence came to light. In death, Toshiro Rahal, master of the free trader *Prospero*, muddied the waters even further, leaving us with the question of *cui bono*. To whom did his demise profit the most?

— Nineteen —

"You're thinking dark thoughts, Chief. I can always tell." Arno, who'd been listening in on my calls from his vantage point just outside my open office door, was studying me with a knowing gaze.

"Do you figure someone is sending us a message?"

"If so, what is it? Good luck proving the allegations now that the sole eyewitness is gone? Or is it good luck exonerating the Marines now that reasonable people might suspect they murdered the sole eyewitness to cover their crimes?"

"How about, careful where you dig? You might be next?"

Arno cocked an amused eyebrow at me. "Are you nervous in the Service, Chief?"

"Last time we stumbled across a body during an investigation, I almost made a one-way trip back to the planet of my birth for a quiet execution by the secret police. Probably after digging my own grave."

"True. But around here, getting shot by a railgun sniper from three kilometers isn't exactly an option."

I gave him a wan smile.

"No, although a needler at two paces in the underground city is. But I digress. If anything suspicious happens to us, Assistant Chief Constable Sorjonen will swoop in like an avenging angel and take Novaya Sibir apart. I daresay that should figure prominently in the mind of anyone thinking about derailing our inquiry. We're just cogs in the anti-corruption machine. There's plenty more where we come from."

Arno made a face. "Still, Rahal's death proves there's more going on than we suspect."

He was right, of course, as always. If events were unfolding normally, I'd be interviewing Toshiro Rahal in this very office. Yet instead, we found him dead six hours ago on the bridge of his own ship, murdered by a professional, one whose movements the joint team still couldn't track by the time we called it a day. Rolfsson and Kutuzov drew a blank with the spaceport security surveillance network, and they were now doing the same as us, analyzing the records for discrepancies that might indicate manipulation. They were also interviewing anyone who was near *Prospero*'s berth between the moment she landed and our arrival.

Still, the killer might have been aboard the ship before she landed — CSI picked up relatively recent traces of several dozen humans. But if not, it would be someone Rahal either knew or trusted. Free traders who do business on sketchy worlds beyond the Commonwealth don't live long if their survival instincts aren't finely honed. A search of the ship, both physically and with high-powered sensors, didn't reveal anyone hiding in a secret compartment, waiting for the police to leave before escaping.

I wrote a report on the day's events for ACC Sorjonen and Admiral Talyn and saw it off before locking my office and heading to the hotel, where I spent an hour exercising away the tensions of the day.

When I entered the bar afterward for my predinner drink, the bartender caught my eye and pointed at the bottle of Siberiak Blue Gin, a delightful discovery I'd made my first night here. I smiled and nodded once, then headed for my usual table in the corner from which I could see the entire room as well as the Yekaterinburg skyline silhouetted by a setting sun that lit the distant horizon on fire.

I sensed someone approach me and, expecting either the bartender or Arno, I turned back toward the room, ready with a welcoming expression. What I saw instead was a tall, squarely built man wearing an expensive, probably hand-tailored business suit in dark gray. He had a rough-hewn face with prominent cheekbones, hooded, deep blue eyes, and blond hair cut so short I could see the pink scalp beneath. He held my gin and tonic in one hand and a glass of dark ale in the other.

"Assistant Commissioner Morrow." His voice was deep, gravelly, as if coming from the darkest recesses of Novaya Sibir's continental crust, and he had a slight accent as if Anglic wasn't his primary language. I got the impression he was a powerful man, one used to getting his way. "My apologies for intruding. I am Sergei Ustinov and appropriated the bartender's duties."

He placed my glass on the table with care, then met my eyes without unease or shyness. "May I join you for a few moments?"

I gestured at the chair across from me, intrigued. "Since you brought my drink, it's the least I can do."

"Thank you for your courtesy, Commissioner." He sat and raised his glass. "*Za Zdarovje.*"

I imitated him, and we each took a sip, after which I raised my glass and said, "*Za Vstrechu.*"

A big smile split Ustinov's angular face. "You've studied the customs of my homeworld. How truly courteous."

I returned his smile with a sly one of my own because I was beginning to suspect who, or rather what, Ustinov was, and my curiosity grew by leaps and bounds.

"What can I do for you, Gospodin Ustinov?"

"First, let me tell you a bit more about myself, if I may?" I inclined my head by way of assent. "I am the chief executive officer of Taiga Import-Export Corporation, and because of that, I enjoy connections in every part of the Novaya Sibir commercial, financial, and industrial community. Of course, like most in my position, I'm also acquainted with people at every level of government. I mention this not to boast, you understand, but so you can appreciate what I am about to say."

He paused and studied me with his intense gaze.

"Understood."

"Good. Now, as you might expect, I know why you're here. Everyone does. I'm also aware of who Toshiro Rahal was, the fact a person or persons unknown murdered him shortly after his ship landed at the Yekaterinburg spaceport this morning, and of his importance to your inquiry. In the import-export business, word can travel far and fast."

"No doubt." I also knew other businesses, many of them less salubrious than others, where word got around quickly on some issues but kept a neutral expression on my face.

Ustinov took another sip of ale, then placed his glass on the table.

"Here is my advice to you, Commissioner. Forget about ever finding Rahal's killer or killers. They are professionals who can slip through any net, no matter how tight, and slipped through it, they did. Find out what really happened on Torga and make sure justice is done. But keep in mind that things are not as they seem, and events may or may not have happened. Finally, take care who you trust. The stakes could be high enough that a few people would do anything to keep you from the truth while there could be friends you're ignoring."

He took another sip, then stood. "Enjoy the rest of your evening, Commissioner."

I watched him walk away and enter one of the smaller side rooms, wondering what Ustinov's little spiel meant. By now, I was reasonably sure he wasn't just another corporate CEO. Organized crime groups loved import-export companies, especially those with their own shipping subsidiaries. I'd check with Skou's OCG section in the morning, but my instincts were rarely wrong. Sergei Ustinov must be a senior member in one of the Novaya Sibir mafia organizations, and if so, he was undoubtedly a krestniy otets, a boss of bosses.

Did this mean he was involved in Rahal's murder? And if so, why would he think the death of the sole eyewitness might stymie my investigation? Assuming, of course, he wanted the allegations disproved. I'd always counted on the records rather than Rahal's testimony as my principal source of evidence. The fact he'd gone to the newsnets with his story rather than the authorities spoke volumes.

Arno joined me a few minutes later, and I recounted the strange conversation with Ustinov verbatim. When I was done, he scratched his beard for a few seconds, then took a healthy sip of the stout that was fast becoming his favorite tipple on Novaya Sibir.

"If there's the slightest suspicion this Ustinov fellow might be connected with OCG, you'll need to complete a contact report and fire it off to ACC Sorjonen in the morning, Chief."

I made a grimace. "Don't I know it? I can see the story now — the head of AC-12 was approached by a suspected krestniy otets in a hotel bar. They had a drink together. No one overheard their conversation. It's a wonderful tidbit for the defense if ever the war crimes allegations go to court, whatever side that defense may be on."

"Which might be the point or at least one of them. Tell me you paid for your drink."

"Oh, fiddlesticks." I signaled the bartender, who came over with a solicitous expression on his face.

"Yes, Commissioner?"

"Gospodin Ustinov delivered my drink, but you put it on my tab, right?"

He nodded. "I indeed charged it to your room. Would you like another one?"

"Sure. And thanks." When he was out of earshot, I gave Arno a tired look. "Thank the Almighty for small mercies. At least Ustinov wasn't trying to make it look like I was taking a freebie from a mafioso. If he is one."

"Your gut instinct is better than most people's certainty, Chief. If your figure he's mobbed-up, then something isn't right about the man. Unless he's one of Admiral Talyn's lot. She uses import-export businesses as a cover for her agents."

"No." I shook my head. "I'm sure he wasn't Fleet, mainly because I met his sort many times during my career, and so did you. That's one reason why both of us are working anti-corruption, Arno. We can sniff them out when most police officers remain clueless."

He took another gulp of his stout. "Unless you want to chew on this new development all evening, perhaps we should drink up and head for supper. Destine and the sergeants are off on their own quest, and I could use an early night with a book and a brandy in my suite. Murders don't get any easier with age."

"Ditto."

The next morning, after a quick breakfast in the cafeteria with my team, I made directly for Chief Superintendent Skou's office to take care of the formalities. With the door wide open, I could see he was alone, and I rapped my knuckles on the jamb.

"May I interrupt you for a moment?"

Skou climbed to his feet. "Certainly, Commissioner. Can I offer you a coffee or tea?"

"I've just come from the cafeteria, so my blood caffeine levels are adequate, but thank you. There's something we should discuss before the day gets any older." I took the chair facing his desk, crossed one leg over the other at the knee, and speared him with a gaze that brooked no evasions or hesitations. "Who is Sergei Ustinov?"

"He's head of Taiga Import-Export. An influential businessman with friends in every part of Yekaterinburg society."

"And a mobster?"

Skou gave me the impression of someone forcibly repressing a snort. "May I ask why we're discussing Ustinov, Commissioner?"

"Because he accosted me in the hotel bar last night." I gave Skou the same rundown I'd given Arno. "And yes, before you ask, I prepared a contact report that will go off to HQ with the daily subspace packet and, since this is your jurisdiction, you'll find a copy in your message queue shortly. Now, who is Ustinov really?"

— Twenty —

Skou sat back with a thoughtful expression, eyes on his desktop, and didn't immediately reply. After a few heartbeats, he looked up at me again.

"What do you know about organized crime in this star system, Commissioner?"

"Only what I read in the package provided by the intelligence division before we left Wyvern. Like most worlds, Novaya Sibir has several OCGs that vary in size, reach, and interests. The largest are connected with groups in other star systems as part of informal networks and tend to be more sophisticated and less brutal. The smaller ones are strictly local, cruder, and more violent. Most run legitimate businesses which serve as a front, and they're tough to indict because they know all the tricks and use top-notch legal advisers. The largest

OCG bosses are de facto oligarchs with extensive contacts at every level of government."

Skou nodded. "In a nutshell. It could describe any of the Home Worlds, no?"

"And most of the older OutWorlds."

"So, you see, there's nothing exceptional about OCGs here, except for one thing. At least in my experience and that of my organized crime section's investigators. They're intensely patriotic, more so than OCG members in other star systems and will go to great lengths in making sure outsiders can't harm Novaya Sibir."

I let out an amused chuckle. "Patriotic mobsters. Nice."

"Now, on to Ustinov. He's one of the top oligarchs, and his company, Taiga Import-Export, is huge. He also sits on a dozen boards of directors and likely owns several of those businesses via layers of cut-outs, subsidiaries, and shell companies. They never told us if anyone ever tried tracking down his holdings, but I doubt it. Ustinov takes pains to make sure his visible dealings are above board."

"Visible?" I cocked a questioning eyebrow at Skou. "Interesting choice of words."

"But apt, as you'll see in a moment. One of the biggest OCG, perhaps even the first among peers, calls itself the Yekaterinburg Bratva, and as the name might indicate, is headquartered and centered on the capital. However, it has tentacles reaching into every part of the planet. We know little about it, and if one is to believe the National Police Service, neither do they."

"And you think they're not being truthful?"

Skou shrugged. "Who knows? The Novaya Sibir groups impose one of the strictest codes of silence in the known galaxy, which is why they've prospered."

"So, you're telling me Sergei Ustinov could be the krestniy otets of the Yekaterinburg Bratva?"

A nod. "That's what the smart money out on the street says. He's never so much as been accused of impropriety, let alone charged, and keeps his dealings as mob boss completely separate from those as CEO of Taiga. Oh, we suspect the company serves as a conduit for smuggling and to move people around, but we can't pin it down, and I don't have the resources for lengthy investigations with little chance of a payoff at the end. You know how tough interstellar, cross-jurisdictional cases are."

"What about the National Police Service?"

"They looked at Taiga closely a few times but saw nothing that would warrant a deeper dive into its affairs, though I suspect Ustinov has a hand in directing law enforcement attention elsewhere."

"To rival groups or bosses who won't submit?"

Another nod. "Almost certainly. Ustinov is a major player, and wherever there's money to be made, his sort looks for the main advantage."

"Legally or illegally, no doubt. Now, why did he approach me last night with rather sibylline warnings?"

Skou grimaced. "I can only surmise it was because of that patriotism I mentioned earlier, and perhaps because of the Siberiak organized crime groups' rather old-fashioned and strict code of honor. Other than that, your guess is as good as mine."

"I assume he's on the side of those who consider the 212th innocent and victims of a smear campaign perpetrated by Senator Olrik on behalf of centralist interests."

Skou made a vague hand gesture. "Ustinov and the other oligarchs keep a strict appearance of neutrality, both in star system and Commonwealth politics. As my organized crime section head likes to say, they can dance around raindrops without getting wet. Does Ustinov dislike Olrik in particular? No idea. But you might recall the theory that a strong central government on Earth and weak star system governments are more conducive to graft, corruption, influence peddling, dirty dealing, and every other sin on this side of the Infinite Void. Both oligarchs and krestniy otets very much prefer that sort of environment, which leads me to believe Ustinov wouldn't be opposed to centralists like Olrik."

"But then there's the patriotism factor."

Skou nodded again. "Which makes guessing his views on Olrik's allegations a risky undertaking."

"In my experience, profits trump patriotism at a certain point. It's not the same point for everyone, but the Ustinovs of this galaxy still have a price, however high it may be."

"Yet on Novaya Sibir, the usual rules don't necessarily apply in the way we expect, Commissioner. The only advice I can give is to take whatever he told you seriously. He's not the sort who'll approach senior federal police officers in the first place, let alone with advice about his homeworld."

"Has he ever spoken with you?"

Skou shook his head. "No. Nor with my predecessor."

I climbed to my feet. "Thank you for your time, Chief Superintendent."

"My pleasure."

Once back in our office suite, I updated my team on the situation and the irony of AC12's commanding officer sending a contact report to the head of the Anti-Corruption Division.

"Should I do some digging on this Sergei Ustinov, Chief?" Arno asked.

As I thought about his suggestion, an idea struck me.

"See what you can find out about the client list of Lieutenant Commander Racitina's civilian law offices, with particular focus on suspected mafia members and people connected to Novaya Sibir oligarchs, such as Ustinov."

"You think she might be closer to them than she lets on?"

I gave Arno a sly grin. "Let's just say I'm curious about these people showing such an intense interest in our investigation."

He tapped the side of his nose with an extended index finger. "Understood."

As so often, I found myself at loose ends, waiting for my team to dig up the next clue I could pursue with the imposing dignity of my office as a senior internal affairs commander. And so I decreed a sixteen hundred hours team update meeting in the main room. Since neither Arno nor Destine protested — I didn't expect the sergeants to say a word — it was probably not a bad idea.

But I should have known events would keep me busy. I finally heard from HQ on Wyvern and ACC Sorjonen, or more likely Grand Admiral Larsson speaking through the Chief Constable who spoke through my boss, left the matter of Racitina attending the interviews up to my judgment. Since Admiral Talyn gave me the go-ahead, I would read Racitina in just before we started off by taking Major Morozov's statement.

After lunch, however, I received a bit of news that left me wondering what would happen next. Senator Olrik had just arrived from Earth on a fast transport, a luxury aviso used by the powerful and wealthy who were in a hurry. Funny, I wasn't warned. It should be common knowledge Olrik was on his way. Unless he kept his unannounced trip home a well-guarded secret. And if so, why? To catch us unawares? It seemed unlikely an experienced political operative of his sort wouldn't know PCB investigators were chosen, in part, because they couldn't be easily ruffled by anyone, no matter how high up the food chain.

When I told Arno about these fresh developments, he let out a grim chuckle.

"May I suggest you avoid the hotel bar from now on? Otherwise, Senator Olrik will buttonhole you, and speaking with him, even though it might be totally innocuous, will appear much worse than you giving Hautcoeur and Ustinov the time of day."

"You're probably right, but it's a shame. The view is superb, and the bartender knows what I like."

"Sure, but at this point, everybody there knows your name, and that's generally not ideal when you're heading this sort of inquiry. Tell you what. We can surely find a store selling that blue gin along with tonic water. You can make your own predinner drink, save a little money, and stay out of sight. Besides, the view from our rooms is pretty good."

I always recognized the voice of reason when I heard it, and I was hearing it now. "Very well. I'll go on a shopping expedition after work. You can tag along and see if there's any of that black stuff on offer."

"The Imperial Stout? I'm sure it's available wherever your gin is sold."

"Deal."

That afternoon, Sergeant Cincunegui reported his first formal findings, those that would form part of the casefile.

"First element," he pointed at the conference room display, which showed lines of data, "is the integrity of the raw video provided by Carla Hautcoeur. Our analysis couldn't find any evidence it was tampered with, not even at the basic code level. Therefore, I can state with over ninety percent confidence it is a genuine recording of events on a world with a G class sun. We ran a comparison of the newsnet recordings with the matching visuals we took from *Prospero*'s core, and I can state with over ninety-nine percent confidence they're the originals from which the newsnet copies were made. We can use both as our comparison baseline when we analyze the visuals provided by the 212th Pathfinders. Our next step, tomorrow morning, is digging through *Prospero*'s logs to ascertain her itinerary during the relevant time frame and determine whether those logs show signs of tampering. We'll let the AI run with it overnight. It'll analyze every bit of data while we sleep. Questions, sirs?"

I shook my head. "No. Thank you for the update. Arno? Destine?"

Both also shook their heads.

"Then we can call it a —" At that moment, my office communicator chimed for attention. Few besides Skou, his operations officer, Admiral Meir, Colonel Freijs, and Commander Racitina had the address for a direct link, so I stood. "Thanks. See you at supper. Or not."

When I slid behind my desk, the communicator indicated it was a private number and wouldn't tell me who. Intrigued, I accepted, and the face of an earnest young woman with short blond hair framing a delicate face appeared. Pale blue eyes beneath brows so light they almost seemed white met mine.

"Assistant Commissioner Morrow? I am Senator Fedor Olrik's executive assistant. Stand by for a link with his private office node."

"No." The word came out before I even had time to think. "My speaking with Senator Olrik at this juncture would be highly irregular and might harm the outcome of my investigation. Please pass on my apologies. Good day."

I cut the link before she could reply and sat back, exhaling slowly. Wonderful. That was just what we needed — political interference from the man who stirred up this entire hullabaloo.

Arno poked his head through the open office door.

"What the heck?" He sounded incredulous. "Does the man not understand the rules governing professional compliance investigations, with political interference being at the top of the list of proscriptions?"

I gave Arno a smirk that was probably tinged with more contempt than it should be.

"He's a Commonwealth Senator, a member of an infinitesimally tiny elite who preside over humanity's destiny, or think they do. As far as his like is concerned, rules are for little people such as us, not one of the anointed."

Arno winced theatrically. "Ouch. You do know when to drive the blade home, Chief. Just be careful. The anointed usually strike first, then wonder why ACC Sorjonen's inquisitors are tearing up their private lives."

"No worries. I'll handle the Honorable Fedor Olrik, Senior Commonwealth Senator for the Sovereign Star System of Novaya Sibir. After all, we Firing Squad officers have nothing whatsoever to lose." Something that was nagging at me finally swam into focus. "How did Olrik obtain the address for a direct link to this office, anyway? The communications center knows not to give it out, nor connect anyone who isn't on my approved list without prior notice."

"A man like him? He has connections, Chief. Perhaps even inside the 47th Constabulary Group. Maybe we should launch an investigation once we're done with this one. That being said, I believe we planned a brief shopping trip?"

— Twenty-One —

Arno and I enjoyed a predinner drink in my suite's sitting room. It wasn't quite as nice as the bar, but it would do. Destine and the sergeants were off on their own again, and, if nothing else, their being in cahoots could only help the investigation's technical aspect.

"You know, Chief," Arno said after savoring a sip of his meal in a bottle, "I'm feeling vaguely insulted by Olrik right now. His presumption is pushing us out of public spaces, and that's just not right. You called him one of the anointed earlier. How about one of the utterly entitled?"

"That too. But acting like the unmovable object to his unstoppable force isn't the way I want to play it at the moment."

He cocked a bushy eyebrow at me. "Not that I consider his sort an unstoppable force — an unbearable farce, perhaps — but you prepared a plan for him, did you?"

"I'm always planning. And in Olrik's case, I intend to keep him as far away from us and the case as possible. He's not a material witness, nor can he present evidence, and he definitely has no standing."

"I'll wager next month's pay and allowances that he firmly believes he has standing." Arno, eyes twinkling with mischief, raised his glass and downed the rest of the Imperial Stout.

"Pass." I finished my gin, and we both stood. "Hotel restaurant, or do we show a sense of adventure like our juniors?"

Arno shrugged. "I didn't go through all the appealing plates in their evening meal menu yet, and what I've tasted so far was more than acceptable. Besides, I enjoy the subdued surroundings, and I daresay Destine and the sergeants are more inclined to livelier places."

"The hotel restaurant it is, but I think we might broaden our horizons tomorrow evening."

"Deal, Chief. I'll ask Destine if she has any recommendations."

The restaurant was as quiet as usual, with dampeners keeping the sound of conversations within every table's virtual bubble, which was just as well since almost three-quarters of the main room was occupied by people in business or evening clothes. I enjoyed the elegant atmosphere even more than the lack of background noise, but then I've always been fond of wood paneling, soft lighting, and tasteful decorations such as paintings by local artists and large images of Novaya Sibir's wild landscape.

The virtual maître d'hotel directed us to one of the smaller side rooms and a table by a west-facing window, which gave us a last glimpse of the now-vanished sun's glow behind the horizon. We consulted the holographic menu that popped up the moment we sat. So far, I'd been sampling the special of the day and hadn't been disappointed. Sure the price was more than what the Constabulary paid us as a meal allowance, but I could afford it. My personal expenses were limited, and an assistant commissioner's salary was generous. I could afford it, along with a glass or two of Siberiak wine.

Our drinks and the appetizers — smoked fish with pickles and black bread — showed up not long after we placed our orders, and we took the first bite.

Arno let out a soft sigh. "Nice. But then, I'm a sucker for this stuff. Say, Chief, do you notice something about our surroundings?"

"Other than the fact we're alone in here?"

"That's what I meant. Considering the main room still has a few empty tables, and they usually keep spaces like this for large parties with reservations."

"Now that you mention it."

We finished our appetizers in silence, but Arno's observation was bothering me more and more. In due course, the main dish, slices of duck breast, medium rare with the skin cooked to crisp perfection, on a bed of egg noodles accompanied by sauteed greenhouse-grown vegetables, arrived. One bite of the duck, and I was in heaven.

"Eating like this will spoil me for the officer's mess back home."

"Then we definitely need to take our evening meals in the same places as Destine and the sergeants. Apparently, they found good eateries where the allowance will cover a full meal. In other words, nothing as fancy as this."

Moments after we set down our utensils in the time-honored way of signaling we were done, the silent and ever so efficient serving droid appeared to clear off our table. It returned shortly after that with cake and coffee to end the meal.

But before either of us took a single bite, two tough-looking bruisers wearing black who practically screamed bodyguard appeared, scanned the room, and took up positions on either side of the entrance. Moments later, a tall, middle-aged man in what surely was an expensive, hand-tailored gray suit entered.

He sported a full head of lustrous black hair parted in the middle, a handsome, square face, cleft chin, and small, perfectly trimmed mustache. Dark eyes set beneath arching brows studied us as he crossed the floor to our table, followed by an unprepossessing aide, a middle-aged man of middling height, with average stature and a bland, forgettable face.

Arno and I exchanged a glance. In retrospect, I should have known Senator Fedor Olrik would find me after I refused his call. Olrik's sort wasn't put off by anyone. Neither of us stood as he approached, and I saw his eyes tighten imperceptibly at what he no doubt considered a lack of respect for his exalted position. I quickly reached into my tunic pocket and switched on the scrambler I always carried to defeat listening devices. Something told me the gray man behind him had a recording device concealed on his person. Before Olrik opened his mouth, I decided I wouldn't allow him to speak first and take control of the conversation.

"Good evening, Senator. As I told your executive assistant, speaking with you would be highly irregular and might harm the investigation. My chief inspector and I were about to enjoy our dessert and coffee, and I would ask that you leave us alone."

Olrik met my eyes, and I saw anger in them.

"Your lack of courtesy reflects badly on the Commonwealth Constabulary, Commissioner Morrow." His voice was deep, his inflection melodious, and his pronunciation precise. "I am a Commonwealth Senator and not used to being so cavalierly dismissed by someone who doesn't even wear a star on her collar."

"Probably because you've not yet met a senior Professional Compliance Bureau officer. Being unimpressed by rank or position is one prerequisite of the job. Having nothing to lose is another. I will say this again in a more direct manner, Senator. You and I have nothing to discuss concerning the case I'm currently investigating. Not now, not ever. And I cannot think of any other matter we might have in common. Therefore, please leave us to finish our meal in peace."

Olrik's expression hardened. "No uniformed jack-in-office has ever spoken to me in this manner. How dare you?"

"Because I can. Now listen closely. The fact you found me, probably arranged for me to be seated in this private room, and accosted me while I was off duty after I already stated I would not speak with you can be construed as an attempt at intimidating a sworn law enforcement officer. And that's a criminal act. Even Commonwealth Senators can't get away with it, so I strongly suggest you back off before I acquaint you with the relevant section of the Criminal Code."

While the aide showed no reaction to my words, one of the two bodyguards, perhaps alarmed at my tone and facial expression, took a step toward us. I immediately turned my eyes on him.

"Get any closer, sunshine, and I will arrest you on federal charges." Since I was wearing an open jacket and my needler in a shoulder holster, I quickly lifted the left side just enough to show the goon I was armed. He froze, and I looked up at Olrik again.

"Please leave. Now."

"Since it's quite clear you're an unreasonable sort, Commissioner, I shall do so. But this isn't the end of it. No one treats a Commonwealth Senator with such disrespect, especially not someone who is still wanted by the Pacifican State Security Police for political crimes."

"Commonwealth law forbids the Pacifican government from extraditing me on grounds not recognized by other star systems or the federal government. When Pacifican State Security tried to circumvent that law, it didn't end well for the officers involved. And that was the last time I'll overlook a threat from you. As per regulations, I will submit a report on this incident to my superiors, who will forward it via official channels to the Speaker of the Senate. Goodbye, Senator. Do not approach me again."

He stared at me with barely contained fury for a few seconds, then spun on his heels and stalked out, followed by his aide, who gave me a brief, but searching look, before turning away along with the bodyguards.

"You still wield that quasi-mystical ability to make enemies, Chief," Arno said in an amused tone once we were alone.

"Bah. Olrik needed taking down a few pegs. The man is overly imbued with his own sense of self-importance."

"You realize he will try to cause trouble."

"I certainly hope he does so."

"Why?"

I gave my winger a sardonic smile. "Because after meeting the Honorable Senior Senator from Novaya Sibir, I'm in the mood for a fight, Arno. Admiral Talyn once told me about one of her husband's favorite expressions, and it's one I rather enjoy, especially when a fool of Olrik's caliber threatens me. It goes something like this — when the devil whispers in my ear, *you cannot withstand the storm,* I whisper back, *I am the storm.*"

Arno clapped his hands once while laughing delightedly. "That's the Chief we love. Olrik does not know what a mistake he just made."

"Let's enjoy our coffee and dessert, then slip out of here. Suddenly, this place carries a cost that goes beyond simply exceeding our meal allowance."

We quickly downed the cake — chocolate and cream — and after Arno took his last sip, he stared into the porcelain cup as if he might divine the future in the dregs. When he looked up at me again, he asked, "What was this rigmarole really about, Chief? Olrik isn't a stupid man. Otherwise, he'd not be a Commonwealth Senator."

I finished my own coffee before replying.

"There are a few plausible explanations. Two really. The simplest is that he let his sense of entitlement overrule his sense of discretion. If he was briefed on my past, which isn't in any official records other than those of the Pacifican State Security Police, I'm sure his people also told him PCB officers, especially senior ones in the Anti-Corruption Division, could tell him where to go without suffering consequences. At the very least, they'd have told him no senior investigative officer will discuss an ongoing case with an outsider, lest they end up speaking with their local PCB detachment commander about perverting the course of justice. But hubris doesn't listen to advice."

Arno nodded. "Plausible. However, I can offer a better explanation, one you were just about to mention, I'm sure. He may be seeking to discredit our investigation by drumming up false accusations of lacking impartiality in our proceedings. We know he'd rather subject the war crimes allegations to a senatorial inquiry he can control rather than let the Constabulary run with it and find out what really happened. Which can only mean he doesn't want us to find out. Or whoever funds his political ambitions doesn't. And that list can be quite long considering the many people the Armed Forces and we pissed off over the years. How does that sound, Chief?"

I smiled at him. "It was indeed going to be my second explanation. If he was hoping to record our discussion and use it as evidence I'm biased, he'll be disappointed."

"Yes, I saw you switch on the jammer. That aide of his was probably carrying a hidden recorder. So why does he not want us to discover the truth? Why risk making a scene and cause trouble that would affect his own credibility?"

"When we uncover what really happened on Torga, we'll find the answer to those questions as well."

— Twenty-Two —

The following morning, I briefed the others on our encounter with Senator Olrik, as per my personal policy that my team should know everything germane to the investigation. Or at least almost everything. Sometimes, I had no choice but to keep quiet on some matters, if only for a time.

Then, I wrote my second contact report of the inquiry, one which would send waves up both the Constabulary and the Armed Forces chain of command. Just to be on the safe side, I encrypted a copy for Admiral Talyn's eyes and walked both messages to the communications center, hoping I'd catch the daily subspace packet before it went out. However, I purposely didn't inform Chief Superintendent Skou since this was clearly a political matter, and the PCB handled those.

Around mid-morning, Sergeant Cincunegui appeared at the door to my office.

"Can I interrupt you for a moment, sir? There's something you ought to see."

I waved him in. "What's up?"

"Can you open the Galactic Newsnet feed? Carla Hautcoeur is interviewing Senator Olrik as we speak."

I touched my workstation's control pad and called up the relevant stream. "How did you come across that?"

He gave me a small smile. "I set up the AI to sniff the public networks when we arrived, feeding it keywords as things happened, Olrik and Hautcoeur among them. It alerted me when both came up in the same instance."

I set the feed to stream from the beginning and projected it to my office display. Arno, Destine, and Sergeant Esadze joined Cincunegui and all five of us watched the interview.

"Good morning, Senator," a smiling Hautcoeur inclined her head toward Olrik, who sat across from her in what I presumed was a virtual studio. "Thank you for accepting Galactic Newsnet's invitation."

"My pleasure, Carla. Appearing before the citizens of Novaya Sibir, whom I am honored to represent in the Commonwealth Senate, is always a privilege."

I had to admit the bugger could exude charisma when he wanted, even though he was, as Arno often put it, shoveling manure with a dragline bucket.

"I understand you've come home, even though the Senate is still in session, for a very particular reason."

"Indeed, and I'm sure you and our listeners can guess why."

"The war crimes allegations against the 212th Pathfinder Squadron, as well as the Commonwealth Starship *Chinggis*."

Olrik, wearing a grave expression, inclined his head.

"Precisely. When Grand Admiral Larsson bypassed the Senate and the Secretary General and asked the Commonwealth Constabulary's Professional Compliance Bureau to investigate, I was immediately concerned about the direction this inquiry would take, absent legislative oversight."

Arno snorted indelicately. "Bypassed. Larsson followed the regulations to the letter."

"And what are those concerns, Senator?" Hautcoeur asked.

"Well, Carla, you probably know the Constabulary and the Armed Forces share a common ancestry and have a similar relationship with the Senate and the Secretary General's Office. And as this case demonstrates, the Professional Compliance Bureau is the Fleet's internal affairs branch on top of being the Constabulary's."

Another snort from Arno. "And that of the entire federal government, save for the Senate."

"In other words, you're saying the uniformed services are a little too close for comfort."

Olrik nodded.

"When it comes to this particular matter, especially so. There have been no war crimes investigations involving the Armed Forces in living memory, making it a matter of extreme importance, one that shouldn't be fobbed off on a mere anti-corruption unit that deals with venal rather than capital offenses. But since my colleagues in the Senate voted to hold off on a legislative inquiry of our own until the Constabulary completes its work, I think it behooves me to examine what the senior investigative officer is doing. Procedural fairness, perhaps even common decency, demands it. The Professional Compliance Bureau has been a law unto itself since its creation. Some would even say it can, at times, go rogue and act in ways that might shock people unaware of the massive power wielded by its officers."

"Which would be most of us."

Another nod. "Oh, yes. Even I was taken aback by the way PCB officers behave."

Destine let out a brief chuckle. "Shot fired."

"Could you give our listeners an example?"

The smile appearing on Olrik's face was positively vulpine, or at least it seemed so to my cynical eyes.

"I most certainly can, Carla. And it is an example that will be close to your listeners' hearts. Upon my arrival yesterday morning, I took steps to communicate with the PCB officer investigating the allegations in question, Assistant Commissioner Caelin Morrow, so I could take up my oversight duties and make sure everything was being done as the Senate wished."

Arno rolled his eyes theatrically. "Bullshit."

"And what happened?"

"Well, she refused to take my call, and rather rudely, I might add. Yesterday evening, our paths crossed by happenstance at a fine Yekaterinburg restaurant." A chorus of derisive laughter erupted in my office, but it stopped the moment I raised my hand. "I approached Assistant Commissioner Morrow in a perfectly conciliatory manner, hoping we could find common ground, but she was insulting and dismissive, treating a Commonwealth Senator with such disrespect it would shock the average person's conscience. Needless to say, we did not find common ground."

"How disappointing that a senior officer would behave in such a manner. A shame you couldn't record the incident for the edification of our listeners."

Arno and I exchanged a glance. My personal jammer had once again done its work to perfection.

"It is. Otherwise, I might lay a complaint about Morrow with her superiors. But Morrow's behavior, her refusal to acknowledge me, and the fact she apparently revels in the PCB's nickname — The Firing Squad — along with a questionable past, make me wonder whether we could be looking at a cover-up engineered by the Fleet with Constabulary connivance. Did you know Morrow and one of her officers have deep connections with the Marine Corps Special Forces community, which includes the 212th Pathfinder Squadron?"

An air of pure astonishment crossed Hautcoeur's face, and I gave her points for decent acting skills.

"I did not, and I'm sure none of our listeners are aware. Isn't that a little incestuous, Senator?"

Olrik allowed himself a humorless laugh.

"A little? Much more than that, I think. I'm sure her superiors chose her as a senior investigative officer because of her connections. If that doesn't make someone with solid common sense sit up and take notice, I don't know what will. And the people of Novaya Sibir show more common sense than most. Perhaps they might make their views known and demand an aboveboard investigation, one in which the senior investigative officer doesn't hide behind regulations, questionable procedures, and the usual Professional Compliance Bureau stonewalling."

By now, my entire team was staring at me with various expressions. Arno and Destine were clearly amused, while Sergeants Cincunegui and Esadze seemed startled by Olrik's vitriol, especially as he delivered it in such a reasonable tone.

"Strong words, Senator."

"But they needed to be said. Many people feel as I do, yet they can't express themselves because they fear retaliation. That's why Commonwealth Senators enjoy parliamentary immunity — so we may speak for those who cannot."

"Thank you for your candid words, Senator Olrik. I'm sure our listeners appreciate them. This is Carla Hautcoeur, Galactic Newsnet special correspondent in the Novaya Sibir star system."

The stream ended, and my office display went dark.

"Last night, you were hoping Olrik would stir up trouble, Chief. I think your hopes are more than fulfilled."

When I allowed myself a pleased expression, Sergeant Cincunegui gave me a strange look. "May I ask why you don't seem alarmed by the senator, sir?"

"He was kind enough to out himself early on rather than play political games behind the scenes, and I always find enemies who make their intentions crystal clear at the outset easier to counter. Please see that a copy of the interview is on its way to ACC Sorjonen soonest. If that means a special, off-cycle subspace packet to Wyvern, then so be it. He'll have read my contact report by the time he views this, so I need not comment on it."

"Yes, sir. Will do. If I may ask another question, didn't Olrik make tactical mistakes last night and just now? I'd think senior Commonwealth Senators were better at these sorts of games."

"And they usually are, which makes me wonder why he's taking such a direct and quasi-libelous approach. Not that I can respond in any way or fashion. I pity the 47th Group's public affairs officer who'll be dealing with this."

"Fear, Chief." I glanced at Arno, who was stroking his grandfatherly beard.

"A distinct possibility. Powerful people who are frightened will lash out in defiance of good manners and good sense, hoping they can transfer that fear onto their target. But fear of what?"

Arno chuckled. "As a newly notorious assistant commissioner told me recently, when we find out what happened on Torga, we'll know the answer to that as well."

My office communicator chose that moment to chime, and I glanced down. It was the 47th Constabulary Group's public affairs officer, a civilian member roughly equivalent to a senior chief inspector.

"If you'll forgive me, folks. The fallout from Senator Olrik's newsnet appearance is already manifesting itself."

I accepted the call and the delicate features of a forty-something dark-haired woman with green eyes appeared on my display. If she felt anxious at what some might term an explosive development, it didn't show.

"I presume you wish to discuss Senator Olrik's interview with Carla Hautcoeur?"

"You saw it, then, Commissioner?"

"Yes, and I'm sorry that you'll be forced to deal with the stinking mess Olrik left on Hautcoeur's carpet. As a PCB investigator, I cannot speak with the media."

"I understand, which is why I'm calling. Please don't take this the wrong way, but how much of what the senator said is true?"

"Does it matter?" Before she could reply, I raised a hand. "I know you can't stand in front of the newsnets without knowing as much as possible. So yes, I refused to speak with him because it could jeopardize my investigation. It's normal procedure in PCB inquiries, especially when politicians try to inject themselves. When he refused to desist last night — and by the way, he engineered the encounter in our hotel restaurant — I became rather direct in a way he likely never experienced before coming from an officer of a uniformed service. That's it. Everything else Olrik said is pure speculation, if not conspiracy theories. I reported last night's incident to my superior, ACC Sorjonen, and a copy of this morning's interview is headed his way as well."

Which reminded me to send another copy to Admiral Talyn.

"It might interest you to know that I'm sure Olrik attempted to record last night's incident and play it for Hautcoeur's benefit, but I carry a service issue personal jammer at all times and kiboshed his plans. That would explain his remarks on the subject."

"Oh." She gave me an astonished stare. "I guess that was lucky then."

"There's no luck involved. I've learned not to trust people. What are your intentions in this matter?"

"I'll prepare a statement on Chief Superintendent Skou's behalf — you'll see it first, of course — and will report up the public affairs chain of command as well, in case the Chief Public Affairs Officer wishes to take action."

"Sounds good. If you come up with further questions, don't hesitate."

"Thank you, Commissioner."

"Morrow, out."

Olrik's declaration of war convinced me he wasn't acting out of pure motives. On the contrary. And that made me determined to take a good look at him while my team dug through the records. It would have to be completely hush-hush. Technically, I couldn't investigate a legislator without specific permission, but since he injected himself into my case, ACC Sorjonen wouldn't object so long as I remained discreet and merely passed my findings along.

That's what I liked about my boss. He was one of the few who preferred that his officers follow the evidence wherever it took them and to hell with the consequences. So long as they did it intelligently.

And at this moment, between Olrik and me, I enjoyed an edge if only because I heeded the old adage, better stay silent and be thought a fool than speak and confirm it.

My communicator chimed again, and I glanced at the display — General Elin. Before the morning was out, I'd no doubt be speaking about the Olrik interview with everyone involved.

— Twenty-Three —

"Good morning, General. What can I do for you?"

Elin wore a grim expression on his face. "You saw Senator Olrik on the newsnet with Carla Hautcoeur, Commissioner?"

I grimaced. "Yes. Quite the theatricals."

"How much was garbage, and how much can he prove?"

The steel in Elin's tone reminded me of Sorjonen, and I hesitated before answering.

"He approached me twice, and both times, I made it clear my speaking with him could jeopardize the investigation. The second time — which he engineered, it wasn't happenstance — he wouldn't back off forcing me to use language he probably hadn't heard from a lesser being since he became a senator, perhaps even well before then. His sort doesn't tolerate opposing points of view. Other than that, the rest of his assertions are outright lies. But the PCB never comments about inquires nor issues public statements, so there is no way of rebutting him."

"More or less what I expected." Elin took on a thoughtful expression. "I'll even bet he tried recording last night's incident, but you somehow blocked him."

"Right on both counts, sir."

"You and I racked up over three-quarters of a century police experience between us, Commissioner. That means we've likely seen humanity's savviest miscreants and its worst. Now, why do you think a slick political operator like Olrik basically defamed the Commonwealth Constabulary's legendarily incorruptible Professional Compliance Bureau and you in particular on a popular morning newsnet feed?"

I studied Elin for a few seconds, wondering what he wanted from this conversation.

"I'll defer to your greater experience, General. What are your thoughts on the matter?"

"He's afraid of you, Commissioner. Don't you agree?"

"Fear certainly motivates him, sir. Whether it's of me personally or of what I might discover remains open to speculation." I shrugged.

"They're one and the same. Olrik is desperate to throw your investigation off course or, better yet, discredit it so thoroughly that your findings would be seen as tainted." He studied me for a few heartbeats. "I think that if you find out what he fears, you'll also uncover the truth about the war crimes allegations."

"Probably, but PCB officers can't investigate Commonwealth Senators on their own initiative. It's one of the restrictions the Senate demanded in return for supporting Grand Admiral Kowalski when she forced the creation of the Constabulary down the government's throat." It was my turn to hesitate as I pondered the wisdom of my next question. "Can you think of anyone who might know things Olrik would rather keep out of the public eye?"

Elin gave me a curious stare. "You plan on striking back at him?"

"I live by the motto, start nothing, finish everything. But joking aside, if Olrik keeps up his current behavior, he will taint my investigation, and I need leverage to make him stop since I can't counterattack directly." An idea struck me, although it could well be a bad one. "Winning a Commonwealth Senate seat is an expensive proposition on many worlds, General. Could one or more of the oligarchs around here know something about Olrik? Leverage in return for financial support. Sergei Ustinov, for instance."

"Why him?"

I briefly described my conversation with Ustinov and Skou's warning he might be the head of a powerful organized crime group. When I finished, he grimaced.

"Ulf Skou is right about Ustinov heading the Yekaterinburg Bratva. We've never uncovered indictable evidence, but we know. My advice to you is stay away from him. He could cause you more grief than Olrik."

"But is Ustinov, as chief executive officer of Taiga Import-Export, one of Olrik's backers? I understand the Novaya Sibir mobsters are surprisingly patriotic and therefore get irked at their star system's senior senator blackening the reputation of a proud Novaya Sibir-based Marine regiment whose ranks teem with Siberiaks."

"They are. But I can't recall Ustinov ever publicly discussing politics, let alone endorsing candidates, so I wouldn't know if he backed Olrik in the past. However, I still think approaching him for information is like playing with an unstable antimatter containment field."

"Understood, sir."

He held my eyes for a few seconds, then said, "I'll see how the President reacted to Olrik's interview, and if it's what I think, I'll ask if he could speak with our dear senator. As you might remember, the Novaya Sibir Duma can initiate the recall of a sitting Commonwealth Senator should a majority of members believe it necessary, and the Duma will entertain a request from the President to consider the matter. But I wouldn't get my hopes up. Olrik rarely listens to the President."

"Thank you, sir. Was there anything else?"

"No. Please keep in mind Olrik is not representative of most Siberiaks, who are polite, respectful people, even though he represents us on Earth."

"Noted."

"Until next time, Commissioner. Elin, out."

I stared at the blank display for a bit while wondering whether the good general tried to tell me something in a roundabout way. And if so, what was it?

Before I could come up with plausible theories, Admiral Meir called.

"What was Senator Olrik on about?" She asked before I could even say hello. "Oversight duties? Not only no, but hell no. I will not stand by and watch him turn this into a political circus."

"Then we agree about something, Admiral. Don't worry. There is no legal way he can come near the investigation, let alone oversee it. And yes, before you ask, we exchanged tense words last night when he wouldn't back off after ambushing me in the hotel restaurant, which explains his attitude this morning."

"Then good for you, Commissioner. The slimy bastard deserves a stiff jacking up by someone he considers inferior. But what he said during the interview will affect your credibility in certain circles. Can you still come up with an impartial result?"

"Without a doubt, although I can do nothing about people who will never accept that my findings will be as close to the truth as humanly possible. Nor can I offer a rebuttal to Senator Olrik. Professional Compliance Bureau officers never speak with the media, let alone hold news conferences. If there is a reason to inform the public at large about the results of an investigation, it will come through Constabulary HQ Public Affairs. And yes, I dispatched a copy of the interview recording to Wyvern. Other than that, I will continue my work while ignoring Senator Olrik's antics. I'm sure a sizeable chunk of Novaya Sibir's citizenry isn't happy with him at the moment, probably more than before he opened his mouth and impugned the Constabulary."

"Oh, you're absolutely right about that. He's a bloody disgrace."

"While you're on the link, sir, I received preliminary authorization to read in Lieutenant Commander Racitina. Once I get the official go-ahead, she will attend our interviews unless the interviewee objects."

"Excellent. If you need anything from me in dealing with Olrik, just call."

"Thank you, sir."

"I'll let Colonel Freijs know about our conversation. I'm sure he'll be pleased to hear about your views on this matter. Meir, out."

It seemed as if the thin, multicolored line was unexpectedly closing a protective circle around me and my investigation. It reminded me of an old proverb — me against my sibling; my sibling and me against our family; my family and me against our clan; our clan and me against the universe. And the clan was assembling. Perhaps something good might come from Olrik's temper tantrum.

But today was not the day. Before I could think about these developments, Chief Superintendent Skou appeared at my office door.

"Can I ask for a moment of your time, Commissioner?"

"Sure." I gestured at the chairs in front of my desk. "Grab a seat, Ulf."

Skou stepped in and closed the door before sitting.

"I face a problem and would like your advice."

"I'm listening."

"Senator Olrik informed me he would visit the offices of the 47th Constabulary Group this afternoon. Or rather, his executive assistant did on Olrik's behalf. I can hardly bar a Commonwealth Senator from a federal building. He's not an ordinary civilian."

"But you can keep him from entering sensitive areas and viewing records that aren't public. You can also decline to discuss any active or closed case whose specifics haven't been made public. There's a procedure for senators to obtain classified or non-public information from the Constabulary, and it involves HQ on Wyvern."

"Yes, sir. I understand that. But you surely saw his interview with Carla Hautcoeur this morning. I don't want to do anything that might make matters more difficult for you or my unit. Senator Olrik can be pushy and unreasonable."

I gave him an amused smile. "He most certainly can."

"What if he demands I take him to you?"

"I'll make myself scarce after lunch. That way, you can honestly say I'm not in the building, and you don't know where I am."

"Thank you, sir."

"In fact, I'll take Chief Inspector Galdi with me, just in case the senator decides that in my absence, he'll speak with my second-in-command."

Skou's face took on a faint air of discouragement. "Isn't it sad we're stuck maneuvering around elected officials?"

"It's been the case since the first of that species appeared, looking for ways to boost their profiles. Why do you think Grand Admiral Kowalski moved the Armed Forces HQ to Caledonia and established the Constabulary's on Wyvern instead of Earth? Senators, Secretaries, and Secretaries General are supposed to set policy and oversee expenditures, not interfere in day-to-day operations. Yet, they'll stick their fingers into every bit of machinery if we let them and muck things up."

When I saw the expression on Skou's face, I chuckled. "Shocked to hear a PCB assistant commissioner utter such words? Don't be. We all too often clean up after someone with more ego than sense throws a wrench into the workings of justice. I won't let it happen here and now. That being said, what's the best way of avoiding Senator Olrik's latest attempt at barging in?"

Skou thought about it for a moment, then said, "How about a bit of sightseeing? Change into civvies, leave the service issue communicators here, hire an aircar and go incommunicado for a few hours."

I cocked an eyebrow at him. "Sounds like you've done this before."

"Me? No." Skou shook his head. "But it is one of the local mobsters' favorite ways of handling business meetings when they don't want us or the Police Service to know. Novaya Sibir isn't a forced traffic control world, so you can go manual, cut your vehicle off from the net any time, and basically vanish."

"I'll take that under advisement. Thank you. Was there anything else?"

"No, Commissioner." Skou stood and drew himself to attention. "With your permission."

"Dismissed."

Moments after Skou vanished from our office suite, Arno appeared and took a seat across from me without waiting for an invitation. He cocked his head to one side in question.

"So, where are we going this afternoon?"

— Twenty-Four —

"Your absence chagrined Senator Olrik, but he expects you to call him first thing in the morning."

Chief Superintendent Skou seemed somewhat embarrassed at passing along Olrik's message. I'd gone straight to his office after Arno and I returned from a self-guided tour of the Angara valley. The Almighty knows I felt guilty at leaving him to face Olrik alone while I took the afternoon off. But Skou didn't seem overly fazed.

"I'll take his wishes under advisement. How was it?"

"No worse than any of his previous visits or those of other off-world grandees. He didn't even ask about your incident room."

"Small mercies." I gave Skou an encouraging smile. "Thank you for the suggestion we take in

Novaya Sibir's natural beauties. If truth be told, the experience refreshed us."

"My pleasure, sir. But if I could express one wish, it would be that Senator Olrik not revisit the federal building during his stay."

"Since he missed me once, he won't try twice. I assume a small entourage recording Olrik's words and gestures for posterity followed him."

Skou nodded. "There was one obvious flack whose covert electronics fried when he took them past our security gates."

I couldn't restrain a burst of laughter. "Chief Superintendent, you're a man after my own heart. If you ever contemplate a change of career stream and think of the PCB, send me a note. I'm still building up my unit."

"Thank you for the offer, Commissioner, but I'm quite happy to finish my career as a regular cop."

"No problems." I gave him an amused smile as I stood. "Thank you for dealing with Senator Olrik. Enjoy the rest of your day."

When I entered our incident room, Arno stood behind Cincunegui, looking at his workstation display while Destine and Sergeant Esadze were busy at theirs. Upon hearing my footsteps, he turned.

"And how's our good chief superintendent?" When I related what Skou told me, Arno shook his head in mock dismay. "Typical attempt at grandstanding and collecting propaganda video for his re-election campaign. Hopefully, once his PR agent realizes what happened, Olrik will refrain from further attempts."

"Don't count on it."

"On the bright side, Teseo and Alina can present our first definitive results." Arno gestured at Cincunegui.

"Then why don't we take a seat at the big table, go through them, then call it a day?"

"You're the chief, Chief."

Once we were seated, I nodded at Cincunegui.

"We analyzed the navigation logs of *Chinggis* and *Prospero*." He turned to Esadze. "Alina?"

"Neither log shows signs of tampering," she said. "My confidence level is above ninety percent. They show both ships present in the Torga system on the same day with overlapping time periods. *Chinggis* was, of course, in orbit and *Prospero* on the ground near a rogue settlement by the name Bakun, which neighbored the cartel base raided by the 212th and destroyed from orbit by *Chinggis*. They are less than five kilometers apart. I quickly checked the frigate's surveillance sensor recordings, and she indeed spotted a ship fitting *Prospero*'s description on the settlement's spaceport tarmac. The sensor chief's assessment deemed her not a threat to the mission."

Destine guffawed. "Little did they know at the time."

"So, there's no doubt the late Toshiro Rahal was able to see the raid."

Cincunegui shook his head. "Not unless one or both logs were falsified in a way we couldn't detect. Granted, there are ways of doing so, but only a few specialists possess the knowledge and ability, and the majority probably work for Naval Intelligence. Certainly, it would take a naval person possessing an extremely high-security clearance to tamper with a warship's logs. The bad guys probably use specialists as well and would find it easier with *Prospero*, but since both records agree right down to the particulars, my inclination is to accept they were both there at the same time."

Arno let out a brief chuckle. "Of all the outlaw settlements, on all of Torga, in all the Protectorate Zone, Toshiro Rahal had to land near the one identified as a target."

I gave him a questioning glance. "That sounds suspiciously like something you adapted from a quote."

He nodded. "I did. But let's allow Sergeant Esadze to continue."

"Teseo thought the illumination in the *Prospero* videos wasn't quite on spec for Torga's sun, but I checked, and both they and *Chinggis'* records show the same spectral class. This means either the astronomical database is a little off, or the recordings didn't faithfully reflect reality, which wouldn't be the first time. That's about it for now, sir."

"Thank you, Sergeant." I turned to Cincunegui. "Anything else?"

"No, sir. Next, I will analyze the 212th's combat recordings while Alina continues to work on *Chinggis*' log."

"Thank you, folks. That's a big step forward. At least now we know we're facing two different stories of events that occurred in the same physical space at the same time. And that means one of them is either partially or fully wrong, and the other isn't."

Arno shrugged. "We've not yet heard anything from the Navy and the Marines, other than a blanket denial they committed atrocities."

"True." I stood. "Thank you for another fine day spent serving the cause of anti-corruption in our beloved Commonwealth. Dismissed."

That evening, Arno and I went out to a small restaurant three blocks over, based on the underground network's grid demarcations, a place Destine recommended. But from the moment we left the hotel, I felt a vague sensation of being watched. It wasn't anything definite, more like a gut feeling, and it took a measure of restraint to avoid looking around, a futile act in any case. Anyone covertly trailing senior anti-corruption officers would be a pro. No one else would dare. And even though we were in civilian clothes, we carried our service weapons beneath our tunics.

The restaurant struck me more as a pub than an eatery. Like so many of its kind, it was below ground level, meaning no views of a wintry Yekaterinburg. This one was industrial chic to boot, a stark contrast to the genteel, wood-paneled establishment where Arno and I dined the previous few evenings.

My winger winced theatrically at the noise level as we searched for an empty table, preferably against a wall, while casing both our surroundings and the clientele for potential threats. What could I say — it was instinct. As was our unspoken rule of never going out alone while off duty, at least not away from our home base. If nothing else, it meant someone at our back, either as a witness or as a fire team buddy.

Like Destine said, the food was plentiful for the price, albeit simple, the black Siberiak tea strong and sweet, and the ambiance lively. Arno and I spent our time people-watching rather than conversing as we waited for our food and while eating. The background noise made anything else less than appealing, and there wasn't much to discuss in such a packed setting anyway, jammer or no jammer.

I felt a mild sense of relief when we left the pub, sated and rather content, and found ourselves once more on a comparatively quiet underground sidewalk.

The crowd in the sheltered network was thinning considerably now that offices and stores were shuttered for the night. The blizzard announced by the weather service probably helped propel people back to their warm homes beyond Yekaterinburg's core as quickly as possible.

As we rounded a corner, I found our way blocked by a woman and two men. The woman, who could be anywhere between twenty and sixty, had that artificial face, expensive wardrobe, and overly elegant coiffure typical to newsnet personalities. The two men, who I immediately assumed were bodyguards, wore neutral expressions beneath close-cropped hair as black as hers was blond.

"Assistant Commissioner Morrow? I'm Gina Graetz of Novaya Sibir Information Broadcasters."

Her words, along with the small video drone, which appeared out of nowhere to hover over her left shoulder, confirmed my split-second assessment. I assumed it was recording and stuck my hand into my tunic pocket to switch on my personal jammer.

"You should know better than to accost a senior Constabulary officer in the street, Ms. Graetz. Now kindly step out of our way."

"Any comments on Senator Olrik's statement about your fitness to investigate the war crimes allegations?" One of the men behind Graetz leaned over and whispered something in her ear. She gave me an annoyed look. "Are you jamming my camera? Because if so, you're violating Siberiak law concerning freedom of the news media."

I knew, right then, that there was no graceful way out of this situation. Even if Graetz and her goons couldn't record the incident live, she would surely recount it later. And she would use my refusal to speak and purported use of a jammer to further the narrative that I couldn't be relied on for a fair, open, and transparent investigation.

"Ms. Graetz, please contact the 47th Constabulary Group's public affairs officer. I cannot speak with you on any matter without prior clearance, as you well know." We tried to step around Graetz and her men, but they blocked us, and I speared her with an icy stare. "Move out of our way before I'm forced to call the National Police Service and see that you're removed, newsnet or not. You may think ambushing federal law enforcement officers on the street in the name of journalistic freedom is an acceptable tactic, but the law says otherwise. Attempting to prevent us from proceeding freely is a criminal offense."

"Ambush?" She gave me an indignant look. "I'm merely seeking the truth, and I see that you're not even acquainted with the concept, just as Senator Olrik believes. Thank you for making his case."

Graetz turned to her goons. "We got what we came for. Let's leave the commissioner and her man to reflect on their lack of honesty."

They stepped out of our way and watched us leave. Her floating camera probably came back to life once we reached my jammer's practical limit of approximately ten meters, meaning she'd have a few seconds of us on the scene.

"So much for avoiding the hotel restaurant in case Olrik returns," Arno muttered. "At least her sort wouldn't be allowed into the hotel, period."

I let out a soft sigh. "No, she wouldn't. And now to write another contact report. The ACC will be tired of them by the time this case is closed."

"So will the 47th's poor public affairs officer."

— Twenty-Five —

Our encounter with Gina Graetz streamed over the Novaya Sibir Information Broadcasters' net at oh-eight-hundred the following day, and she did a reasonably murderous hatchet job on me. She specifically mentioned my use of a jammer in contravention of Novaya Sibir law and announced that NSIB legal staff would pursue the matter with the National Police Service.

I knew they wouldn't get far because local law didn't override Commonwealth law, which allowed Constabulary officers to jam recording devices if they found reasonable grounds to believe said recordings might jeopardize a federal investigation. Considering her quasi-libelous reportage, no honest judge in the sector would even consent to hear a case against me on the matter.

"I guess your evening sucked, sir," Cincunegui said after I switched off the feed.

I shrugged. "There wasn't anything I could have done differently. An ambush, by definition, is unexpected and demands an instant reaction to limit the damage. Since this was a no-win situation for us, I figure it went about as well as possible. Graetz won't make new friends with her hit piece, but it is a further sign of Senator Olrik's desperation to discredit our work for unknown reasons — because there's no doubt in my mind he set this up. Let's get back to it. The sooner we complete the job, the sooner we'll be away from here."

As I expected, the parade of calls started shortly after the stream ended, beginning with General Elin.

"Good morning, sir. I assume you just saw Gina Graetz impugn the integrity of my investigation."

He nodded once. "Me, the President, and a large segment of the population. NSIB sent out warnings to subscribers that there would be an explosive reportage this morning."

I gave him a crooked smile. "Something exploded all right, sir, but probably not what Graetz expected, though she doesn't know it yet."

"Did you threaten her with charges of interfering with a federal law enforcement officer, and did you use a jammer?"

"I merely informed her that preventing us from proceeding was a crime, and she did try to bar our way with her goons—"

"Producers, but never mind. Sorry for the interruption."

"And I don't take kindly to anyone doing so, especially after ambushing me in public. As to the matter of a jammer, I can neither confirm nor deny, but local laws about their use don't apply to us."

"I see. Well, there's nothing I can do with this one either, though I suspect for you it was merely water flowing off a glacier. Cold, unpleasant, but quickly gone. There's another matter I wanted to discuss. An anonymous informant tipped us off about Toshiro Rahal's murderer."

"I'm listening, sir."

"The informant never identified him or herself, and we weren't able to track the origin of the message. But my organized crime folks figure that it came from one of our larger OCGs, perhaps even the Yekaterinburg Bratva, based on the method and wording. In any case, the informant pointed at someone we'd long suspected was a high-priced fixer for hire, the sort who moves around like a ghost. Or, in this case, wearing the uniform and carrying the credentials of the Novaya Sibir Customs and Excise Department — it's how he entered *Prospero*'s berth without detection. We're still looking for accomplices in the spaceport security division or access to nodes he shouldn't."

"Did you bring him in for questioning yet, sir?"

Elin grimaced. "No. When my people entered the apartment named by the informant, they found our man dead of unknown causes. The medical examiner will conduct a postmortem this afternoon, but people like this fixer don't just up and die in their living room one day for no reason. However, we compared his DNA to the traces found in *Prospero*'s bridge and found a match from a recent deposit, which would indicate he was aboard."

"Do you think someone killed him so you'd be unable to trace his employer of the moment?"

"A good possibility, although if this was a mob hit made to look like death from natural causes, it might be a warning as well — don't murder witnesses in a federal case without the top krestniy otets' permission. They're rather touchy about that around here, and Ustinov told you to forget about finding Rahal's killer. Besides, the local mobsters surely weren't happy that your sole third-party eyewitness could no longer testify. Sadly, chances are we'll never know for sure."

"You think Rahal's murder wasn't commissioned by an OCG?"

Elin shook his head. "It wouldn't make sense considering how they think and operate, but anything is possible if the profits outweigh the risks by a sufficient margin. Except, I can't see any profit for them in eliminating Rahal unless they were paid to hire the fixer. Some of our OCGs will farm out jobs on behalf of other parties, but they take a healthy cut."

"Meaning it's basically a dead end."

"I'm afraid so. The chances of finding whoever took out Rahal's killer are one in a million, worse odds than you'll find in any casino on the planet."

I gave him a wry smile. "Aren't most casinos run by OCG front groups?"

"Yes." He smiled back. "That's it, Commissioner. I'll let you deal with this latest journalistic smear attack in your accustomed manner."

"You mean by ignoring it?"

"Yes, and I envy you that ability. The National Police Service can't quite tell the news media to go forth and multiply without actually uttering a single word."

I let out a chuckle. "This job offers a few perks."

"That it does. Until the next time. Elin, out."

Moments after his link faded away, Admiral Meir, the next on the list of expected callers, appeared on my office display.

"What the hell is going on with you and the news media, Commissioner? Two hatchet jobs in a row are a bit more than coincidence, I'd say. Is someone attempting to destroy your credibility?"

"Possibly. But that's something I can't worry about. I'm keeping my superiors up to date, and a copy of this last one is on its way to Wyvern. They'll decide what, if anything, should be done."

"I daresay you show more patience than I would in your place." Meir paused for a second. "Tell you what. I can offer a set of suites in the transient officer accommodations on the base, a secure incident room, a private and equally secure connection with the 47th Group's HQ, and access to the mess for meals. That way, you won't be ambushed by nasty journos again."

"Thank you for the offer, sir. But it would be best if we don't set up shop on an Armed Forces base at this juncture."

She nodded. "Understood. I figured that would be your answer, but I was duty-bound to offer."

"We will take greater precautions if that reassures you, sir."

"It's your show. I'm just an interested bystander, and I won't ask about your progress. Enjoy the rest of your day."

"Thank you."

"Meir, out."

Skou and his public affairs officer were next. But the only thing I could tell them was that we'd do the same as before — he would issue a statement that the Constabulary would make no comments while the investigation was ongoing, and she'd tell the Chief of Public Affairs at HQ.

When we assembled around the conference table that afternoon, both of my forensic analysts seemed excited. However, they kept the same stoic expressions as before, which presaged actual movement in the case.

"Let's hear it, Sergeant Cincunegui. I sense you've found something of note."

"Yes, sir. We finally found a real discrepancy between *Prospero*'s files and the 212th combat recordings." He pointed at the primary display where a split image appeared. "The still on the left comes from the 212th, taken as they were extracting after eliminating the compound's cartel garrison and rescuing captives. The one on the right comes from *Prospero*, supposedly taken immediately after *Chinggis*' kinetic strike to vaporize the installation. I can say with over ninety-five percent confidence that the second image wasn't taken on the same day, even though it bears a chrono stamp from two hours after the raid."

I examined both images, wondering what difference, other than the compound still standing on the left and replaced by a crater on the right, made Cincunegui come to that conclusion.

"Sorry, Sergeant, I can't see it."

"And you wouldn't, sir. But the AI did. The illumination in both images is noticeably different due to cloud cover and other atmospheric factors. They certainly weren't taken within two hours of each other. We ran a projection of what the illumination and shadows would look like in the hours following the raid, based on atmospheric conditions at the time, and came up with a notably different result. Most telling, the second image was taken in the afternoon when the raid happened at around oh-six-hundred hours local time. The shadows, short and faint as they are, don't lie."

"Meaning Toshiro Rahal's recordings were made after the fact and what they show is a reconstruction of events rather than the raid itself?"

"That's what it looks like, sir."

Arno raised a hand. "I'll play devil's advocate here, Chief. None of this means the 212th didn't play fast and loose with the rules of engagement."

"No, but it discredits the recordings on which the war crimes allegations are based. However, that won't be enough, considering how the newsnets inflamed the situation. It's a shame *Chinggis* broke out of orbit the moment she recovered her Marines and the cartel victims. If she'd stuck around and watched the site of the strike, she might have witnessed cartel survivors working on a lie. It makes me wonder who, among them, thought to exploit the situation via Toshiro Rahal. Perhaps one or more visiting VIPs from higher up in the food chain were enjoying the fleshpots of Bakun and escaped notice." I smiled at Cincunegui. "Excellent work, Sergeant. Was there more?"

"Yes, sir," Sergeant Esadze said. "*Chinggis*' log noted the arrival of sixty-seven humans rescued from the cartel compound, but nothing whatsoever about their identities, not even the slightest hint at age, sex, or planet of origin. The combat imagery taken shows a precision strike on the cartel base, which didn't cause damage much beyond its perimeter. If civilians died they would have been within the walls, and as Teseo will tell you, those who died at the hands of the Marines were armed and fighting back. Besides, the destruction was so comprehensive, there wouldn't be any bodies left to display."

"Another reconstruction."

She nodded. "Clearly. The 212th came nowhere near Bakun, as evidenced both by the visuals and the telemetry covering the entire raid from launch to recovery and entered in the frigate's log."

"And that shifts the focus away from the *Prospero* recordings for the time being."

"What about the so-called victims of atrocities those recordings show?" Arno asked. "Shouldn't we figure whether they were crisis actors or actual victims murdered solely to support the war crimes allegations?"

"I'll send an interim report to ACC Sorjonen informing him of this development. If he wants us to pursue that angle, or the matter of how and why the recordings were made, then fine. Otherwise, we'll examine the actions of the raid's participants to decide whether they violated the rules of engagement or otherwise committed actions that might be construed as criminal, which is the reason we're here. Was there anything else?"

Both sergeants shook their heads.

"What would you like us to look at next?" Cincunegui asked.

"Carry out an in-depth examination of the 212th's combat imagery. Find out if there are deletions or manipulations, that sort of thing. Then, I want each recorded action analyzed in light of the ROE. Chief Inspector Galdi and Warrant Officer Bonta can help with that. We need to be as familiar with the raid as possible before we begin our interviews. And with that, let's hit the gym. I think we can use a good workout."

— Twenty-Six —

When I returned to my room after an hour-long cardio and weight training session, I found a square paper envelope placed on the dayroom's coffee table. It bore no writing, nor did it appear sealed, and at first, I thought the hotel staff put it there. After all, they were the only ones who should be able to enter guest rooms at will.

But before I could reach for the envelope, I hesitated. Considering the turmoil around this case, perhaps touching a mysterious apparition without precautions wasn't the best idea of the moment. Like the rest of my team, I traveled with a service issue sensor, though I rarely carried it unless needed. My jammer took up less space and was more valuable. But on this occasion, I retrieved it from my locked luggage in the bedroom closet, entered my personal activation code, and brought it back to the dayroom.

Paper within paper, ink, and nothing else the sensor could detect. I dug out a pair of gloves from my personal crime scene pack and slipped them on, then carefully picked up the envelope, lifted the flap, and extracted a folded sheet. I unfolded it to formal and well-rounded handwriting, the sort you don't come across often.

Dear Assistant Commissioner Morrow,

The man who murdered Toshiro Rahal was hired by off-world interests. He did not know who they were, but they paid well. Unfortunately, that is all he said before merging with the Infinite Void. His fee for the job was recovered and anonymously donated to the Yekaterinburg District Orphanage. Keep up the good work.

A friend.

After a moment of contemplation, I took images of the note, then slid it back into the envelope and placed the envelope in an evidence bag. General Elin's forensics people would likely find nothing to so much as hint at the sender, but it was now part of the Rahal murder case.

I had little doubt as to the missive's provenance. It could only come from Sergei Ustinov, or more accurately, his people, since the CEO of Taiga Import-Export would keep his public persona well away from the Yekaterinburg Bratva he supposedly ruled like a mafia don of old. And that being the case, I knew it would be child's play for one of them to enter my suite undetected, or more likely with the connivance of hotel staff in the Bratva's pay. Going through the hallway security sensor records most probably wouldn't tell us anything, but I'd leave that up to Elin's investigators as well.

But now I owed HQ and Admiral Talyn yet another contact report. I didn't know who'd tire of them first, ACC Sorjonen or me, but I was fast approaching my limit. When Arno joined me for supper in my suite's day room, I showed him the image I had taken.

He let out a soft grunt and asked, "Krestniy Otets Ustinov's handiwork, I presume?"

"That would be my guess. His people captured Rahal's killer and interrogated him. I presume he didn't survive the experience, meaning he was likely conditioned."

"Which makes him a heavy hitter in the underworld."

"Or a mercenary hired by the *Sécurité Spéciale*. And if not them, then perhaps one of the zaibatsus that run their own black ops organizations. I'm sure Admiral Talyn's people can figure it out, which is just as well — I certainly don't intend to pursue the matter." I took a sip of my drink, wondering about my unknown correspondent's motives. "Why would the Siberiak mob be helping us? Or at least attempting to? It must be more than just patriotism."

Arno shrugged. "Could be they have a bone to pick with Senator Olrik and figure us as a way of ensuring he's impeached and replaced with someone who doesn't proclaim centralist preferences."

"Why would the local mafia be against centralists? You'd think they would prefer weaker star system governments. Or it's a personal matter. Someone simply doesn't like Olrik and wants him gone. He's hardly a pleasant individual. A scandal involving fake war crimes allegations supported by doctored evidence will be enough to make Olrik persona non grata among the Siberiak electorate."

The door chime sounded at that moment, and the security display showed a blocky service droid faintly reminiscent of a miniature transport shuttle hovering in the corridor with our supper. I admitted it, and we both watched as the machine extruded a set of arms, set the small dining room table, then produced covered plates from its locked warming compartment. Once done, it floated back through the door and vanished, its mission done.

"Shall we?"

The following day, I tracked down Chief Inspector Rolfsson, the Constabulary half of the team investigating Toshiro Rahal's murder, gave him the mysterious letter and a statement concerning how I found it and what I did. Then, I prepared the contact report and fired it off to my boss and Admiral Talyn, wondering what they'd make of the idea mobsters might be helping us while a Commonwealth Senator was peddling a false narrative supported by faked evidence. The irony of the situation did not escape me.

What General Elin thought about it, I couldn't tell. By the time late afternoon rolled around, he hadn't called, although I was sure the murder investigation team made him aware of the letter by now. When we gathered around the conference room table, both sergeants and Destine looked at Arno, who cleared his throat.

"A productive day, Chief. We analyzed the 212th's combat imagery for the entire raid. Teseo and Alina found no evidence someone might have tampered with the videos, so we can assume it's a clean record. Destine and I studied each use of weapons and found nothing that indicated a deviation from the standard Special Forces rules of engagement in the Protectorate Zone. The operation was a more or less normal raid against a cartel compound, and none of the deaths recorded can be classified as civilian under the rules that make armed organized crime members legitimate military targets.

"Did they give us every bit of imagery taken? That is the one thing we can't tell. There may be incidents that aren't in the official record. If so, unless someone confesses, we'll never find out. But we watched the Marines liberate and evacuate what looked like victims of human trafficking, and they took still images of every cartel member killed, presumably for the intelligence database.

"We saw no cartel survivors. I selected the most relevant sequences for our interview preparation, which I assume you'll want to carry out tomorrow. There's no reason we should watch every clip."

"In that case, we're visiting Joint Services Base Wolk the day after. I'll let Commander Racitina know. If she'll be stuck to us for the duration, she might as well do something useful, like arrange for an interview room and warn the witnesses."

That evening and the following day passed without hiccups. No interventions from Olrik, Elin, the local Bratva, or the newsnets, and nothing from either Talyn or Sorjonen other than a formal acknowledgment that Racitina could sit in on the interviews. Arno and I ate in my quarters. As before, neither Destine nor the sergeants became the target of the newsnets, the mafia, or anyone else intent on influencing our investigation as they headed out into the underground network.

If nothing else, I was thankful that the various intervening parties left my people alone. But then, I knew wearing an assistant commissioner's rank insignia was a magnet for those intent on scoops, a leg up, or mischief.

I spent the day reviewing the visual recordings from the 212th Pathfinder Squadron, as well as those from *Chinggis* until I was as familiar with the raid as anyone in Major Morozov's command post or the frigate's combat information center. And even I, with my two years as Constabulary liaison officer in the 1st Special Forces Regiment accompanying C Squadron on several operations, couldn't find a violation of the ROEs.

Granted, many civilians would find those rules rather harsh — on the cartels, reivers, pirates, and other assorted scum. But as the immortal saying went, the good citizens of the Commonwealth slept safely at night because rough men and women kept the two-legged animals at bay by whatever means necessary. A few cartel members shot and killed without hesitation by Marines could easily save a few hundred civilians from a fate worse than death. And that sort of math worked for those of us who'd seen the worst of humanity up close, out on the Rim and in the Protectorate Zone.

"So, Chief?" Arno asked, dropping into the chair across from me, coffee cup in hand, during the afternoon break.

"What we found was a clean operation conducted under Grand Admiral Larsson's rules of engagement. People might disagree with those ROEs, but the Marines kept to them. The only civilians in the records are those who were evacuated, in other words, victims. But we still need corroboration from the witnesses to make sure there aren't any gaps in the evidence. By now, I'm sure they've re-watched the raid from end to end ad nauseam, so we'll need to probe for missing bits, but bugger if I can come up with obvious questions. But there's one thing I noticed about the civilians they rescued."

Arno gave me a knowing look. "I was hoping you'd pick up on it. The ones we spotted were children."

"Precisely. Not a single adult. Perhaps not even a single teenager."

"A shame we can't ask about the true nature of the mission on Torga. I'm sure it wasn't a hot pursuit of an obvious pirate. The answer to that would wrap up the case, at least where our superiors are concerned."

I winked at him in a conspiratorial fashion. "We may not be able to ask officially, but that's never stopped me before."

"No, it hasn't. Mind you, the answer still won't explain Senator Olrik's vendetta. What he thought he might gain is beyond me at the moment. Any old fool should know we'd find out Rahal's video was a fabrication once we dug through the official mission records. I suppose he and whoever else is in this with him figured the lie would propagate faster than light while the truth was still getting its boots on."

I shrugged. "They figured the mission records would never be released to an outsider because of their security classification, leaving the fabrication as the only publicly available so-called evidence. Except they didn't count on us seeing those records."

"Which makes me wonder what they'll do next once their scheme collapses."

"Ours is not to wonder what or why, Arno. After we present our findings to ACC Sorjonen, that's it. We go home with no one being the wiser until the Chief Constable formally announces the results of the investigation."

Arno snorted. "If ever. It might just end up with Grand Admiral Larsson putting a flea in the Senate Speaker's ear to rein Olrik in. After that, the story just fades away as the newsnets receive orders to pretend the allegations never happened. If nothing else, the great zaibatsus who own them know when to cut their losses."

"Cynic."

"Realist. We've had this little debate before, Chief. I'm just an old idealist who was mugged by reality. The zaibatsus own at least half of the Senate — the Home World half — and they own the major newsnets. They'll back off and look for another way of driving a wedge between the Fleet and the OutWorlds."

I cocked an eyebrow at my long-time winger. "Is that what you think they're doing?"

"In part." He nodded. "I was thinking about it last night, and it makes sense. But I'm sure that's not the entire story."

"No, it's not. If I'm right, blackening the Fleet's reputation is a target of opportunity, not the main reason for this circus."

"And that would be?"

As I explained my theory, I became increasingly convinced I was right, but I would need Sonier and Morozov's confirmation.

— Twenty-Seven —

Lieutenant Commander Racitina greeted Arno and me by the main entrance to the Support Group HQ at precisely oh-eight-hundred the next morning. After snapping off a salute, she said, "Good morning, Commissioner, Chief Inspector, I've arranged for us to use the secure client-solicitor interview room in the JAG offices. It's proof against eavesdropping, but you can still record."

"Thank you, Commander. We'll be taking notes, but no recordings for security reasons."

She ushered us into the building and toward the stairs. "Major Morozov is waiting in my office. Commander Sonier is across the quadrangle with Admiral Meir's staff. The rest of the witnesses from the 212th are on call in their barracks."

"And I need to read you in before we start with Major Morozov. We can do that in the interview room."

Once in the JAG offices, we left our overcoats in the main closet and headed straight for the interview room, whose door sign said 'Occupied. See LCdr Racitina for details.'

The interview room wasn't exactly cozy by any means but nowhere near as bleak as the standard police version. Its walls were painted a soothing cream color and illuminated by gentle lighting. The floor was covered in the same light gray patterned tile as the rest of the building. Several scenes of military life hung above the sideboards while a large display covered the far wall where I'd expected a window. A wood-topped oval table occupied its center, with three padded upright chairs on each side. A recording station sat on one sideboard to the left while a jug of water, glasses, a coffee urn, and cups occupied the other sideboard.

Arno and I sat in front of the recording station and pulled out our pads. I handed mine to Racitina.

"You know how this works. Read the entire text, then make the declaration out loud and thumb at the bottom."

She nodded and took my pad. Her eyes moved over the text, then she looked up at me.

"I, Lieutenant Commander Katy Racitina, Commonwealth Navy Reserve, Judge Advocate General Branch, do hereby declare that I understand the strictures involved in being granted the clearance Top Secret Special Access Codename *Reilly*. I also understand and acknowledge that if I reveal any information covered by the clearance without authorization from the classifying officer, Assistant Commissioner Caelin Morrow, Professional Compliance Bureau, Commonwealth Constabulary, or misuse said information, I will be prosecuted under the Official Secrets Act."

Racitina thumbed the declaration and handed back my pad. I checked to ensure the signature corresponded to the biometrics on file, then saved it.

"The way this will work is that I don't want you to intervene or interrupt. If you have concerns with my or Chief Inspector Galdi's questions or the witnesses' answers, please raise a hand and wait until I give you the go-ahead. Otherwise, I expect you to stay silent. Do you understand?"

She nodded. "Yes, Commissioner."

"I'll be using the display to go through the visuals. How do I control it?"

Racitina pointed at the touch screen embedded in the tabletop in front of me. "Just place your data chip there and follow the instructions. It works like any other system."

"Thank you. Any questions?"

Racitina shook her head. "No."

"Then please fetch Major Morozov."

She left us alone in the interview room for less than a minute before reappearing with a stocky, broad-shouldered, dark-haired man in his late thirties. He wore a black Marine garrison uniform with a major's single diamond and oak leaf wreath at the collar and a set of gold Pathfinder wings with combat jump stars on his chest. His blue beret, worn at a rakish angle, was adorned with the crest of the 21st Regiment. Morozov's hooded, deep blue eyes rested briefly on Arno, then on me or, more precisely, my silver Pathfinder wings as he came to attention on the opposite side of the table and saluted.

"Major Dagon Morozov reporting to Assistant Commissioner Morrow as ordered."

I returned the salute, then gestured at the chair across from me. "Please sit. You understand why you're here, correct?"

"Yes, sir. You're investigating allegations that the 212th Pathfinder Squadron committed war crimes during a mission on Torga." His tone, like his expression, was carefully neutral, though his eyes held a spark of something. Irritation, perhaps?

"Precisely. We reviewed the visual records provided by your unit and the frigate *Chinggis* covering the raid you conducted and will ask you questions for clarification. At this point, we will not record your answers other than in our notebooks, as this is not an interview under caution, let alone an interrogation. Feel free to elaborate on your answers since we are here to understand what happened on that day, not assign blame, let alone lay charges. Grand Admiral Larsson alone will decide the next steps. We are merely acting as the Armed Forces' internal investigations unit. Do you understand, Major?"

He inclined his head. "Yes, sir."

"This investigation is classified Top Secret Special Access Codename *Reilly*. Nothing we discuss here this morning shall be shared with anyone else, not even members of your unit who hold TSSA clearance."

"Understood, sir."

"Were you involved in collating the recordings for us after I spoke with Colonel Freijs?"

"Yes."

"And what we received included every bit taken from the moment the 212th's dropships left *Chinggis* until they returned."

"Yes."

"No omissions, accidental or otherwise?"

"No."

"Then begin." I produced a data wafer and placed it on the touch screen. A few taps and the primary display came to life with the first of the 212th's combat imagery recordings. "Please take me through the raid step by step."

Over the next hour, Morozov interpreted every bit of video for us with an assured voice, never faltering, as we watched his Marines wipe out cartel members with extreme prejudice, drain the compound's computer core, and liberate bedraggled civilians. Arno, in his role of curious cop who never served with Special Forces, asked several questions designed to elicit responses that might contradict the visual evidence or the after-action report filed with SOCOM, but Morozov remained steady and always on target. By the time we were done, I knew he'd told us nothing but the unvarnished truth. There was no sign the 212th violated the rules of engagement.

"Thank you for your candor, Major. You're dismissed."

Morozov stood, saluted, and left the room.

"Serious sort of character, isn't he?" Arno asked no one in particular.

A smile lit up Racitina's face. "He's known as Deadpan Dagon in the 21st Regiment on account of his sober mien."

"Well, he wasn't holding back, which is to his credit. Can we see Commander Sonier now?"

"Yes, sir."

Racitina left the room. Several minutes passed before she returned with *Chinggis'* captain, who looked just as composed as her Marine colleague, as she saluted me and sat. I gave Sonier the same spiel as Morozov and had her take us through the operation from the moment her ship launched the 212th until they recovered the dropships and struck the cartel compound with a kinetic penetrator rod.

Then, we discussed *Prospero* sitting on the ground at Bakun, and she confirmed the free trader was noted by her CIC and classified as not representing a threat. *Chinggis'* last scan of Torga before going FTL showed *Prospero* still on the landing strip.

Neither my nor Arno's questions could uncover the slightest inconsistency. Sonier was as confident and as firm as Morozov.

"That's it, Commander, thank you."

"Will you be interviewing members of my crew?"

"I'm not planning to do so at the moment."

"Good. They're due shore leave, and I'd rather not send them off only to recall a bunch halfway through their downtime. Can I go now?"

"Yes."

"Sir." Sonier stood, saluted, and left on her own.

"That's two for two, Commissioner," Racitina said. "Who's next?"

"We'll see the 212th's battle captain before lunch, then the sergeant major and the four troop leaders after lunch."

None of them brought anything new to the investigation. The battle captain and the sergeant major corroborated Morozov's description of the raid, as did the four troop leaders, albeit on their own, smaller scale. By the time sixteen hundred rolled around, I was ready to draft my report. There would be no use in speaking with anyone else. The evidence was overwhelmingly in favor of neither *Chinggis* nor the 212th violating their ROE. Which meant someone went to great effort and expense creating a false narrative, but that would be a separate investigation. Perhaps even something for Admiral Talyn's people to resolve in secret.

As Racitina escorted us down to the main entrance, she asked, "Is that it, sir?"

"Pretty much. As you saw, there really wasn't any need for the witnesses to have counsel present. We're hardly ogres when we're simply looking for facts rather than interrogating suspected criminals after we arrest them."

She smiled. "Good to know. And truthfully, I enjoyed the experience of seeing how you corroborated the recorded evidence. It's always a treat watching pros in action. I suppose I can go back to my civilian practice now."

"Yes. And before we part ways, a reminder that you cannot discuss anything related to this case with anyone."

"Understood, sir. Everything I've heard and seen comes under the same strictures as client-solicitor privilege. That being said, it was a pleasure and a lesson, Commissioner." She drew herself straight and saluted.

I returned the compliment. "Goodbye, Commander Racitina."

Once in the car, I switched on my jammer while Arno got us on our way back into town.

"After-action review tonight or tomorrow, Chief?"

"Oh, tomorrow, once I've drafted my report. Probably in the afternoon."

"You know we only answered half of the question, right?"

I nodded. "Yes, but it's the one they tasked us to answer. I don't think this is the sort of case where we can afford mission creep without authority because of the visibility."

"Will you tell anyone that we didn't find evidence to support Olrik's allegations?"

"Sonier and Morozov, certainly, to put their minds at ease. Meir and Freijs as well. But that's it."

"Not Elin?"

"No. He'll find out the same as everyone else — once our superiors issue a press release. Military personnel, I can swear to secrecy by invoking the fires of Mount Hades on Parth. A Sovereign Star System police chief, not so much."

Arno gave me a curious look. "Mount Hades? I didn't know such a place existed."

"That's because I just made it up. Sounds more dramatic than Desolation Island, which does exist."

"True." He smirked. "How about we throw caution to the wind, enjoy a drink in the hotel bar and eat in the restaurant for a change, seeing as we're done but for the paperwork?"

"After I hit the pool and do a few lengths."

"Of course. I shall visit the cardio center and pay for my sins of gluttony in advance."

— Twenty-Eight —

That evening, Arno and I enjoyed a drink at the bar with no one present taking notice of us. Seeing as how we'd decided on the war crimes allegations, even though no one other than Racitina knew about it — and even she could only surmise based on the interviews — the paranoid in me expected an appearance by Olrik and his tame newsnet personalities. Or perhaps one of Novaya Sibir's leading mafia bosses. But we sat in splendid isolation admiring the dancing ribbons of an aurora borealis kiss the northern horizon now that a shattering cold snap was descending on Yekaterinburg.

"Nice view," Arno remarked after swallowing a healthy sip of his favorite Imperial Stout. "Not something we'd enjoy on Wyvern, let alone Cimmeria."

"True. But I'll take a more temperate climate and a less active sun any day of the week."

"I was only speaking as a tourist, Chief, not as a would-be immigrant. My views on a warm environment versus a cold one are no secret." He'd obviously seen my eyes quartering the bar's main room every few seconds. "Expecting company?"

"Dreading, more like. Why, I couldn't say. It's not like anyone has a clue as to where we're at with the case."

"If I hadn't been your winger for so long, I'd say guilty conscience, but knowing better, perhaps you realize that even though the official investigation is done, more looms on the horizon, and you're searching for signs to confirm it."

"Or I'm merely tired, and as you might remember, fatigue makes me somewhat paranoid. Perhaps this time, it's catching up before I tap out."

"A full day of interviews and note-taking can sap one's energy. Especially considering what we knew going into them." Arno took another swig of his stout. "But I still think you're looking beyond the horizon for what comes next because you know it isn't over until it's over."

"Or until the ACC recalls us for the next job."

"That too."

We finished our drinks in silence, then, by common accord, we stood and walked across the floor to the hotel restaurant.

The moment we entered, Arno let out a soft grunt. "Uh-oh. I guess even paranoids are right sometimes. Now, why would he dine with a large party in the middle of the main dining room?"

I spotted Senator Olrik, Carla Hautcoeur, and a half dozen other local notables, three of whom were Duma members and the rest corporate chief executives. However, if Ustinov was anything to go by, at least one of them might be a krestniy otets in his leisure time. Olrik's bodyguards and the bland-looking aide who'd scrutinized me the other evening sat at a smaller table to one side, keeping their boss and everyone else under scrutiny.

"To be seen, Arno. Novaya Sibir's senior Commonwealth Senator is showing everyone he's perfectly at his ease in public, even though he stirred up a major controversy."

At my request, the maître d' led us to a corner table from which we could watch the Olrik party without being too obvious. The closest diners were sufficiently distant that they couldn't overhear a quiet conversation thanks to the dampening fields.

Once we were alone, I reached into my pocket. "Jammer's on, Arno. We can talk."

"Good. So, you figure Olrik is living large as a way of warding off the inevitable? He must know the evidence on which he based his allegations is fake from top to bottom and that we'll inevitably find out."

"In fairness, the good senator wasn't counting on an investigation getting access to top secret military data when he launched his campaign, the sort of data we can use to discredit Rahal's recordings." I absently scanned the menu for the day's prix fixe. "Mind you, Olrik won't know for certain we got said access unless someone close to the case spoke out of turn."

Arno scoffed. "An operator like him is probably evaluating worst-case scenarios. This sitting in full view with a coterie of notables is pure bravado if you ask me."

"Looks like he saw us."

Olrik and Hautcoeur, heads together and staring in our direction, were obviously exchanging comments about us, judging by the disdainful smiles they wore like badges of honor. Both nudged the people beside them. They, in turn, gave us nothing more than brief, unfriendly stares. Arno and I did our best to ignore them as the service droid appeared with our wine glasses and appetizer plates.

Under the adage that the best revenge was living well, we'd both taken the five-course prix fixe with wine pairing and enjoyed our meal in the leisurely fashion of those without worries. In fact, glimpsing Olrik out of the corner of my eyes, I could read concern on his face as he surreptitiously watched us converse and laugh like the two old friends we were.

When we finally left after a sinfully delicious slice of cake and a rich, dark espresso, I could feel Olrik's eyes burning holes in my back. If we'd shaken him by our air of insouciance, so much the better.

The following day, I made sure everyone was clear about which of the case report's appendices to write and sat behind my desk to compose the main narrative. As I'd already written the principal sections in my head the previous evening and since getting up this morning, it proved a reasonably pain-free exercise. Of course, the meat of the findings would be in the appendices detailing every step we took and every conclusion we made based on the evidence. We were ready to parse each other's work for mistakes, inconsistencies, and the like by lunch.

When we regrouped later that afternoon, I went through my usual process of asking for comments, starting with the most junior in rank, Sergeant First Class Alina Esadze.

"Raise any points you may think of, Sergeant. This report has to be absolutely perfect, and even assistant commissioners make mistakes."

"Yes, sir." She seemed just a tad uncertain.

"Am I right in guessing you're not normally asked to comment on case reports?"

Esadze shook her head. "No."

"I see. The standard operating procedure in the teams I lead is to dissect what I've prepared for the boss. It reduces the chances of my overlooking something or, worse yet, getting a small but important fact wrong. ACC Sorjonen forgives many things but never sloppy, incomplete, or error-ridden paperwork. Our reputation isn't only based on incorruptibility but getting everything unquestionably right." I pointed my hand, palm up, toward her in a go-ahead gesture.

But Esadze offered no comments. Neither did Cincunegui, Destine, or Arno.

"So, we agree. There is no evidence the frigate *Chinggis* or the 212th Pathfinder Squadron violated their rules of engagement, let alone committed war crimes as defined in the Commonwealth Criminal Code and the Code of Service Discipline during the raid on Torga."

One after the other, they nodded.

"Then this investigation is suspended until further notice. I will see that an encrypted version of the report goes out to Wyvern as soon as possible. We will keep this incident room and the evidence we collected until HQ closes the case formally. But in the interim, take a breather, do some sightseeing, and relax. Arno and I will deal with the local military chain of command tomorrow. And thank you for your excellent work. You're a credit to the Constabulary and the Professional Compliance Bureau. Lock up your things and get out of here."

I read the report one last time in splendid isolation, then produced two encrypted copies, one for ACC Sorjonen and one for Admiral Talyn. I walked them to the communications center and waited while the duty officer sent both via special subspace packets.

On my way to the hotel, that familiar post-investigation wave of fatigue washed over me, and I contemplated the joys of a nap before supper. But considering the previous evening's rich meal, I opted for a solid forty-five minutes of vigorous swimming, which left me ready for a light dinner and an early bedtime.

The following day, I called Admiral Meir and Colonel Freijs to arrange for a private meeting with them, Sonier, Morozov, and Racitina in the secure JAG interview room we'd used two days ago. Once again, Racitina greeted Arno and me at the Support Unit HQ's main entrance when we arrived shortly after lunch and announced everyone was already there. We found the four officers sitting at the oval table, coffee cup in hand, engaged in desultory conversation, which faded away the moment I entered.

"Good afternoon, everyone. Thank you for coming." Arno and I took two of the three remaining seats while Racitina took the third. I glanced around the table, meeting their eyes. "I concluded my investigation into the war crimes allegations brought forth by Senator Fedor Olrik and submitted my report to HQ on Wyvern late yesterday afternoon. What I am about to say is covered by the same Top Secret Special Access

Codename *Reilly* as the rest of the case. Nothing can
be discussed even among yourselves once we're done
here until your chain of command makes my
findings public. I trust you understand."

The tension around the table rose perceptibly, not
in small part because of my flat tone and neutral
expression, but they nodded.

"My report states unequivocally that we found no
evidence whatsoever that Commander Sonier or
Major Morozov, or any of the Armed Forces
members under their respective commands, violated
the rules of engagement in effect at the time of the
raid on Torga. We, therefore, disproved the
allegations. Further, my report states that there are
enough discrepancies between the combat imagery
taken by *Chinggis* and the 212th to indicate the video
submitted by Senator Olrik and provided to him by
the late Toshiro Rahal via Galactic Newsnet might
be in part or in total a fabrication created for an
unknown purpose."

Freijs let out an indelicate snort. "Hardly
unknown, Commissioner, and not just in part."

I gave him a silent look for a few heartbeats.
"Perhaps, Colonel. But I can only comment on
matters about which I'm sure beyond any
reasonable doubt. And in this case, it is a fact the
evidence does not support the allegations. As such,
my investigation is closed. A decision on whether
the suspected fabrication requires a separate inquiry
will be made by someone much senior to me."

"What happens now?" Meir asked.

"Everyone carries on with their duties as if this never happened. In due course, you'll receive instructions from Fleet HQ. I will, however, suggest *Chinggis* and the 212th return to their patrol route as soon as possible, Admiral, although they're owed time ashore. Get them out of the public eye and away from the newsnets while my report wends its way up my chain of command and across to yours. The fact I'm no longer working on the case will become known soon enough — especially once we climb aboard a Constabulary cutter headed for Wyvern — and everyone will clamor for even the slightest hint about the result. Do not, under any circumstances, comment on the matter or its outcome, and do not allow anyone from the frigate or the squadron to do so. That will be for someone with more stars on their collar."

After a moment, Meir nodded. "I understand, Commissioner. Don't worry, we'll make sure everyone here stays perfectly stumm."

"With the caveat that I might not be able to answer all of them, do you have questions?"

Freijs raised his hand. "What are you going to do about that lying bastard Olrik and his scheme to defame the finest Marines and spacers in the Fleet?"

I gave him a faintly amused look. "Me? Nothing. My work here is done. Beyond that, I can't comment. Anything else?"

When no one said a word, I locked eyes with Meir. "Admiral, I'd like to speak privately with Commander Sonier and Major Morozov before leaving."

After a few heartbeats, she nodded reluctantly. "Very well."

Then she stood, imitated by Freijs. "Thank you, Commissioner, and don't take this the wrong way, but I hope we never see you again."

I chuckled. "That's pretty much what everyone says, Admiral."

Neither of them offered their hand. Instead, they nodded and filed out behind Racitina. I closed the door and turned to Sonier and Morozov.

"Alright. Time to tell me what your objective on Torga really was."

— Twenty-Nine —

Sonier gave me an arch look. "I don't understand what you mean, Commissioner. And I'd be more comfortable with Commander Racitina present if you're going to cover ground we already mined exhaustively."

I held her gaze for a few seconds longer than most people consider comfortable. To her credit, Sonier never wavered.

"As I said, the investigation is over, and my report is sitting on my commanding officer's desk at Constabulary HQ by now. Nothing I wish to discuss at the moment will affect the outcome. But your answers may influence events that don't affect either of you. So, I need the full truth." I'd already figured out the answer but wanted to be sure I was right.

"I'm not sure I follow," Morozov said.

"Or I."

"Trying to hang war crimes allegations around your necks was nothing less than an attempt by party or parties unknown to turn a routine raid inside the Protectorate Zone — one of many, albeit none of them are ever acknowledged — into an atrocity. Those responsible didn't do it primarily to discredit the Fleet. It was overly elaborate and surprisingly amateurish for a concerted effort at blackening your reputation. This means there's more, and that, in turn, means this isn't over, not by a long shot, at least not for the folks who are using the intel you collected to work their way up the cartel's food chain and find its backers. And that is something which might involve me and my team or another Constabulary unit since we've worked with the Fleet on similar issues before, the sort involving both organized crime and national security.

"Therefore, I need to know what the Torga mission was really about. Clearly, it wasn't a pursuit in the heat of battle as per the official statement, but a carefully planned and executed operation in a star system beyond the Fleet's remit under the Treaty of Ulufan. I served in a Special Forces squadron in my younger days and can tell from your data. So, why did you raid that particular cartel compound on that particular backwater planet?"

"Your security clearance isn't sufficient," Sonier replied. "With respect."

I gave her the coldest of my smiles, one which could stop electrons from orbiting around their atom's core in Arno's considered opinion.

"A senior Professional Compliance Bureau officer investigating classified events at the behest of the Grand Admiral has the clearance she needs for everything related to said events, Commander. Now tell me about the Torga mission. In detail. I won't put anything in writing, let alone add it to my official report."

"Why?"

"It's clear the primary reason Senator Olrik pushed the allegations was to cover up the cartel activities on Torga by pre-emptively discrediting the Fleet's actions. This would give the cartel's backers a chance to destroy evidence that might link them with serious criminal activity. Attacking the Armed Forces' reputation was, in military parlance, a target of opportunity. It, therefore, means the reason we ended up dealing with Senator Olrik's allegations in this fashion was because the Fleet cannot reveal certain details, so Naval Intelligence's ongoing work hunting those backers wouldn't be compromised."

When Sonier's eyes widened, I gave her a grim smile.

"I was chosen for this case because I've cooperated with Naval Intelligence before and know how things work in the deepest depths of black ops. That being said, the Fleet is the only thing standing between humanity and a third migration war, so I'd rather it not be embroiled in political garbage pushed by the likes of Senator Olrik and the centralist faction. Especially not when the primary goal is keeping the venality of our elites hidden. Now, the actual story, if you please."

Morozov and Sonier exchanged a glance.

"It was a planned raid," the former said. "Intelligence uncovered the terminus of a new human trafficking operation, and we — *Chinggis* and my squadron — were the closest strike team to the target. These days, we act as quickly as possible in such cases where before, it would be left to the 1st Special Forces Regiment. This is ever since the regiment's Ghost Squadron discovered that the victims of a particular human trafficking cartel ended up as supper for a rather primitive non-human species."

I nodded. "It involved one of our undercover officers. She almost died at the hands of those non-humans."

"Then you understand the urgency of going after actionable intelligence. Our orders were to sail to Torga, liberate the victims, gather what intel we could, destroy the cartel's installations, and terminate cartel members with extreme prejudice."

I cocked an eyebrow at Morozov. "Terminate?"

"The era of taking cartel members back from beyond the Commonwealth sphere as prisoners is over, except in certain circumstances. Since we can't convince them to stop engaging in the slave trade, the only solution is eliminating every last one until they're gone. In this case, the victims we recovered were mainly under twelve years old and destined as playthings for the most depraved sentient beings in the galaxy, so we hoisted the black flag." He paused, studying me to see if I caught the reference. When I nodded, he continued. "We also recovered information from the cartel base, which will allow Naval Intelligence to track the abductors, those who run the transport network, and their financiers. A Navy Q ship took the victims off *Chinggis* in deep space."

"And neither Admiral Meir nor Colonel Freijs is privy to the real reasons for the raid?"

"No. When Naval Intelligence or SOCOM issues immediate execute orders, they bypass the battle group and regiment. Our after-action reports up our regular chains of command are redacted as per mission instructions. Only operational control at HQ on Caledonia gets the full story."

I contemplated Sonier for a bit. "Then you understand the war crime allegations were to smear you and destroy your credibility before the truth emerged. Or at least before Naval Intelligence leaked part of the actual story to discredit the cartel's respectable backers, the sort no one can touch because they're in the highest of places."

"Such as the Senate, sir?" Morozov asked. "But how can you prove that?"

"I'm not sure it'll be up to me, Major. I completed my assignment. My guess is, whoever's behind the trumped-up war crimes allegations didn't expect Grand Admiral Larsson would immediately ask us to investigate and pre-empt their entire scheme by putting the PCB on the case. It's probably a given that Toshiro Rahal was murdered at the schemers' behest because they feared he'd tell the truth under Constabulary interrogation. They probably hired one of the local bratvas, or if the plotters were high enough in the food chain, ordered the *Sécurité Spéciale* to do it. You know who they are, right?"

"Yes, sir. What we call the opposition in the Special Forces community."

I nodded once. "Just so."

"When will Olrik find out it failed?"

"In due course. And with that, we're done here. Our job was determining whether you violated the rules of engagement, nothing else. And you didn't. Thank you for your cooperation. I don't doubt that they'll slap my casefile with a top secret special access designation, so you're not to discuss it even with each other. But as far as the Constabulary's Professional Compliance Bureau is concerned, you're cleared of the specified war crimes allegations. We will not revisit them."

"Understood, sir, and thank you." Morozov glanced at Sonier, who nodded.

Arno and I stood. "Goodbye, and may you enjoy many more years of hunting bad guys."

Both sprang up and came to attention. Morozov cracked a smile and said, "The same to you, Commissioner. I guess the only actual difference between us is the color of our uniforms. Safe jumps."

We shook hands and walked out of the secure conference room where Lieutenant Commander Racitina waited to escort us out.

"Everything's good, Commissioner?"

"I have the answers I need." We picked up our overcoats in the JAG suite reception room and headed down the stairs.

Once at the main entrance, I considered Racitina for a second or two. "Mind if I give you advice from the other side of the table, Commander?"

"Sure."

"Choose a single legal career path. Either resign your reserve commission or transfer into a non-legal job, or join the Fleet as a regular legal officer. Being a civilian criminal lawyer and a reserve JAG officer doesn't work unless you stick to defending spacers charged with drunk and disorderly while on shore leave. You can't afford too many more situations like this one before someone wonders about the wisdom of a partner in a large firm with certain interesting clients also practicing law for the Fleet."

"Yes, sir." She smiled at me. "Apropos of nothing, Saga's stepmom sends her best. Good hunting, Commissioner."

She saluted, turned on her heels, and vanished into the corridor.

Arno gave me a quizzical glance. "Saga's stepmom?"

It took me a few moments to make the connection. The only Saga I'd met in recent times was a Marine Corps intelligence analyst and the apple of her father's eye. Said father, Colonel Zack Decker, married Rear Admiral Talyn in a military wedding I'd never forget for its splendor, camaraderie, and downright fun. And that made her Saga's stepmother.

"I believe the commander was referring to my friend Hera, Zack's spouse."

"Well, I'll be superannuated," Arno muttered. "Another of the Navy's secret squirrels. No wonder the admiral had no problems with you reading her into the investigation."

"And I'll bet Racitina suggested to the AJAG that she be involved in her legal capacity so she could monitor us and hear what we hear, for Admiral Talyn's benefit, of course. Now I feel like a fool for attempting to lecture her. That'll teach me. I suppose we can both guess what Racitina does for Naval Intelligence in her civilian career." I couldn't help but grin. "She hid it well."

"That she did. Mind you, we feed the admiral highly classified information as well occasionally, which makes us colleagues of sorts."

I growled at him. "Don't remind me. Sometimes the degree to which we anti-corruption officers cozy up to Naval Intelligence is just a little disturbing."

"In a good cause, Chief, as you told those frontier roaming youngsters just now. There can't be a better one than avoiding a third ruinous civil war."

"True."

Once back in our car, I switched on my jammer while Arno lit up the power pack and got us in gear.

"I'll entertain any idea or thought, no matter how outrageous."

He grinned, eyes locked on the control screen. "Such as secretly investigating a Commonwealth Senator without authorization?"

"The possibility occurred to me. Crimes were committed, that of attempting to slander the Commonwealth Armed Forces, which is a form of sedition, and perverting the course of justice by knowingly proffering charges based on falsified evidence."

"Shouldn't we leave that up to Admiral Talyn, though, Chief? She has more appropriate resources than us mere cops."

"We're here, and the proverbial is about to hit the force field — with a little help. Who knows what facts will emerge, maybe something that might be lost if we wait for ACC Sorjonen or Admiral Talyn's direction? I know our commanding officer encourages the sort of initiative most senior officers consider too risky, provided we obtain results. The admiral is no different."

"Then we go on the hunt for a specific Siberiak senator." The grin returned. "We've not cuffed one of his sort yet."

"Are you keeping track of every coup you count?"

"Sure. Aren't you? Besides, what else will we do once our report makes the rounds and the powers that be decide how they'll deal with the newsnets and the centralists' false accusations? It could take weeks, and you know how good I am with idleness."

"You think I should finally accede to Olrik's demands, meet with him, jammer switched on, and let him know we figure he's full of it?"

"Could be fun, Chief." Arno turned his head and gave me a look that many might qualify as slightly maniacal. "We fixed Mission Colony on our own. Why not fix this mess as well? I doubt the Grand Inquisitor will mind if we present him with a neatly wrapped present. So long as no one finds out we're investigating a Commonwealth Senator until we present the Chief Constable with enough evidence for a chat with the Speaker of the Senate, we're golden."

"Then how about we stampede Olrik into making a fatal mistake."

A brief grimace crossed Arno's face. "That could be dangerous if he has one of the bratvas in his back pocket or a zaibatsu operative on call."

"Or the *Sécurité Spéciale* in support, if this is larger than just covering up human trafficking financed by highly placed people in business and government."

"Okay. We don't stampede him. We merely make him increasingly paranoid until he stumbles."

"A better plan, Chief. What if we don't uncover any evidence before HQ recalls us?"

"Then I discuss our suspicions with ACC Sorjonen and let him take it from there. But I will let Admiral Talyn know what we're up to right away. She has resources we can only dream of and enough influence at court to see us employed in the service of a good cause."

— Thirty —

When I returned to our now empty incident room, I composed a message for Admiral Talyn, telling her about my intention of scrutinizing Senator Olrik's role in the trumped-up war crimes allegations while my report wound its way up to the Chief Constable and across to Grand Admiral Larsson. As a lark, I added a comment to the effect that Lieutenant Commander Katy Racitina sends her regards. Since the missive was encrypted and for her eyes only, I figured I could risk it.

Moments after I returned from the communications center, having seen my message off on a priority basis, the 47th Group's public affairs officer called.

"Commissioner, Gina Graetz, that reporter with Novaya Sibir Information Broadcasters, put up a stream concerning your investigation a few moments ago. I think you need to hear it. What she relates is rather inflammatory. I've forwarded the link to your office workstation. Let me know what, if anything, you'd like us to issue in return."

Her expression was so solemn I gave her a crooked smile. "That bad?"

"You be the judge, Commissioner."

"In that case, we'll talk later. Thanks for warning me."

I called up the feed in question and sat back when Graetz's irritatingly perky face appeared on my office display.

"In new developments today, sources close to the Constabulary investigation into war crimes allegations against two Novaya Sibir-based Armed Forces units tell us Assistant Commissioner Caelin Morrow, of the Professional Compliance Bureau's Anti-Corruption Twelve, is preparing to submit her findings. If she hasn't yet done so."

My eyebrows rose by their own volition. Who spoke out of school?

"For commentary on this, I contacted Senator Fedor Olrik, who first raised the allegations in the Senate and demanded a full inquiry." The image dissolved into one where Olrik and Graetz sat facing each other over a low coffee table — a virtual reality construct, no doubt. "Senator, what are your thoughts on the news that Assistant Commissioner Morrow concluded the investigation?"

Olrik gave her a smile that didn't quite reach his eyes. "I, for one, will be glad when this charade is over. Then, we can conduct a properly constituted inquiry by a committee of senators empaneled for the express purpose of examining the Fleet's increasingly illegal actions on our frontiers and beyond it."

"Do you think Assistant Commissioner Morrow will produce a finding of not guilty?"

He chuckled. "That would be for a court to decide, obviously. But I do expect Morrow to exonerate the individuals involved, so they never face the justice they so richly deserve. It's been clear to everyone watching with an impartial eye that having the Constabulary — even the much-vaunted Professional Compliance Bureau — investigate these allegations is akin to putting a poacher in charge of a wildlife sanctuary full of endangered species. In other words, not just negligence, but madness."

"If the outcome is as you expect, do you contemplate taking legislative action and achieve true justice via the Senate?"

Olrik's smile became positively vulpine. "Just watch me."

"Thank you for taking a few minutes to discuss the matter with me, Senator."

"Always a pleasure, Gina."

The image faded out, leaving me to stare at a blank display. Did Olrik just declare his intention to stay with what he surely realized was a rapidly disintegrating ship? Or was he counting on a surprise to derail the conclusion of this case?

I mentally parsed the evidence one more time and didn't find a single flaw he might exploit. If he persisted, I was convinced Grand Admiral Larsson would share the comparison we prepared between the actual video and Toshiro Rahal's faked recordings. But that was not my problem at the moment. Dealing with Olrik in the immediate, on the other hand? Did the leaked information that I was done come from someone attempting to help me find an opening I could exploit, say, someone like a Naval Intelligence operative with dual civilian and Navy legal careers?

The more I thought about it, the more I figured someone like Admiral Talyn and even my own boss were keen on me ending this business here and now before Olrik lit a fresh fire in the Senate, where he enjoyed immunity. And that meant finding out why he went to such great lengths in smearing Fleet units publicly when he knew the evidence didn't support his allegations. But how? I called the public affairs officer back and told her we would ignore Gaetz's so-called reportage and Senator Olrik's comments.

That done, I stood, shrugged on my overcoat, then walked around the incident room to make sure everything was secure before heading off to the hotel and its gym. Perhaps a slow jog on one of the virtual reality trainers would help my brain give birth to ideas I might discuss with Arno and Destine, something that would drive Olrik into making mistakes we could exploit.

When I entered the cardio facility, I found Arno power walking in one of the trainers. He gave me a quick wave without missing a beat. Based on the sheen of sweat on his brow, he'd been at it for a while. I started my routine, but Arno made his presence known halfway through. Since I figured he wouldn't interrupt me for no good reason, I paused the simulation but kept the treadmill going.

"What's up, Arno?"

"You saw Gina Graetz's latest hit job?"

"Yep. And I spoke with the public affairs officer about it. As usual, no comment."

"That's what I wanted to know. We can discuss the matter later. Sorry for interrupting you, Chief."

"Think nothing of it."

An hour later, Arno and Destine filed into my sitting room, both with their favorite predinner libation in hand, and sat across from where I was enjoying a cold gin and tonic.

"So," Arno took a sip of his stout, "who'd you think these sources close to the investigation might be?"

"It's not the sergeants or us. We understand the consequences of unauthorized leaks to the newsnets. That leaves Meir, Freijs, Sonier, Morozov, and Racitina."

Destine grimaced. "Unless one of those five spoke to a family member, friend, colleague, or other unauthorized people after our meeting."

"Doubtful when it comes to the admiral, Colonel Freijs, Commander Sonier, or Major Morozov. My impression of them is that they're professionals who understand when it's time to shut up. No, my money is on Racitina doing so under orders from Naval Intelligence."

Arno frowned at me.

"Why would she do that?" But before I could reply, he snapped his fingers and pointed at me. "To provoke something while our report winds its way through the corridors of bureaucracy. Of course. But what?"

"That's what I've been struggling with since I heard the newscast. Will someone else pursue the Olrik angle now that we've done our job to exonerate *Chinggis* and the 212th? Or is this meant as our opening to do what we were already planning, absent orders to the contrary?"

"I'll take the latter explanation, Chief. Now we need a plan to use that opening."

"And therein lies the first challenge. Any suggestions, be they outlandish or otherwise insane, gladly received."

An amused grin split Arno's beard. "How about you approach him while he's glad-handing the public under his propaganda fluffer's floating eye and ask point blank whether he dropped out of the human trafficking business after the Marines raided Torga."

I cocked an eyebrow at him. "Didn't you say earlier that stampeding Olrik might not be the best approach?"

"You asked for outlandish."

"I'll consider it the throwaway course of action, staff college style. But it points in the right direction."

"We leak a few tidbits to the newsnets?" Destine suggested.

"Not without express permission from upstairs. That's one line I won't cross on my own because it might easily stir up more than we can handle without top cover from the ACC. And it can create utter chaos."

Arno grunted. "Zero out of two. We must be getting closer to the answer."

I gave him a sardonic look. "Only you can turn a double negative into hope."

"Everyone possesses at least one useless talent, Chief. In my case, it's more than one, but who's counting? Still, I'm not sure an indirect approach is possible."

"You're probably right on that score. The local cops have nothing on Olrik, and we can't dig into his affairs using our Constabulary credentials, which we would need to access the criminal intelligence database. Naval Intelligence probably has a dossier, but I can't ask for a copy directly. Admiral Talyn knows what we're up against, and if she deems it fit, she'll pass along anything we might need, but since she likely won't see my report for a day or more and a reply would take at least another, we're on our own."

"And where does that leave us?" Destine asked.

"With me goading Olrik into acting rashly, but in such a manner that no one can accuse me of provocation. Perhaps Gina Graetz's little reportage can give me an opening."

Arno scratched his voluminous beard.

"If your gut feeling that Sergei Ustinov is involved, insomuch as his mobsters, if such exist, interrogated and killed Toshiro Rahal's murderer, perhaps you can coax him into helping — subtly. Maybe he has something against Olrik. It wouldn't be the first time a star system business tycoon, let alone a major OCG figure, clashed with his home world's Commonwealth Senator."

Destine leaned forward and frowned. "Isn't the presidential levee tomorrow, sir? It might be a good way of running across Olrik by happenstance. He's sure to be there. Perhaps Sergei Ustinov will be as well."

"I didn't bring my full dress uniform with accouterments, and the 47th's quartermaster stores are closed."

Arno, who sensed reluctance at my attending one of the premier social events of the Novaya Sibir's winter season, gave me an avuncular smile.

"But you brought your service dress tunic with shoulder boards, ribbons and devices, and your service dress boots. You'll cut quite a dashing figure, especially with the service issue fur hat, and that'll do just fine around here, I think, especially since you're the most senior Constabulary officer on the planet, and if Skou isn't on the guest list, the only one present." He pointed at my communicator, sitting on the table between us. "Go on and send General Elin a message. The President said you should go through him if you changed your mind about the levee."

"It might be a bit late for——"

"Chief, we're aware you hate socializing, let alone hobnobbing with grandees, but this is really overt undercover work."

Knowing he was right, I picked up the communicator and sent General Elin a quick missive, asking whether it was too late to attend tomorrow's levee. When we finished our drinks and were preparing to head for the restaurant, I received a reply. The general would pick me up in his staff car at thirteen hundred hours in front of the hotel. All that remained was to gussy up my service dress tunic as best as possible and shine my boots to a high gloss.

— Thirty-One —

The next day, shortly before thirteen hundred hours, Arno gave my silver-trimmed gray uniform the sort of inspection that would make the Sergeant Major of the Constabulary proud. After flicking imaginary specks of dust from my silver-edged shoulder boards, each with the oak leaf wreath and three diamonds of my rank, he stepped back, gave me a last once-over, and nodded.

"You'll do fine, Chief. Too bad you didn't bring your full-sized medals, but that fruit salad topped by the jump wings will prove you're not just a paper pusher in fancy clothes." When I put on my fur hat, he stepped further back and smiled. "You could even pass for a Cossack. Too bad it's no hats during the reception."

"Thank the Almighty. Wearing this thing in a ballroom filled with hundreds of people isn't my idea of a fun time."

Arno wagged a finger at me. "You're not going there to enjoy yourself. Just keep sipping on the same glass of champagne."

"I ate a solid midday meal and took a metabol pill. It'll take more than I can consume to impair my faculties."

Glancing at myself in the mirror, I had to admit Arno was right. My trousers tucked into my boots and lightly bloused over their tops, as per winter service dress uniform regulations, gave me a certain rakish cavalry air that would attract attention in a mass of sober civilian suits and National Police blue. I glanced at the time and grabbed my overcoat.

"Enjoy your afternoon, Chief."

"I thought I wasn't there for fun."

"That's not what I mean, and you know it. Enjoy giving Olrik quiet conniptions."

"Oh, I will."

Moments after I reached the hotel's main entrance, a sleek, black staff car with a blue plate bearing the four stars of a National Police Service general on its nose and a miniature version of the NPS Chief of Police flag on the left front fender pulled up. As I hurried out into the shatteringly cold air under a brilliant winter sun, the aft passenger door opened, and a uniformed arm beckoned me aboard. I climbed in and took the rear-facing seat, across from a smiling General Elin.

"Glad you could make it, Commissioner. These levees can always use a bit of off-world color to liven them up."

"I'm sorry I'm not wearing the proper accouterments, sir. We rarely bring a full set of uniforms to cover every occasion when we travel for an investigation."

"Understood. And I'm sure the President will graciously excuse you." He studied me for a bit. "Was Gina Graetz blowing smoke, as usual, yesterday, or did you wrap up the case, and that's why you changed your mind about the levee?"

"I sent my findings to my superiors the day before yesterday, sir. Which means unless I receive orders to the contrary, I've completed my mission and am free to partake in social events."

Elin nodded once. "I see. Asking you about the outcome is no doubt a waste of breath."

"Yes, sir. Sorry. I can't divulge anything about the case. That privilege belongs to Assistant Chief Constable Sorjonen, although I suspect in this instance, it will most likely be Grand Admiral Larsson who makes my findings public."

"My contacts tell me *Chinggis* and the 212th received orders to resume patrol duties on the Rim frontier. Is it true?"

"I was not aware of that, sir. And even if I were, I couldn't possibly comment."

A faint smile creased his face. "Then Gina and Senator Olrik are on the right track, are they? You cleared them with proper PCB methods?"

"Again, sir, no comment. But I can categorically state we don't whitewash anyone, not even the highest and mightiest who live on human worlds."

"Glad to hear it."

We turned onto the main boulevard linking the Presidential Palace with the Duma and slowed. I glanced over my shoulder ahead of us and saw dozens of police officers in heavy parkas and fur hats directing traffic. They were separating ground cars into one long column headed up to the central portico, where they disgorged passengers and a quasi-empty strip leading to the underground parking. We were directed to the latter without hesitation, which explained the car's identifying plate and flag, and sped past the slow-moving column.

When he noted my interest, Elin said, "This is why I picked you up, Commissioner. Otherwise, you'd be stuck waiting, both here and inside. With me, you'll enjoy the luxury of leaving your coat and hat in the car rather than a clogged cloakroom. And you'll greet the President and his spouse ahead of the other guests."

"Then I owe you doubly, sir."

"We old cops have to stick together."

Once in the parking garage, we were guided to a spot near the inner doors where the driver parked us. Both Elin and I climbed out, removed our overcoats and hats, and tossed them into the car. Elin glanced at the driver and said, "Keep your communicator open, but otherwise, go enjoy the hors d'oeuvres and cake in the enlisted staff mess. We should be done by sixteen hundred."

While Elin spoke with his driver, I glanced around and saw a burnished, expensive-looking black ground car with a small plate identifying it as belonging to one of the star system's Commonwealth Senators. A man was standing beside it, watching us, and I recognized the aide I'd seen shadowing Olrik. He stared through me with a bland expression, as if I wasn't really there.

"Yes, sir." The senior corporal snapped to attention and saluted.

Elin returned it with a nod, then gestured at the doors leading to the grand stairwell. "This way, Commissioner."

As we headed up, I snuck a few glances at Elin's dark blue, full dress uniform, with enough gold braid around the collar, cuffs, and shoulder boards to dazzle even the most jaded civilian. He wore full-sized medals on his left breast, but at that moment, I was glad mine were back home. Wearing them would make me look a bit over-adorned in his company. As it was, my rows of undress ribbons took up as much space as his gongs.

Once at the top of the stairs, a staff member in a severe, high-collared black suit checked us off on the guest list and pointed us toward what Elin whispered was the presidential room, where Antonovich would receive the very, very important personages before greeting the lesser guests.

The buzz of conversation increased as we neared the tall, open doors at the end of the corridor, and I felt Elin brace himself. Then, I saw President Antonovich, regal in a formal black afternoon suit, wearing the white-blue-red sash of office over his right shoulder, standing just inside the door. Next to him was a tall, elegant woman with snow-white hair, a patrician face, and lively eyes. They were smiling as they spoke with someone who'd become my primary target in the last twenty-four hours — Senator Fedor Olrik, senior representative of the Novaya Sibir Sovereign Star System in the Commonwealth Senate.

After bowing to Madame Antonovich, Olrik moved deeper into the reception room, which, as I later understood, connected directly with the ballroom via vanishing walls that hadn't yet been retracted. Elin stepped up to Antonovich and formally bowed his head.

"Mister President."

Antonovich held out his hand. "Thank you for coming, General. May this winter bless you and yours with happiness and good fortune."

As they shook, Elin replied, "Thank you, Mister President, and may I offer the same back to you?"

"Certainly. And I see you brought our off-world guest. Delightful."

Elin moved over to Madame Antonovich while I imitated him by coming to attention in front of the President and bowing my head.

He held out his hand. "I'm so pleased you could join us, Commissioner. May this winter bless you and yours with happiness and good fortune."

We shook, and I gave the same reply as Elin, word for word.

"I do hope you'll enjoy yourself." He turned to Madame Antonovich. "Dear, may I introduce Assistant Commissioner Caelin Morrow of the Commonwealth Constabulary?"

That was my signal to take one step to the right. I bowed my head again. "Madame."

"A pleasure to meet you, Commissioner. Your reputation precedes you." She held out her hand, and the strength and firmness of her grip surprised me.

I gave her a friendly smile. "Hopefully, what you heard is good, Madame."

She smiled back. "I certainly think so, but not everyone shares my opinion. Do enjoy the levee, Commissioner, and welcome."

That was my signal to move on, and I joined Elin, waiting for me a few paces away.

"Madame Antonovich is quite gracious, isn't she?"

"Absolutely." Elin nodded at a table laden with champagne glasses. "And a learned scholar — she's dean emeritus of the Yekaterinburg University School of Quantum Engineering. Though I suspect once the President retires, she'll drop the emeritus and return to the classroom, though perhaps not as dean. She's not the type to oust the incumbent."

"You seem to hold her in rather high esteem, General." We both picked up a glass.

"As do most Siberiaks — because of her kindness, love for others, and joyful disposition. If Madame Antonovich nurtured political ambitions, she could easily succeed her husband and win on the first round of balloting at that. But she's content with charitable work while President Antonovich is in office." Movement attracted Elin's attention. "Speaking of charity, or lack thereof, you noticed Senator Olrik ahead of us?"

"Indeed."

"Well, brace yourself. He spotted you and is making his way over."

For a fraction of a second, I felt unprepared to confront Olrik. Somehow, I'd hoped for at least ten or fifteen minutes to acclimatize myself. This was my first foray into a high-powered crowd in longer than I could honestly recall. But then, the feeling passed. After all, Olrik was my sole reason for attending the levee. Were it not for him, I'd likely be out and about, enjoying a rare afternoon of freedom with my team.

As I kept an eye on Olrik out of the corner of my eyes, I saw Sergei Ustinov, and he was openly staring at the senator, or so it seemed from my vantage point. But I couldn't make anything of the business tycoon's bland expression.

"Ah." Elin touched my elbow. "There's the Minister of Public Safety. Come, let me introduce you to her."

I briefly glanced back at Olrik as we moved away and caught a flash of irritation crossing his sculpted features. Perfect. The more I could annoy him before we spoke, the more receptive he'd be to my attempts at spooking him into doing something rash.

Elin approached a middle-aged woman wearing a dove gray formal suit and her long black hair braided into a flat tress hanging down her back. Aqueous green eyes peered at us from a face dominated by high, remarkably sharp cheekbones framing a pert nose as we entered her field of view. The two men who'd been speaking with her fell silent and moved aside as Elin said, "Madame Minister, may I present Assistant Commissioner Caelin Morrow of the Commonwealth Constabulary? Commissioner Morrow, Minister of Public Safety Petra Jaakkola."

She turned to me and held out her hand. "A pleasure, Commissioner."

"Likewise, Madame."

Jaakkola released my hand but held my eyes. "General Elin has been keeping me aware of your work. It can't be easy under the circumstances."

"We deal with every sort of case in the Professional Compliance Bureau, Madame."

"I'm sure you do. If General Elin hasn't mentioned it yet, I was once a member of the Constabulary — just one five-year hitch in my early twenties, to be sure — before coming home and joining the National Police Service. I know a bit about the difficulties and challenges your line of work entails." She gave me a tight smile. "I spent three years as a captain in our Professional Standards Branch before retiring to enter politics, so I ask whether Gina Graetz's assertions, let alone Senator Olrik's, have any truth to them."

"As I told General Elin on the way here, Madame, the claim I plan on covering up any crimes committed by the Armed Forces is patently untrue."

"Yes. You're the Last of the Incorruptibles. We studied your ethos and methods closely in Professional Standards, and I'm sure that the senator's assertions could be considered libelous under other circumstances. As it is, I shall consider the source and judge accordingly." Her eyes slipped to one side. "And speaking of the man, he's paying more attention to you than to Minister Durakin, which won't endear him with old Gustav, who isn't one of his fans."

"Perhaps I should say hello." I allowed myself a mischievous smile.

"I'm sure the senator would enjoy that, but I can see your fellow Commonwealth uniformed services officers over by the buffet table. You should do like them and stake out a defensive position near the best finger food in Yekaterinburg's social calendar."

— Thirty-Two —

I left Elin with his minister and wandered over to where Meir, Freijs, and the Novaya Sibir Regiment's commanding officer, a Colonel Gus Zelenko who I hadn't met yet, were chatting with a pair of senior National Police Service officers wearing three stars on their shoulder boards.

My fellow Commonwealth officers wore full dress uniforms — Navy blue, Marine black, and Army rifle green — splendid enough to make me seem rather dowdy, like the poor cousin of our extended family. Meir moved back slightly when she caught sight of me to make room in their circle and nodded politely.

"Commissioner. Sampling a bit of Novaya Sibir's official hospitality before heading off for your next case?" She asked, smiling.

"Something like that, sir." I greeted Freijs and introduced myself to Zelenko and the two police generals, one heading the service's human resources branch, the other in charge of procurement. "President Antonovich was kind enough to invite me."

"Jumper, eh?" Zelenko nodded at my wings. The gruff, raspy-voiced colonel also wore a set complete with combat jump stars, proof of time spent in the Marine Corps before coming home and transferring to the Army. "Makes you part of the tribe and puts you among those who know what it's really like out there on the frontiers. Unlike some grandstanding idiots."

I followed Zelenko's undisguised glare of contempt and saw it land on Senator Olrik a half dozen meters away by an hors d'oeuvre table. He gazed back at the Army man with a stony expression. No love lost there, either.

One of the Police Service officers, conscious of the sudden tension in the group, waved his half-full champagne glass at us. "Can't remember the last time we saw a full spread of senior Commonwealth officers at a presidential levee. Makes for a colorful display."

The other Siberiak general turned to me. "Is it true you've completed your investigation, Commissioner?"

I nodded once. "It is, sir. I sent my report to my superiors, and I'm now awaiting fresh orders which might take me home to Wyvern or send me straight to a new case on the other side of the Commonwealth."

"Quite the itinerant lifestyle, isn't it? I'm not sure it's something I could handle."

Zelenko grunted. "Few people can, and many of those end up not being able to do it anymore at a given point, me being a prime example. Twenty years was my limit, and I'll bet my light-years traveled don't add up to a fraction of Commissioner Morrow's."

Aware that Olrik was watching, I allowed myself a smile. "Traveling keeps me away from HQ and the demons living in the bowels of the demented bureaucracy. Better still, moving from case to case keeps me one step ahead of those whose toes I've stepped on."

The chuckles I received were a little louder than my quip deserved, but it triggered the desired effect. I watched Olrik's face tighten as he heard and saw the uniforms enjoying my company.

"Demons from the bowels of the demented bureaucracy. Good one. I must remember to use that in polite conversation someday," one of the Police Service generals said, grinning. "People will never believe it came from a Professional Compliance Bureau commissioner."

"Feel free with the attribution, sir. We do have a sense of humor, albeit an often dark one." I quickly related one of Arno's favorite jokes, then said, "If you'll excuse me for a moment, I'd like to sample the finger food."

"We're staying right here," Zelenko said, raising his glass.

I deliberately ignored Olrik as I threaded my way across to the table, but I could sense his eyes on me. He would make the approach; I was sure of that. I had seconds left to abort my move before committing myself, for better or worse, on a path that could spell disaster if I didn't handle it properly. Perhaps even the sort that might make ACC Sorjonen, with his high tolerance for risky business, wonder about my future in anti-corruption. But as I reached the table and saw Olrik come toward me from the corner of my eyes, my doubts vanished, leaving nothing but an icy determination to uncover the truth.

"Assistant Commissioner Morrow, how nice to see you at the President's levee before your departure from Novaya Sibir, now that you've wrapped up your investigation."

As I turned toward him, he smirked. "You wrapped it up, right? Otherwise, you wouldn't be enjoying a grand old time with the uniformed crowd over there, as if this was the officer's mess and not the Presidential Palace."

Between the buzz of conversation, people giving him a wide berth, his proximity to me, and his low tone, I was sure no one else could make out his words.

"Well," I gave him an amused smile and pitched my voice for his ears only, "I guess there's no harm in admitting that I completed my investigation into the allegations you raised against *Chinggis* and the 212th and sent my report to Wyvern."

"And it'll be a complete and utter whitewash, no doubt."

"As I'm sure you know, Senator, the Professional Compliance Bureau works only with facts supported by evidence and doesn't care on whose toes it steps in the process, nor whose ox it gores. We clear the innocent and charge the guilty, no matter who they are, who they work for, or their station in life. End of story. But this particular one isn't quite over just yet. Oh, we resolved the war crimes aspect, but not the matter of who, what, and why regarding the cartel activities on Torga that attracted military intervention in the first place. And the subsequent attempts to deflect public attention. They bear a direct relation to your allegations and the actions of the Fleet and need answers before we can lay the issue entirely to rest."

I placed a few bite-sized Siberiak delicacies on a small plate, then looked up and smiled at him. "You wouldn't know about what was happening on Torga, now would you, Senator? A respectable elected official such as yourself."

Without waiting for an answer, I turned back to my uniformed companions and walked away, thinking to myself, shots fired. I could almost feel

Olrik's eyes firing lasers into my back. But when I rejoined Meir and the others, Olrik had disappeared into a crowd growing ever larger now that the walls separating the reception room from the ballroom were gone and Antonovich was receiving the mass of invitees.

I met a stream of government ministers, Duma members, and private sector grandees throughout the afternoon, enough to sap my endurance for social events. It seemed as if everyone who mattered was keen on meeting the Constabulary officer who'd either cleared or condemned *Chinggis* and the 212th. Until Grand Admiral Larsson pronounced himself on my report, it was the internal affairs version of Schrödinger's cat.

Shortly after fifteen-thirty, General Elin wandered over and said, "I think it's time we call it a day, Commissioner."

I gave him a grateful look. "If you say so, sir."

Within minutes, we were settling into his staff car, both of us sighing with relief. I felt like I could nap for hours upon returning to my hotel suite. There was no trace of Olrik's vehicle, meaning he'd left before us, which suited me. The last thing I wanted was one more confrontation today.

"Does President Antonovich hold many levees?"

"Four a year, on the solstices and equinoxes. Mercifully, he doesn't hold one for New Year's Day, preferring to let everyone else hold theirs. Of course, it means I receive visitors in the Central Police

Service Mess. But you surely won't be around by that time."

Since it was still over three weeks away, I shrugged. "Doubtful."

"I saw you speak with Senator Olrik. He seemed rather worried afterward, and you looked just a tad pleased. Anything you can share?"

I gave Elin a sly smile. "When he pestered me about the results of my inquiry, I reminded him it represents only part of the entire issue — the war crimes allegations. The matter of why a military strike force raided Torga and who was involved on the other side, both the cartel and their backers inside the Commonwealth, remains under investigation. He seemed somewhat taken aback at the idea."

Elin watched me in silence for several moments. "You're much like my own internal affairs people, Commissioner. You reveal nothing without a purpose in mind or speak without forethought. The fact you said what you did to Olrik, and now to me shows you plan on looking at his potential connection with the Torga business and might look to the National Police Service for a bit of help here and there."

"You may well think that, sir, but since I can't officially investigate a Commonwealth Senator without express permission, I'm in no position to offer any comments."

After another pause, he nodded. "Understood. If you need anything from the National Police Service to help make the rest of your stay on Novaya Sibir as pleasant an experience as possible, please let me know."

"Thank you, General."

Back at the hotel, I'd barely unfastened my tunic before Arno and Destine stood in front of my door requesting admittance so I could tell them everything. After I let them in, I pointed at my mini-bar.

"If one of you would be so kind as to make me a gin and tonic while I go change, I'll give you chapter and verse. I spent the afternoon nursing a grand total of two champagne flutes."

"Consider it done, Chief," Arno said.

I vanished into the bedroom, carefully hung up my uniform, and then slipped on civilian clothes suitable for a meal in the hotel restaurant before rejoining my two wingers. Arno handed me a glass, then sat beside Destine across the coffee table from my favorite sofa.

When I finished speaking, Arno let out a soft whistle. "You definitely fired the opening salvo across his bow, Chief. But was letting Elin in on it a wise decision?"

"I figure him as one of the good guys, and I'm rarely mistaken, especially when they're at the top of their own food chain. If I'm wrong, then so be it."

Destine frowned. "But surely, Olrik is aware we can't investigate a Commonwealth Senator without the permission of the Speaker of the Senate, sir, and if the Speaker gave us the go-ahead, Orlik would be cognizant of it by now. If he figures we're coming for him next, then he'll know it's unauthorized, meaning he can turn the tables on us at the slightest misstep. Or worse. We'll become the rogue PCB officers who damaged decades of a carefully constructed reputation for always staying between the lines."

Arno nodded vigorously.

"Destine is right about that, Chief. If your little conversation planted a seed of worry in Olrik's twisted mind, he might just become dangerous." When he saw my expression, Arno sighed. "Which is what you're counting on."

"Sometimes, poking the bear is the only way to lure it into a trap." I gave them a quick smile. "Don't worry. I'm doing this on my own, so if it goes wrong, I'll be the only one taking the blame. It's why they pay me more than you."

Arno scoffed. "Perish the thought, Chief. We've been doing this together for so long by now that we're all in with you."

Destine jerked a thumb at him. "What the chief inspector said, sir."

— Thirty-Three —

I went to the office the next morning to check my
message queue, but curiously, there was nothing
from either ACC Sorjonen or Admiral Talyn. After
debating whether to write a contact report for my
brief conversation with Olrik, I decided on the
prevaricator's favorite scheme and sent one to
Talyn, but not my boss. That way, if she had designs
on Olrik, Talyn could either provide backup or
warn me off, and, if ever I screwed up, Sorjonen
could state, hand on heart, he didn't know I was a
rogue officer.

Since I was wearing civilian clothes, now that my
official inquiry was over, I decided to continue my
exploration of downtown Yekaterinburg beneath
the surface. At around ten, my communicator
buzzed with a message from Racitina. Would I be

free to join her for a cup of coffee at a place which, as I found out moments later, was in the underground level of the Yekaterinburg courthouse, across the street from the high-rise where her law firm had its offices? Intrigued, I accepted and made my way there.

The moment I entered the cafe, my nostrils took in such a blast of delightful aromas — coffee, mocha, dough, marzipan, and the Almighty only could tell what else — that a faint grin tugged at my lips, and I felt my stomach give off a soft rumble. As my eyes scanned the room, a familiar face looked up from her plate in the far corner, where she sat in splendid isolation — Katy Racitina, wearing a smart civilian suit.

I made my way over, and she pointed at the chair across from her. "Please join me, Commissioner."

"Thank you. Back at your civilian job?"

"Yes." A holographic menu appeared in midair, and Racitina said, "I recommend the pirozhki filled with fruit and the house tea blend."

"Done." I ordered, tapped my personal payment wafer on the table's reader, and sat back. "How are Saga and her stepmother?"

"Doing fine. Thank you for accepting my last-minute invitation. A few things are in motion, and I felt it prudent that we didn't wait."

"Should I turn my jammer on?"

Racitina nodded. "Now that you've ordered, yes."

I reached into my jacket. "Done."

"I understand you spoke with Senator Olrik at the levee yesterday."

"You were there?"

Racitina shook her head. "No. But acquaintances who are aware I was involved with your inquiry were, and, as one of them said, he seemed rather spooked when you walked away from him looking like an ice tiger who'd cornered a mountaineer."

"He pestered me about the results of the investigation. And on a whim, I reminded him I'd dealt merely with the rather narrow matter of the war crimes allegations. Because of that, many unanswered questions remain about the reasons for the allegations, the raid on Torga, the nature of the cartel destroyed by the Fleet, and the identity of the cartel's backers inside the Commonwealth."

Racitina gave me a quick smile. "Do you think our dear senior senator harbors a guilty conscience?"

"The mere fact of sitting in the Commonwealth Senate gives you one. There are no clear consciences in federal politics. But beyond that? Who can say? Perhaps Olrik was more deeply involved than simply calling for an inquiry based on recordings broadcast by a newsnet belonging to the most powerful zaibatsu in human space. Recordings handed over by a free trader who was killed shortly after landing here to testify in my inquiry."

"And you intend to investigate him?" Racitina held up a hand before I could open my mouth. "Yes, I realize you can't do so on your own initiative. But if we stuck religiously to dictates issued by politicians so they can commit crimes any way they want, the Commonwealth would eventually be embroiled in another civil war. Don't tell me you've never overstepped your legal bounds in the pursuit of true justice."

"Then I won't. But as I told my team, whatever I do by myself in the coming days is my responsibility alone."

"Would you like some assistance? If you're about to break the rules, you might as well go all the way."

I studied Racitina for a bit, wondering how much I could trust her. Sure, she had access to insider knowledge if she was aware I'd met Saga Decker, but a good spy could uncover enough to let me believe she moonlighted for Naval Intelligence. Of course, she would hardly be the first part-time operative or deep-cover agent employed by Admiral Talyn, but still.

"What can you offer?"

A smile crossed her face.

"I sense you're a little leery." When I didn't immediately answer, she added, "Call it defense attorney's intuition."

"We didn't exactly get off to a good start, and your civilian practice — or at least that of your legal firm — involves representing what we cops call OCGs."

"Organized crime groups. Yes, I'm aware of that acronym. The National Police Service uses it as well, and a little too freely. They may consider a few of our clients as high-level OCG executives, but they've never been able to prove it. So as far as we're concerned, they're merely successful businesspeople who attract the wrong sort of police attention. Not that Novaya Sibir doesn't have its share of mobsters, but my firm won't represent them. Besides, they employ their own legal counsel, the sort we generally avoid at Bar Association parties."

"Fascinating as that is, what manner of help were you thinking about?"

Her smile widened. "Many of our clients really don't like Fedor Olrik. They see him as living in the pockets of the big interstellar zaibatsus whose head offices are on centralist-controlled worlds. Olrik doesn't enjoy a reputation for supporting Siberiak business interests ahead of those based on wealthier worlds."

I chuckled. "You mean he prefers off-world organized crime to the native sort."

For a moment, I thought she would correct me again, but I was mistaken.

"When you put it like that, Commissioner, it's not too far from the truth. The National Police Service may not find evidence Olrik is involved in shadier dealings than is normal for a Commonwealth Senator of his sort. But certain Siberiak entrepreneurs whose interests are in off-world trading know things. Not actionable in a legal sense, certainly. Otherwise, the police might have received anonymous tips of the sort that fingered Toshiro Rahal's killer."

"And not actionable in the Saga's stepmom sense either? I'm surprised."

"Certain downfalls are better triggered in full view of the public, *pour encourager les autres.* Isn't one of the PCB's principles that justice must not only be done but seen as being done, at least in a manner those targeted will understand without ambiguity."

I raised a hand, palm facing downward, and wiggled it from side to side. "Yes and no. More than a few of our cases never reach the public disclosure stage for various reasons, mainly because it would serve nothing."

This time, she gave me a sly look. "You mean when you can't find evidence for an unimpeachable case but are convinced the guilty party is guilty and can be persuaded to fade away quietly."

My return smile was rather wry. "It happens. We seal those investigations under what we generally term for the good of the Service."

"I'm sure you'll agree Fedor Olrik can't just fade into that good night after what he's done — both the war crimes hoax and what he's been up to with his cartel-adjacent financiers. That was really nasty stuff on Torga."

"And I'm the one to bring him down under the glare of the newsnet video drones?"

"Nobody else is in the right place at the right time, Commissioner. Besides, you're itching to do it.

Otherwise, you wouldn't have poked the bear yesterday. I've watched you long enough to understand you do nothing without giving it a lot of thought."

"Funny. General Elin said the same thing after we left the Palace."

"And he's nobody's fool. Unfortunately, he's also not in a position to help. Olrik still has plenty of supporters in the planetary government and the private sector segment that profit from zaibatsus elbowing Siberiak corporations aside."

I gave her a nod. "Figures. What about OCG supporters?"

"That's where it gets interesting. Those in the know—"

"Meaning your firm's clients who aren't OCG executives?" I bit back a smirk at the last moment.

"No comment. Those in the know say he enjoys the support of at least one Bratva, a violent group engaged in activities that more mainstream organizations eschew — human trafficking being chief among them."

"Does that OCG have a name?"

"The Irkutskaya Bratva. They own most of the illegal activities in the Irkutsk Oblast under the informal terms that divide Novaya Sibir into exclusive gang territories. It's not a large group, compared to the Yekaterinburg Bratva, seeing as how Irkutsk is a minor district capital. Still, since the city has its own spaceport, they can conduct off-world activities without paying tribute to more powerful OCGs."

"And Olrik is in cahoots with them. Interesting."

A serving droid with my tea and pastry trundled up at that moment, and I switched off my jammer in case it interfered with the machine's proper functioning. After it deposited my order and left, I turned the jammer back on, then took a bite of the pirozhki, a hand-sized pastry pouch. Almost immediately, an explosion of warm berries filled my mouth. My reaction must have been amusingly visible because Racitina grinned.

"Told you it was good. Now wash it down with the tea."

I complied, finding the sweet, black brew at just the right temperature. "Lovely. We're clear to talk again."

"Olrik is apparently a close friend of the sister of Irkutskaya's leader, close enough to suspect they share more than just an appreciation for fine art, expensive wines, and refined company. How they keep it quiet enough even the police aren't aware is a mystery. I've heard people claim he used the Bratva for nefarious purposes. However, there is no evidence whatsoever, unless you count the fact he won an overwhelming majority of the votes in the Irkutsk Oblast. And his tally in the adjoining districts was also rather high compared to the rest of the star system."

I took another bite of my pie and another sip of tea while watching Racitina. "Interesting backgrounder. Is that what you do for our common friends? Keep tabs on Siberiak organized crime?"

"Among other things. I'm something of a stringer for them rather than a full-timer — they recruited me shortly after I became a JAG reservist — but one of my main lines of interest is OCGs with known off-world correspondents and interests."

"So now that I'm aware of Olrik's dark side, where does that leave me? If the aim is taking him off the board openly, despite the fact I can't officially investigate Commonwealth Senators without specific permission, then he needs to experience a complete public breakdown that discredits him forever. Triggering that is a tall order for an anti-corruption cop."

"And that's where certain friends of friends come in." She emptied her cup. "Tell me, Commissioner, did you visit Saint Innocent's Cathedral yet? It's one of Yekaterinburg's crown jewels, dating back to the founding of Novaya Sibir. Saint Innocent's is magnificent in the early afternoon when the sun blazes through the stained glass behind the altar. Say, around fourteen hundred hours."

— Thirty-Four —

The idea of accepting help from a suspected OCG to bring down a Commonwealth Senator was probably the most bizarre in a career replete with the strange, the unusual, and the outlandish. But having poked the bear, my only other choice was waiting for the riposte. However, now that I knew Olrik had underworld connections, a potential counterattack before I dug into his unsavory side might well prove more perilous than I initially thought.

That made the rest of my morning stroll less a time to enjoy the city and more an exercise in spotting potential surveillance. I'd already decided I wouldn't share any of this with my team, not even the loyal Arno. Hoping Senator Olrik would trip over his own feet out of anxiety while we waited for orders from home was one thing. But accepting the help of what I suspected were underworld figures in a bid to expose him was quite another. The list of things that could go wrong was endless, and any of them would leave me facing a full disciplinary hearing, if not criminal charges.

I took the midday meal by myself in the federal building cafeteria, grateful for a relatively quiet half-hour in a secure environment so I could ponder over how the next steps would unfold. And how I'd keep knowledge of my actions from my team. When I resumed my aimless tourism, I wasn't any wiser than before. I hoped Racitina was not only the real deal as undercover Naval Intelligence operatives went — even part-timers or stringers, as she called it — but also capable of delivering.

As suggested by Racitina, my footsteps took me to a set of large, heavy wooden doors standing open shortly before fourteen hundred hours. A blue sign with gold leaf lettering above the opening announced, both in Cyrillic and Latin, 'Saint Innocent's Cathedral,' or at least I assumed that's what the Cyrillic said as well.

I was curious, since I'd never visited an Orthodox house of worship, I entered and climbed the large, curving wooden staircase polished by countless feet that led out of the underground network.

At the top of the stairs, I stepped into a narthex whose walls were made of carved stone. Massive inner doors stood open on my right, revealing the cavernous nave and the altar beyond. Smaller but still impressive doors on my left led to the street. They were shut, of course, it being well below freezing outside.

A gentle aroma of incense and beeswax tickled my nostrils as I entered the silent nave. Though I wasn't familiar with Orthodox rites, I stopped and bowed my head respectfully before slowly making my way along the right-hand aisle. A few people occupied pews here and there, while others knelt, hands joined in prayer.

I found an empty row about halfway to the altar and sat, collecting myself. My eyes scanned what they could without moving my head around like a crass tourist. The cathedral felt too holy for that sort of thing. Instead, I focused on the images above and behind the altar, marveling at the way their painters reproduced something that seemed to belong in a pre-spaceflight church on Earth.

As I absorbed the atmosphere, I felt a sense of peace envelop me, as if the Almighty were touching my soul. How long I sat there in a state of quasi-meditation, I couldn't say. And because of that, I didn't sense the approach of a large man wearing an elegant overcoat who stopped by my pew and slid in beside me.

"This is a place where one feels refreshed in the spirit of the Almighty, isn't it, Commissioner?" Sergei Ustinov asked in a reverent whisper.

"Without a doubt. This is magnificent," I replied in the same tone.

"It is the oldest Orthodox cathedral in the entire human diaspora. Only those on Earth are older."

"And not quite as saintly?"

"Little on Earth seems to acknowledge the glory and the mercy of the Almighty these days. People who spend too much time on the cradle of humanity lose their faith and their salvation."

"Such as Fedor Olrik?" I asked.

"Yes. Such as he. But Fedor was never a saintly man to begin with. Ambition has always been his primary driver — the urge to accumulate power, fame, wealth at the expense of his soul. Politics on Earth simply stripped what little good he possessed in the first place, especially after he aligned himself with the centralists instead of faithfully representing his native star system."

"He wouldn't be alone among the Commonwealth Senators to become less than they were. Something about being part of a tiny group holding the destiny of countless billion humans in its hands will twist even the saintliest. But your junior senator, Jumakiz Ruslanova, she hasn't lost her soul yet, has she?"

Ustinov shook his head. "No. Thankfully, she started off in a better place than most and comes home to reflect as often as possible instead of wallowing in the pleasures of the capital."

"You're aware I completed my investigation?"

A nod. "Yes. Friends of friends told me, and since other friends hinted that both *Chinggis* and the 212th Pathfinder Squadron received orders sending them back on patrol, I can only surmise you found no basis for Senator Olrik's allegations. You need not answer, Commissioner. I'm aware you can't discuss the matter, especially not with a civilian such as I. However, am I right in thinking the wider ramifications of what happened on Torga and why the false allegations remain unexamined?"

"They do."

"Am I also right in thinking Senator Olrik's insistence on pushing the allegations while attempting to discredit you makes him a person of interest?"

"You may think so, but I'm not in a position to answer that question either."

Ustinov didn't immediately reply, and his eyes remained fixed on the altar. Finally, he said, "You've shown respect to this cathedral, Commissioner, something Senator Olrik never did because he never visited, let alone attended any services."

"Really? Glad to hear it. I know nothing of the Orthodox faith, and my own is rather tenuous."

"And yet you behaved respectfully since entering the nave. That means a lot to those of us who worship here. We are many, although only a fraction of the faithful on Novaya Sibir, but they too would prefer your fellowship to that of Fedor Olrik."

"Then I am honored."

Ustinov let out a grim chuckle. "In certain circles, an honest cop is preferable to any politician."

"How does that hoary old joke go again? Ah yes. Don't steal. The government doesn't like competition."

This time, Ustinov's chuckle held a hint of amusement. "You're rather unusual for a Constabulary internal affairs investigator."

"Why? Because I have a sense of humor?"

"Because you take risks, the sort that gets other cops investigated by your colleagues."

"I'll only end up on the wrong side of the interview table if I fail."

Ustinov nodded. "Success excuses almost anything. Failure, on the other hand... It is much the same in the business world."

I forcefully repressed the urge to ask which business he meant. Mafia bosses were unforgiving no matter the star system. But then, many chief executive officers, especially those running zaibatsus, were so as well. It was a brutal universe for failures, no matter where.

He reached out and took a small, printed psalter from the rack attached to the pew in front of us.

"Only the Almighty forgives without question." Holding the psalter in his left hand, he tugged at the flat red cord stuck between two pages with his right and opened it at the place thus marked. His hand briefly hovered over the open book, then he said, "One can always find the truth in this book."

Ustinov held it out to me, and I glanced at its pages.

"I'm sorry, but I can't read Cyrillic script."

"It doesn't matter. If a picture is worth a thousand words, what can we say about a thousand pictures?"

I finally noticed a small data wafer nestled against the red cord and understood his meaning. I took the psalter and palmed the wafer.

"Nothing you might see is admissible before anyone other than the Almighty, but he will judge when the time comes."

Ustinov rose, stepped out into the aisle, and bowed toward the altar, making the sign of the cross. Then he turned on his heels and walked away. I remained seated for a few more minutes, psalter in hand, senses reaching out for any signs that we'd attracted interest. I carefully put the psalter back and stood when nothing struck me as unusual. I bowed to the altar before heading back toward the narthex and the stairs.

There was no other choice than return to our incident room in the federal building and see what was on the data wafer. As I crossed the underground, I exercised my fieldcraft skills to check for surveillance but found none. The incident room was, as I expected, silent and empty and would stay so until we dismantled it once HQ accepted my report and recalled us.

I settled at Sergeant Cincunegui's workstation and rummaged through my memories of how he'd dealt with Carla Hautcoeur's data wafer. There was no question of my involving him in this. Sure, accepting information from suspected underworld figures was an accepted part of policing, but these were extraordinary circumstances. Ustinov's inadmissible images were for my eyes only.

After checking the wafer for nasty surprises, I placed it in the isolation reader and waited until the segregated workstation called up the file directory. Images. Hundreds of them. None of the image files had any metadata that I could detect, meaning not even a hint of provenance. I opened the first, not knowing what to expect. But the moment I saw its contents, I knew that if the rest were of the same nature, I'd need Arno and Destine's help to get through them before our recall orders arrived. A quick sample showed more of the same until the last fifty or so, stills from covert video surveillance. The latter turned my stomach and stiffened my resolve to trigger Olrik's downfall.

But why would Ustinov give me this data instead of using it to bring Olrik under his complete and utter control? Who wouldn't want to own a Commonwealth Senator? Unless, of course, any attempt at blackmailing Olrik could rebound on the blackmailer. If my suspicion Olrik was owned by the centralist faction was correct, then they could probably call on nastier operatives than Ustinov, people capable of wiping out the Yekaterinburg Bratva. And that told me Ustinov was hoping I'd remove the troublesome senator he couldn't touch.

Nothing ever came for free.

I sent a recall message to Arno and Destine, asking them to meet me in the incident room without the two sergeants, then tried to figure out a way of classifying the images. I put the video stills in a separate folder, which I would forward to General Elin and the Constabulary's Human Trafficking Division under the notation that I'd received the images anonymously. At least they could identify the visibly underage victims and maybe find them while notifying the families — if they have any. My wingers showed up together less than thirty minutes later, both wearing civilian clothes, although I knew they carried their service weapons and communicators.

"Finally decided to let us in on your shenanigans, Chief?" Arno dropped into one of the chairs around the conference table.

"I'd rather not, but things are changing." Over the next hour, I related my conversations with Racitina and Ustinov and showed them a sample of the financial records contained on the data wafer. "There's no way I can analyze everything in our remaining time on Novaya Sibir. Our recall orders could show up at any moment."

"No sweat. We can work through the night if necessary."

"If you need any added motivation."

I called up a few of the video stills and saw my wingers' faces harden as only a cop's can when faced with evidence of sexual exploitation.

"Olrik is a dead man walking," Arno growled. "We know he'll never face proper justice. What Ustinov gave you is the fruit of the poisoned tree. But it explains why Olrik threw himself wholeheartedly behind the war crimes fraud. His financiers, who were desperate to muddy the waters while they scurried for cover, did not give him any choice."

"I'm sending the stills to Elin and our lot. Hopefully, they can use them to solve missing persons cases. Perhaps a vengeful soul might even leak a few so that the stench of corruption attaches itself to Olrik and ends his political career under a cloud if we fail. But I won't hand them over until we have our go at him. Shall we get started?"

— Thirty-Five —

Destine went out to fetch the local version of a boxed meal from one of the nearby pubs shortly before eighteen-hundred hours, and we took a quick break to refuel. We weren't past the sorting stage yet, which meant we would probably not carry out much of the analysis before breaking off for the night.

Just after twenty hundred hours, the incident room door opened, and Master Sergeant Cincunegui poked his head in.

"Told you, Alina," he said to the person behind him. "It's a work party and they didn't invite us."

Both entered, and Cincunegui wandered over to where I sat at his usual workstation. He peered over my shoulder and watched me work for a bit while Esadze did the same with Arno.

338

"I think we can help make this go faster," Cincunegui finally said. "If you tell us what's going on and why you kept us away, Commissioner. There are ways of extracting raw data from images to analyze it with the tools at our disposal. Doing so manually, as you no doubt intended, would take days, and HQ might recall us at any moment."

I glanced up at him over my shoulder. "I didn't want you and Alina involved because I'm exceeding my orders and authority to a point where I could face serious disciplinary action, perhaps even criminal charges. Arno and Destine shouldn't be involved either, but I needed help, and this is one of those things where we higher ranks assume the responsibility so that we can shoulder the blame."

Cincunegui nodded. "I appreciate that, sir. But if you plan on tackling Senator Olrik with what you have right there, you need our help. We're senior noncoms. We know the score. Succeed, and we're good. Fail, and we take our lumps. It's an inevitable part of dealing with the serious scum."

"Take his offer, Chief," Arno said. "Maybe even show them the video stills."

"Very well." I swiveled my chair around to face Cincunegui and Esadze and gave them an abbreviated version of what I told my wingers. When I finished, they glanced at each other and nodded.

"We're in, sir. And we'd like to see those stills the chief inspector mentioned."

After I showed them a few, Cincunegui pointed at his workstation. "May I, sir? We need to stop that despicable bastard before he hurts anyone else."

I called it quits moments before the clock struck midnight. At this rate, we wouldn't be any good analyzing the complex data provided by Ustinov.

"Let's secure the incident room and pick this up tomorrow morning, folks."

"Aye." Arno pushed his chair away from his workstation and rubbed his eyes. "I'm seeing things that aren't there. But correct me if I'm wrong. Does Olrik have anonymous numbered financial accounts in every corner of the known galaxy?"

"Of the Commonwealth for sure, Chief Inspector," Sergeant Esadze replied. "The bugger is stinking rich."

"I'll bet it isn't even his own money," Cincunegui said. "He dies, and his heirs won't see a single cred. It'll go back to the shadow financiers who've been using him as a front. Our Senator Olrik took the golden ticket to fame and fortune, not knowing it didn't cover a return trip. I've seen the pattern before. We both have. It's borrowed money."

Esadze nodded. "Oh, isn't that the truth? Though it's a shame we can only see the client's side of the records, not the bank's. Otherwise, we'd know who's been so generous toward the senator and could ask why. But it would take a federal superior court judge's warrant and heavy-duty legitimate evidence, which we don't have."

Arno grunted. "Another game rigged in favor of the corrupt buggers at the top."

"Most of them are." I climbed to my feet. "And on that note, I invoke *sufficient unto the day are the evils thereof.* Lock up and go."

Sensing that Arno wanted a few words, I invited him into my suite, splashed single malt into a pair of glasses, and handed him one.

"Do you think it's a good idea doing what amounts to a mobster's dirty work, Chief? Because that's what this is, stripped to the essentials. He can't use that evidence to get at Olrik without facing serious repercussions. Us, on the other hand." Arno shrugged.

"Don't think the thought hasn't crossed my mind." I took a sip of the Glen Arcturus and reveled in the path it burned down my throat. "But as I once read, if a plan is stupid and it works, it isn't stupid, or words to that effect. Or, as per our military cousins, one of the fundamental principles of war is selection and maintenance of the aim. That aim is rendering Senator Fedor Olrik incapable of committing any further crimes on behalf of his masters. Any stratagem which helps us achieve said aim without fatally compromising our ethos is fair game. After all, we don't know that Sergei Ustinov is a mobster."

"Many would call it a specious argument, but fine. So be it. What's the next step once we know every financial detail about Olrik's corrupt existence? We already concluded the video stills of his depraved persona won't take us there if his patrons carry out a counterattack on the evidence's credibility."

I winked at Arno, took another healthy sip of whiskey, and said, "Ruin him."

"Easier said than done." His eyes narrowed, and he stared at me over the rim of his glass. "I bet you don't know what you'll do next."

"Nope. Other than forwarding everything we discovered to Naval Intelligence. They can drain those accounts, but it'll take a while before they receive our data and act on it. The joys of communicating across interstellar distances."

"In that case, let's do something with the video stills."

I grimaced. "Since it's impossible to prove provenance, Olrik and his handlers will immediately claim they're fabrications created by the Fleet as revenge for raising the war crimes allegations. Their tame newsnets will make sure the accusation sticks, thereby cratering the Fleet's reputation among centralist sympathizers. In other words, releasing the video stills will create the same political effect the centralists wanted from twisting the Torga business into something sinister. Worse yet, we'll waste a unique chance for the human trafficking investigators to achieve something useful with the images. You can count on the cartels and their clients shuttering everything the moment the evidence becomes public. And that, in turn, will spoil the ongoing operations by Naval Intelligence against them."

"True." He nodded slowly. "Okay. The stills are completely out. More's the pity. Exposing Olrik as a depraved sociopath would be quite a coup."

"The goal isn't for us to expose Olrik, Arno. We not only won't be believed but we'll be castigated for conducting an unauthorized vendetta. No, the only way is to make him do it on his own, hopefully in a way that'll cause his supporters, apologists, and financiers to abandon him. Nothing else will work. But what I can't figure out is how."

Arno drained his glass and stood. "We won't find an answer at this time of night, certainly not after hours squinting at columns of numbers. Goodnight, Chief, and thanks for the wee dram."

"Goodnight, Arno."

I spent a few minutes staring into my glass after he left before emptying it. My eyes found the bottle of Glen Arcturus standing in splendid isolation on the sideboard, and the urge for a second serving almost overcame me. Yet even the finest single malt in the galaxy held no answers, and the Glen Arcturus, while good, wasn't one of them. But it was among the best an assistant commissioner could afford without raising questions about her lifestyle.

I woke at dawn the next morning tired, grumpy, and no wiser than before. The sensation our time was running out didn't help my mood as I tried to decide between wearing my uniform or civilian clothes. After opting for the latter, I made my way to the federal building just as the cafeteria was opening for breakfast. Apart from a few of the 47th Group's overnight duty personnel and early risers like me, it was as sparsely populated as the underground network, at least the stretch I could see as I crossed over from the hotel.

By the time my team rolled in, I'd sent off the first batch of analyzed data to Admiral Talyn, hoping her people could at least begin something while we continued our work.

"Did you come up with any good ideas in your sleep, Chief?" Arno asked as he dropped into the chair across from my desk.

I shook my head. "Not a single one."

"We were talking at breakfast — Destine, the sergeants, and me — and before you ask, no one could overhear us." He patted his civilian jacket's lower left pocket, indicating he'd used his jammer. "Teseo suggested we send Olrik a few of the bank account extracts with a notation to the effect that we know what he's doing. Perhaps even add one of the stills just for shock effect. Anonymously, of course. Teseo and Alina can set things up so the message's origin and routing can't be traced. Not exactly a hundred percent under regulations—"

"How about not even a bit absent a proper warrant from a federal judge?"

Arno ignored my interruption. "But since we're merely overstepping our bounds and not engaged in criminal pursuits, the risk of consequences is infinitesimal, as is the risk of getting caught. Teseo is pretty confident he can bamboozle the best forensics analysts in the Service. Considering he's one of the forensic analysts who specialize in catching his crooked colleagues..."

I considered the suggestion, aware that Arno wasn't the only one watching me. Destine, Esadze, and Cincunegui, out in the main room, also waited for my reaction to the latter's idea.

"Right. At this point, delving a little further into the realm of the unauthorized won't increase our risk factor. Set it up. I'll go through the data and decide what we send."

Just before lunch, Cincunegui left his workstation and stuck his head through my open office door.

"Can I interrupt you for a moment, sir?"

"Sure." I gestured at the chair in front of me, but he stayed where he was.

"The untraceable routing to Olrik's personal home address is ready to go. I tunneled through the 47th Group's anonymous darknet node to access the public streams. It's what their investigators use when they communicate with informants. I've also encoded the message shell using the biometrics on file for Olrik. It should minimize the risk of someone else opening it. The only thing left is the content."

"Take the Cimmeria First National Investment Fund statements, and the video still marked image six. That should put the wind up his skirts."

Cincunegui grinned. "Those would be my choices as well, sir. The message will go out in a few minutes."

I'd chosen the investment fund statements because First National was little known beyond a very select elite among the moneyed galactic citizens and because Cimmeria itself imposed the strictest banking confidentiality rules in the Rim Sector. How Ustinov obtained them would likely stay a mystery, and I wasn't about to ask. However, the fact someone had the statements, and the image — one of the few where Olrik's face was clearly identifiable — should frighten him.

"Message on its way," Cincunegui called out less than five minutes later.

— Thirty-Six —

"Where is Olrik's home, anyway?" I asked as we sat around our usual corner table in the cafeteria, munching on sandwiches, jammers on.

"He owns a penthouse apartment in downtown Yekaterinburg, the sort even an assistant chief constable couldn't afford without a healthy trust fund in support," Arno replied. "And what the brochure mockingly terms a chalet high above the ski resort of Kamen, two hundred kilometers northwest of here. Though it's not noted anywhere in the records, I suspect Olrik, or more likely his backers, owns a chunk of Pik Kamen, the mountain itself, through countless holding company layers. And that chalet is more of a mansion built into the mountainside at a respectable height. Almost a fortress of solitude, if you ask me. Apparently, that's where he's been since just after the presidential levee."

"I think you'll find Olrik's heirs won't get Pik Kamen as their legacy either," Cincunegui said around a mouthful of stew. "Like his money. Same old story. He gets to live in the lap of luxury for as long as he obeys his masters."

When I gave him an amused look, Cincunegui grinned. "It's amazing what you can learn about the dirty and the dead by simply analyzing the data they generate, Commissioner. Guys like Olrik, they live in borrowed mansions, with borrowed funds, and on borrowed time."

"Want to join AC12, Sergeant?"

"Thanks, but no thanks, sir." Cincunegui shook his head. "Alina and I sample a greater variety of cases as loaners from the support unit."

"Fair enough."

"But so far, it's been both unusual and fun."

Arno let out a grunt. "Unusual is normal for us. Fun, not so much."

"Oh, I don't know, Chief Inspector. From the stories Destine — Warrant Officer Bonta — told us, you've investigated plenty of entertaining cases over the years."

"Entertaining does not equal fun. Besides, most, if not all, of our investigations lately involved murders, and they're never a laughing matter."

Cincunegui inclined his head. "Point taken."

We finished our meal and headed back up to the incident room. No sooner did we enter that Cincunegui's step faltered as he fetched his communicator from his jacket's inner pocket.

"The message was delivered to both locations but only read at the Pik Kamen address."

I nodded my thanks. "And now we wait."

But it wasn't long before my personal communicator chimed. Its display didn't provide the caller's identity, but I knew it was Olrik. Only he would call me over a private link at this very moment.

I switched it on, put it in speaker mode, and placed it on the conference table. "Morrow."

Without preamble, a smooth voice said, "We need to talk, Commissioner."

"I'm not sure that we do. Why this sudden call?"

"Please don't take me for an idiot. It demeans both of us. A car will pick you up in front of the Saint Innocent's Cathedral main steps in one hour and bring you to my chalet, where we can discuss the matter without being overheard."

"Bold of you to assume I'll voluntarily place myself in your power."

"You want answers to certain questions. I can give them. And then we can negotiate an arrangement by which we both get what we need."

I looked up to see Arno frowning as he shook his head.

"And you'll guarantee my safety?"

"Come now, Commissioner. I'm a Commonwealth Senator, a public official like you. Of course, you'll be in perfect safety with me."

Arno was shaking his head with increasing vigor. He clearly didn't want me to accept the invitation, but this was likely our only chance.

"Very well, Senator. One hour, Saint Innocent's Cathedral."

"I look forward to our conversation. Olrik, out."

With the link cut, Arno's disapproval switched from silent to unmistakably vocal.

"No, Chief. You're not walking into Olrik's lair. At least not without a troop from the 212th Pathfinder Squadron in tow."

"I am, and I have one hour to prepare, so no further discussion, please. Sergeant Cincunegui?"

"Commissioner."

"Please use your anonymous routing setup and send a copy of the video stills to the National Police Service's child exploitation unit. No signature, no provenance. Transmit another copy, encrypted this time, to our Human Trafficking Division back home, under my signature with the notation that a full explanation will be forthcoming upon our return to Wyvern."

"Yes, sir."

"What about sending everything to Admiral Talyn?" Arno asked. "Teseo can't use your private encryption key. I think there's time for you to run up a message for her."

A flash of insight struck me, and I smiled as I understood that my subconscious figured it out overnight and was waiting for the right moment to spring it on me.

"Not necessary. I realized that the Novaya Sibir mafia couldn't have collected everything Ustinov gave me. Their tentacles may extend everywhere on this world and in many parts of human space, but deep inside the Cimmeria First National Investment Fund, to name one secretive off-world institution? It reeks of naval spook work. No, I'm willing to wager that some of what Ustinov gave us came to him from Admiral Talyn's people. We simply joined a long-running game and became the catalysts to conclude it. And if not us, someone else would do so at another time and in another fashion."

"This was always the endgame?"

I nodded. "Ever since Olrik leveled the war crimes accusations. We clear them, then take Olrik on without direct Naval Intelligence involvement. Admiral Talyn counted on my stubbornness and inability to let Olrik escape unscathed."

"But why didn't they do it themselves?" Destine asked.

A shrug.

"I couldn't say offhand, but since this is Hera Talyn we're talking about, it's probably part of her master plan — wheels within wheels. She merely brought a part of it forward the moment Olrik began playing his role as a front man after the Torga raid to divert attention from the cartels' backers." I turned to Destine. "Can you visit the 47th's armory and see if they can issue me a tracking implant? Something the average cartel or mafia goon can't detect with civilian grade sensors?"

Arno pointed at me. "Excellent idea, Chief. Otherwise, how can we back you up? Maybe Destine should see if they carry something unobtrusive that can record or transmit conversations."

She gave us a nod. "On it." Then she vanished into the corridor.

"What shall Alina and I do, sir?" Cincunegui asked.

"I'm sure Arno will draft you once I'm aboard the car Olrik is sending. Keeping tabs on me while I enter enemy territory has become something of a specialty for him."

Destine returned five minutes later with two small packages in her hands. "The armorer didn't give me any guff or ask questions, for that matter. I don't know if it's the PCB mystique or because he took Chief Superintendent Skou's admonition that we get what we need when we need it to heart, but this stuff is Class Two and therefore accountable."

"Did he tell you the best place to inject the tracker?"

She shook her head. "No, but the instructions with the injector cover that. As for the listening device, how would you like new earrings?"

"Let's equip me. I have a little over thirty minutes before it's time to leave, and I want you to check both pieces with police-grade sensors once I'm wearing them."

We finally settled on placing the tracker in the web between my left thumb and forefinger. Destine pulled a ring from her hand and slipped it over my left thumb. It was a little tight, even though her fingers were larger than mine, but not uncomfortably so.

"Copper. Squeeze your thumb against your hand, and it should help distract sensors. They will check." Next, she pulled a pair of stud earrings from the other pack and exchanged my own for the recording devices. "They're dormant and therefore indistinguishable from the regular sort until you activate them. One at a time, please. The battery charge is limited. Squeeze the backer twice in quick succession for on and twice again for off."

Destine stepped back, pulled her police issue sensor from her pocket, and scanned me as she slowly walked around my office.

"Good. I can't pick up anything untoward. Just keep your thumb against that hand."

"Will do." I glanced at the office display and nodded. "Time to head out."

I slipped on my service issue overcoat, stripped of insignia, so it looked little different from those worn by Siberiaks working in downtown Yekaterinburg and my fur hat, which no longer bore the Constabulary's *Fiat Justicia* badge.

"Don't do anything foolish, Chief," Arno said as I crossed the incident room.

"Am I ever foolish?"

"No comment," he growled back.

I left them with no goodbyes as if I were merely headed back to the hotel for an hour in the gym. A cold gust of air and the brilliance of a low sun bouncing off snow and ice greeted me as I left the federal building via the ground level main entrance. I turned right and headed toward the cathedral at a measured pace, wondering how long I would feel the comforting heft of my service issue weapon in its shoulder holster. Presumably, Olrik's people would relieve me of it the moment I climbed aboard his car, but I had to play the game and carry it, nonetheless. My sidearm was a Class Two item, like the tracker and recorders I wore, but under the circumstances, I wouldn't fill out anything more than a loss report for it either.

Having seen the inside of the cathedral, I had a greater appreciation of its external grandeur and simplicity. The gilded domes, shimmering in the mid-afternoon light, seemed like beacons calling on faithful not only from across the planet but the entire star system. But I was pretty much alone on the sidewalk, breath coming out in great clouds while the tip of my nose and my cheeks were slowly freezing.

A low-slung, silver car of impeccable pedigree, more splendid than the one I saw at the levee and likely costing as much as three times a deputy chief constable's annual pay, slowly came around the corner as I reached the portico's steps. It glided to a halt in front of me. No doubt another of Olrik's 'possessions' he wouldn't leave to his heirs.

The aft passenger doors opened, and the face of what was unmistakably a bodyguard poked out. "Assistant Commissioner Morrow? We're your ride to Pik Kamen. Please climb in."

I did so and found myself in a cabin of uncompromising luxury, with cream-colored leather upholstery, wood paneling, discreet displays, and what could only be a bar tucked away between the rear-facing seats. As soon as the doors closed, the goon pulled out a civilian pattern sensor and aimed it at me while frowning at the display. I made sure my thumb was hard up against my hand and hoped Destine's ring would obscure the tracking implant.

"You'll need to hand over your weapon, Commissioner," the man said in a gravelly voice. "We'll return it when we're back in Yekaterinburg."

I reached into my parka, withdrew the needler using only my thumb and index finger, and held it up, barrel pointing at the floor. The man took my sidearm and slipped it into one of his overcoat pockets. Apparently satisfied, he nodded once to himself and stowed the sensor before sitting back and watching me with lifeless eyes.

We headed west along main arteries until the city petered away, then silently lifted off, proving it was an aircar and worth at least three times my original estimate. If not more. As soon as we reached travel altitude, the car turned northwest toward the mountains and the region's many ski resorts, which should be in full swing considering the time of year.

By the time we got closer, I could see dark shadows already spreading across the valley floors as the sun reached for the horizon. Lights were coming on along the streets and on the facades of houses, hotels, restaurants, and stores. The mansions and boutique hotels perched higher up on the mountainsides were still bathed in glorious sunshine, and skiers dotted the upper slopes like ants scurrying downhill.

As the aircar slowed and shed altitude, I could see its nose was now aiming toward Olrik's chalet, or rather its landing pad. The misnamed mansion, all stone, steel, and transparent aluminum, seemed carved out of the mountain, roughly two-thirds of the way to Pik Kamen's summit. And it was huge. I could make out at least three separate floors, multiple balconies, covered areas, and even openings in the mountain above and below. It was a villain's lair if I ever saw one and certainly unaffordable on a Commonwealth Senator's salary.

I knew from Arno's research that it was served by a large antigrav lift in a vertical borehole that reached halfway down Pik Kamen to where the winding surface road ended. But I was just as happy to travel via aircar.

Moments before we landed on the pad, a door cut into the living rock slid aside, and our driver took us into a hangar large enough for a few shuttles, along with the assortment of aircars parked on one side.

The outer door closed as we came to a stop on a yellow marker, and at the guard's urging, I climbed out. An inner, person-sized door opened, and Senator Fedor Olrik stepped through, followed by two men in black tactical clothes carrying carbines.

"Welcome to my home, Commissioner."

— Thirty-Seven —

Olrik ushered me into a gleaming foyer where a thin, serious-looking, middle-aged woman with shoulder-length blond hair and blue eyes took my parka and hat.

"I'd hoped you might wear your uniform with those impressive Pathfinder wings, Commissioner."

"Since I'm officially on hiatus until my recall orders show up, the uniform wouldn't be appropriate, Senator."

"But you were carrying your service issue needler."

I nodded. "Yes, and I'm also carrying my credentials. Those two never leave my side unless, of course, my host would rather I not be armed."

"A mere precaution by my vigilant security staff, I assure you."

Butter wouldn't melt in his mouth, and I was wondering whether my message had rattled him and he was hiding it well or whether he was so confident that it could only mean I'd walked into a trap of my own devising.

"But I noticed you're not carrying that jammer whose legality on Novaya Sibir is highly questionable."

"There's no need when I'm off duty."

"I see. Well, rest assured I record nothing my guests say. That would be the height of rudeness. Please come with me."

I followed Olrik into a spacious room overlooking the Kamen valley far below. Sofas and chairs upholstered in white leather were grouped here and there around tables topped with what seemed like slabs of pure jade, while equally white rugs covered the gray marble floor. The sun flooded through a wall of windows, softening the cold decor which consisted, along with the furniture, of expensive standing lamps, statues whose provenance I couldn't guess, and lustrous, black sideboards. The latter were topped by small objects whose purpose was as mysterious as the statues' origins.

The entire effect felt contrived as if furnished and arranged solely to impress visitors and not as a space to relax and enjoy the view after a long day. But that was probably the point. Olrik surely received his guests here, keeping them away from the more private parts of the mansion.

As he walked over to the windows, he glanced over his shoulder.

"This view never ceases to enchant me. You're someone who used to jump out of aerospace vehicles in flight. Does that mean you're also a fan of gazing upon the world from high up?"

"It's a vastly overrated sensation, in my opinion. At least after the first few times. Then, like anything else, it becomes part of the job."

Olrik gazed out over the terrace and into the valley below, his back to me.

"It's sad that you no longer see the magic in contemplating creation from a height few enjoy." After a few moments of silence, he turned around. "Can I offer you something? I understand you're partial to gin and tonic and are a fan of our very own Siberiak Blue."

I gave him a sardonic smile. "You're well informed, but no thanks. I'm not in the right frame of mind to enjoy a drink at this point."

"All business, even though you're on hiatus. Why am I not surprised?" He gestured toward one table grouping. "Let's take our ease."

Once we'd settled, Olrik sat back, legs crossed at the ankles, one elbow on the chair's arm, fingers splayed along his jawline, and contemplated me.

"What are you trying to achieve, Commissioner?"

I fondled my left earlobe, switching on the device hidden in the tiny gold ear stud. "Me? Nothing. My work on Novaya Sibir is done."

"Then what was the purpose of your message with the statements from a numbered account on Cimmeria and the obviously fabricated image of depraved behavior even you police officers can't just casually distribute without opening yourself to criminal charges?"

"I never said I sent you a message, Senator." Now that I was recording, I had to make sure my statements didn't veer far from the truth in the unlikely event they became evidence.

"Come now, Commissioner. Someone expertly disguised the routing and point of origin, something I would expect from the professionals on your team. And our little chat at the levee gave me the impression you weren't quite done yet. But isn't the little note 'I know what you're up to' rather puerile for a senior anti-corruption officer?" When I remained silent, he asked, "How did you get those fabricated files? Did one of your data specialists create them from whole cloth?"

"My people fabricate nothing, Senator. They work solely with the available evidence."

"Oh. You're saying those files you sent me are evidence now? They're certainly not admissible in any court of law in human space."

I put on a languid expression. "Why would I send you evidence in the first place? You're a civilian. And evidence of what? My investigation into the war crimes allegations is over."

"Enough." The word cracked across the room with the energy of a chemically propelled gunshot. I was pleased by my showing no reaction whatsoever. "Time to stop playing silly games, Commissioner. What were you hoping for when you sent me those files?"

I kept my tone gentle, though I injected a hint of amusement that would further annoy him.

"Hoping? Didn't you ever hear the expression hope is not a valid course of action? A good investigator goes on facts, and at this moment, I'm picking up the fact that you're rather disturbed by those files you keep mentioning. If they're fabrications, then you could simply laugh them off, but you're not doing so. Care to tell me why?"

"By the Almighty, but you're annoying, Morrow. How you ever reached the lofty rank of assistant commissioner remains a complete mystery to me."

"Hard work, honesty, integrity, a desire to put service before self. You know, impulses foreign to every federal politician, bureaucrat, judge, and cop I've investigated and arrested."

"Careful now. One could misconstrue your statement as an accusation against me, and as you well know, Commonwealth Senators are beyond your remit. Furthermore, keep in mind I don't take kindly to libel."

I inclined my head. "Noted. Now, why am I here?"

"You're here so we can discuss what you're up to with those files you sent. I assume they were a sample, and you have more." When I didn't answer, his face tightened. "I'm trying to do you a favor. Playing with fabricated evidence, no matter who gave it to you is as perilous as manipulating antimatter. One misstep, and it blows up in your face. Let's work this through to make sure neither of us faces career-ending consequences."

"Funny you should mention fabricated evidence blowing up in one's face. My investigation concluded with one hundred percent certainty that *Chinggis* and the 212th Pathfinder Squadron did not engage in acts exceeding their rules of engagement on Torga. Moreover, the evidence put forward by Toshiro Rahal was entirely fabricated. It means you compromised your integrity by pushing a lie, one which will explode in your face within the next few days once the facts are released. And you knew from the start it was a lie. Will it end your career? Probably. You won't survive a recall election, and the Siberiaks will hold one no matter what you do."

I waved my arm at our surroundings. "And all this will no longer be yours. You've become an embarrassment to your patrons."

"The only embarrassment right now is you, Commissioner. Tell me what you have, and we can negotiate a truce that'll make sure both of us walk away unharmed. Otherwise, I'll see that you become a permanent guest of the Commonwealth on Parth."

"Won't happen. I'm walking away from this unharmed. You, however, are finished. Oh, you'll never stand before a judge, much less see the inside of a cell. But the people who financed your rise and demanded you push those extraordinary allegations to cover their crimes and yours will inflict a suitable punishment. If you're lucky, it'll be a quick death." A pause. "And you know it, which is why you've been in panic mode since returning to Novaya Sibir. The irony is, if you'd remained on Earth and let this work its way through, we wouldn't be talking to each other right now. The storm would pass. You'd be wiping a few egg splatters from your face, and then you'd carry on."

"They didn't give me a choice," he replied through clenched teeth.

I cocked an amused eyebrow at Olrik's choice of words, wondering whether he was aware he'd just revealed more than he should.

"Everyone has a choice. Well, not everyone. Those who, like you, take the golden ticket to unearned fame, fortune, and power give up the ability to control their destinies."

A snarl twisted Olrik's lips, and for the first time, I saw him as he truly was — possessed by his own demons.

"And you've just done the same thing, Morrow." He tapped the communicator on his left wrist and said, "Execute Plan Horus."

I gave him a curious look. "Sounds dramatic."

But Olrik didn't reply. Within seconds, a trio of bodyguards appeared, and he gestured at me. "Take her to the guest suite."

"Yes, sir."

Since I didn't want to give him the pleasure of watching me struggle, I stood and followed the goons. As I passed through the foyer, I saw the woman who'd taken my coat and hat pull them on, and something about her face caught my attention. She now bore an uncanny resemblance to me, but I couldn't linger to examine her. One of the men grabbed my elbow and guided me along a passage heading into the mountain.

The guest suite turned out to be an interrogation room, complete with a restraint-festooned flip-up table in the center. However, a nagging part of me suspected they might use it for other, no less disagreeable activities. The goons tied me to the table by the wrists and ankles. Then they left without saying a word.

According to my internal clock, I remained alone for over half an hour before Olrik entered, along with the same bland, unremarkable man I'd seen hovering around him in the hotel restaurant and by his car in the Presidential Palace garage. Now that I got a good look at him and his soulless eyes, I knew he could only be an intelligence operative. Whether from one of the zaibatsus, ComCorp being the most obvious, or the *Sécurité Spéciale*, I couldn't say. But he was likely Olrik's minder, making sure the senator kept to the approved script because he was nothing like any of the other security people I'd seen.

I turned my eyes on Olrik. "What do you want?"

He gestured at the man. "This is, among his many other responsibilities as part of my entourage, an interrogation specialist who will see that you tell how much of this so-called evidence you obtained, what its contents are, and who gave it to you."

"Really? You expect me to talk?"

"Yes, Commissioner, and then I expect you to die."

— Thirty-Eight —

"It's sad, you know. We could come to an agreement, a lucrative one even, but so be it. Since you won't cooperate freely, you'll do so forcibly and then shuffle off into the Infinite Void. A suitable stand-in wearing your coat, hat, and face is already on her way to Yekaterinburg. Witnesses will see her climb out of my car in front of the cathedral, then she'll mysteriously vanish. People do from time to time on Novaya Sibir. The weather and the mafia have a way of ending lives prematurely."

I chuckled with derision. "You really think that'll work? My people will figure out the subterfuge right away and come for me."

He shrugged. "By then, you'll be dead, and your body will be hundred of kilometers from here, at the bottom of a deep ravine where no one in their right mind ever goes."

Something in my eyes must have attracted the interrogator's attention. His words further confirmed he was a professional, someone far superior to the average goon in black guarding Olrik.

"She has a tracking implant. Recall your decoy so we can transfer it."

"How do you know?"

The man didn't reply. Instead, he placed his briefcase on a side table and opened it before examining me from head to toe.

"Now we can do this the easy way or the hard way. Tell me where it is, and I'll extract it painlessly. Refuse, and I'll cut your clothes off and violate you in every way imaginable as I search. Makes no difference to me."

I thought about it for a few seconds, then figured there was little I could gain by remaining silent.

"Left hand, in the web between my thumb and forefinger."

"By the copper ring. Good choice. Standard security sensors wouldn't pick it up. You're quite a pro, Commissioner." He studied my face again. "And I'll bet those ear studs aren't innocent either."

He reached out, removed both, and carried them over to his briefcase, where he dropped them into what I figured was a small Faraday box. Next, a scalpel appeared in his hand, and he turned back to me.

"This will sting, but you won't bleed much."

He crouched by my left hand, found the tracer implant by touch, then sliced. It stung, but I didn't flinch.

"Could you find me a small tray or plate, Senator? It wouldn't do to interrupt the signal while we're waiting for your decoy's return, so I shan't put it in a dampening box."

Once the tiny sliver of electronics sat beside the briefcase, the man flipped me into the horizontal position and once again studied me with those soulless eyes.

"Tell me, Commissioner, are you conditioned against interrogation?"

"Yes." At that moment, I felt genuine fear invade every cell of my body. The conditioning would inhibit me from responding to chemically aided interrogation and kill me if the interrogator persisted. That left torture, which would also kill me, but much more painfully, because it was equally ineffective.

"A challenge then." He turned to Olrik. "It is probably best if you don't witness the next step. Once she responds to questions, I'll call you."

Suddenly, a realization hit me, and I began giggling uncontrollably as if I was already reacting to the interrogation drug and mere moments from cardiac arrest, even though he'd not yet prepared the injection. Conditioning only worked to prevent me from revealing classified information that could affect the security of the Commonwealth. Evidence of a senator's corrupt lifestyle wasn't even classified, just closely held by the senior investigative officer — me. And I could declassify it right now for a worthy cause, my survival.

"What's wrong with her?" Olrik asked.

"Nerves? The knowledge she'll die shortly?" The man shrugged. "I'm not a psychologist."

I stared up at Olrik. "What do you want me to tell you? Everything about the files we received anonymously? Turn on your recorder because this will take time, and your brain isn't good enough to remember everything."

"Pardon?"

"You don't need old dead-eyes here." I jerked my chin at the interrogator. "What are you, by the way? zaibatsu intelligence or *Sécurité Spéciale*? No matter. You won't make it off Novaya Sibir. Now back to you, Senator Scumbag. Ready?"

My captors looked at each other silently as if unable to process my unexpected manic behavior.

"Why the sudden desire to cooperate?" Olrik finally asked.

"Because I'd rather not give the *Sécurité Spéciale* goon a chance to enjoy himself by torturing me, and because it doesn't really matter what we have on you, Olrik. If I don't make it back in one piece, it's headed for the darknet. And no matter how hard you try, the stench of corruption will forever stick to you like a second skin."

It wouldn't be leaked on the darknet, of course. We couldn't just release the files without approval, not even as unattributed leaks, but he didn't know that. I began reciting the list of the financial statements and their general contents from memory before Olrik could answer. As I spoke, I could see his face lose its color and knew the information was sufficiently accurate to spook him like never before.

After a bit, Olrik held up his hand to still me and sent the interrogator out of the room with instructions to inject my tracker into the decoy when she returned.

Once we were alone, he said, "Keep talking."

"Why? Didn't you hear enough to know it's over? Even killing me won't stop what's coming. Your only hope of survival is turning informant and pleading with a judge to grant you witness protection."

One part of my brain poked the other and reminded me of the video stills. No judge would allow witness protection for someone engaged in the sexual exploitation of minors. But I needed not mention that at the moment. Not when I was in effect pleading for my life.

"But killing me means any chance of you making it out alive is gone. First-degree murder of a police officer is an automatic death sentence. And if you could plead it to life on Parth, you'd end up on

Desolation Island, which is nothing more than a prolonged death sentence."

Olrik, rubbing his face with his hand, eyes everywhere but on me, paced back and forth at the foot of the interrogation table, a man in crisis unable to see the faintest glimmer of a painless resolution.

"Let's walk away from this together, Fedor." I hoped my use of his first name would help snap him out of the growing despair I read in his eyes. He knew he was cornered, and that made him even more dangerous. "I'll help you find a solution to your predicament, but I need your cooperation. How about you start by flipping me upright so we can talk more easily?"

"No." He shook his head in a jerky motion. "No more talking. You did this to me. If you're gone, it goes away. You, your team, everyone who's seen those files will be dead by tomorrow morning. We'll blame one of the mafia organizations. Yes. That's it. I'll call my friends. They'll make it happen."

"Are you sure the Irkutskaya Bratva will risk open warfare with the Yekaterinburg Bratva over me, Fedor? No. They won't want to come anywhere near my team or me. It's over."

"Shut up!" His shout echoed off the walls as he glared at me with manic eyes, face twisted into a rictus of hate.

At that moment, I understood Olrik's public persona was nothing more than a thin veneer hiding a weak character, the sort unscrupulous people could manipulate at will. And that weak character was fast losing its grip on reality.

The door opened, and the interrogator entered unbidden.

"Our decoy?"

"She won't be necessary, Senator." The man reached into his open briefcase, withdrew an object, and slapped Olrik's exposed neck.

"You see, I caught everything you said since you sent me out of this room." He tapped his ear, indicating he wore an invisible earbug. "I couldn't trust you alone with Morrow."

Olrik stared at him uncomprehendingly, then he collapsed.

The man gave me a thin smile. "This is your lucky day, Commissioner. Moments ago, Senator Olrik proved he'd outlived his usefulness, something I've suspected for a while."

"So, you are his minder, making sure he does as he's told."

A nod. "Everyone obeys someone else. Fortunately for you, my orders are to avoid major disruptions and do so at my discretion. I've decided killing you and your people would be unproductive, if not wholly inadvisable. There would be nothing to gain and much that can be lost."

"What about Olrik?"

He glanced at the senator. "My leaving him alive would be highly disruptive. By the time your team gets here, they'll find his body far down the slope, an apparent suicide, and this place empty save for you. So you don't waste your time or that of the Police Service's CSI, I'll tell you right now you won't find evidence, at least nothing admissible, let alone actionable. Besides, with Olrik dead, the chalet's ownership reverts to a numbered corporation with no known links to the senator."

"His goons and the decoy?"

"They'll vanish momentarily, and not even the National Police Service's best will find them or me. I've heard of you, Commissioner, and you know how the game is played. This round is yours, fair and square. I personally wouldn't have chosen Olrik as my tool — he's much too weak of character — but then, I'm just a field operative like you. Neither of us makes policy."

He poked his head out the door, issued a command in a language I couldn't understand, and two of the black-clad men entered. They picked up Olrik's unconscious body and took him away. Then he produced my tracker, holding it up to the light between his thumb and index.

"I'll leave this here for your people to home in on. Within the next two hours or so, it'll briefly transmit in emergency mode before running out of juice now that it's no longer being powered by your body. That should suffice."

"Why are you ensuring my survival? I ruined your employer's scheme."

"Oh, Senator Olrik did so by pushing ahead even when it was no longer advisable. Though I daresay, the ultimate responsibility lies with those who devised it in the first place rather than take their lumps and rebuild after a suitable interval. Throw a few minor people to the wolves, that sort of thing. But such is greed. As I said, I don't make policy, though it seems I pick up the pieces afterward more and more often. Like right now. I'm sure you do so as well. At least with Olrik dead, the last bits of that failed scheme die with him." He closed his briefcase.

"And how will I explain this?"

Another smile. "I'm sure you'll find something likely and close enough to the truth that it won't bruise your ingrained sense of honesty. We won't meet again, Commissioner. I'd wish you good luck, but you already have enough as it is."

Then, he too vanished into the corridor, and though I picked up faint noises over the following ten or fifteen minutes, a deep silence soon enveloped the mountainside mansion. Lying in the same position on a metal surface became rather uncomfortable after a while, though I didn't bother fighting the restraints. It would have been wasted energy.

Almost two hours later, or at least that's what I figured, I heard faint footsteps, and I called out. Within moments, a pair of Marines in light combat armor and visored helmets appeared, carbines held at the ready. One of them tilted his head slightly to the side, in the unconscious gesture many make when speaking over a helmet radio, while the other walked over to the table and unfastened my restraints before helping me stand.

No sooner was I on my feet that Arno burst in, wearing borrowed police armor, and brandishing his sidearm.

"Chief! You're a sight for sore eyes. What the hell happened? There's no one here but you."

"I think you'll find Olrik's body on the mountainside below the chalet's main terrace. The rest of his people left a couple of hours ago, or rather the people minding him because they weren't his employees but those of his owners. What's with the Marines?"

"These are Pathfinders from the 212th. I called Major Morozov after you left to ask if he could spare a troop, and he was most happy to oblige. We've been watching this place since about an hour after your arrival, waiting to see if you needed help. I guess Olrik's security team left via the antigrav shaft — we saw no aircar other than the one that picked you up leave, and that was almost three hours ago."

I quickly gave Arno a rundown of events as he led me to the aircar hangar, where a Marine dropship sat like a giant, malevolent beetle.

"How do we let the police know about Olrik?" He asked as we buckled in with the extraction team.

"Anonymous call. What else? It's best if we keep quiet about my presence here when he died. I'm not supposed to be in contact with him, remember?"

"I'll see that Teseo handles it. He's good at hiding his tracks."

The dropship moved out onto the platform and lifted off into the clear night sky, a small black shape invisible to the human eye and even more so to Novaya Sibir's civilian traffic control system. The Pathfinders' craft was about as stealthy as they came.

"So that's it, then, Chief? Olrik gets away with it in death?"

"Yes. And by the way, Teseo was right. He didn't own any of it. If we check the titles to the chalet and penthouse tomorrow, we won't see his name anywhere."

Arno let out a soft grunt. "I guess he got his golden ticket punched with extreme prejudice by the people who owned him."

I nodded. "Mind you, it worries me that I'm beginning to believe it's the way the dirty ones should always find their end."

He shrugged. "If it makes the next potential ticket takers think twice?"

"They won't."

"I just hope Naval Intelligence will be able to drain his bank accounts before they too change ownership. Confiscating that kind of cash will hurt."

"I'll let Racitina know what happened the moment we're back in Yekaterinburg. I'm sure there's a contingency plan in place to trigger a series of actions upon notification of Olrik's death because I'm equally convinced this was the desired outcome. There could never be an arrest, nor a trial, let alone a custodial sentence on Parth. Then, I'll send what will hopefully be my last message to the ACC from Novaya Sibir."

After a few minutes of silence as our dropship flew nap of the earth back to Joint Services Base Wolk, where Destine waited with our borrowed car, Arno asked, "How often will we do Naval Intelligence's dirty work, do you think, Chief?"

"As often as necessary, so long as we do our duty as anti-corruption investigators because we too are soldiers in the shadow civil war."

When we landed on the tarmac of the 21st Marine Regiment's Aviation Battalion in total darkness, I nevertheless saw a rigid figure standing to one side, arms crossed. Major Morozov was making sure his people came home in proper order and one piece.

The aft ramp of our craft dropped, and we disembarked along with the troopers detailed to protect us. I walked toward Morozov and noticed another shadowy figure, the troop leader converging on us from another dropship.

When I reached Morozov, Arno a respectful three paces behind me, I stuck out my right hand.

"Thank you."

He gripped me just under the elbow, forearm to forearm in the jumper's grasp, and we held each other's gaze.

"Leave no one behind, Commissioner."

"Damn right." I turned to the troop leader, who'd raised his helmet visor, and we exchanged the same grasp.

"Thank you."

"Thank your chief inspector, sir. He called it right on the nose. You and your people are okay in our book."

The command sergeant drew himself to attention and saluted.

"Take care, Jumper."

Even though I was in civilian, I returned the compliment.

"And you."

With that, the Marine turned on his heels and marshaled his Pathfinders. I was about to speak with Morozov again, but he also drew to attention and saluted.

"If you ever need to refresh your jump status, Commissioner, look us up." Then he stepped off into the darkness and joined his people.

A ground car pulled up and came to a gentle halt precisely in front of us. The passenger doors opened, and Arno ushered me in.

Destine, sitting at the controls up front, glanced back. "Everything good?"

"The best," Arno replied as he settled in, side-by-side.

"What are the sergeants doing?" I asked.

"They've been monitoring the traffic control, police, and general frequencies, Chief, covering the extraction force with judicious misdirection, jamming, and other mischief. When I ordered the Marines in, Cincunegui made sure no one and nothing saw us enter or leave the chalet. If either of them goes to the private sector after retirement, we're in trouble. They can and just have shuttered the better part of a planetary police surveillance network."

"Remind me to write up a commendation once we're on the way home. That skill should be recognized if only so we can make sure they don't do it again without authorization."

Arno chuckled. "Will do, Chief."

"Not that I'm complaining, mind you, but why did you figure I'd need help?"

"Do you really want me to answer that?" Arno asked. "Considering our common history."

"Better not."

"You got that right. The day we don't prepare for the worst won't be your best, Chief."

— Thirty-Nine —

"Why did you help me, Gospodin Ustinov? I can't believe it's merely because you're a good citizen concerned with the truth. You are many things beyond that. Or so I'm told."

The Siberiak executive and presumed mob boss' smile, faint as it was, held no warmth. He took a sip of his vodka tonic and carefully placed the glass back on the table.

I'd entered the bar to wait for my team when I spotted him alone at a corner table and invited myself over. Ustinov simply gestured at the empty chair as he studied me with those piercing eyes of his.

"I suppose you deserve candor after this, Commissioner. Getting the truth out there because Olrik and his masters threatened the future of my beloved Rodina was one of my concerns, yes. He favors off-worlders to the detriment of his fellow Siberiaks. But I also sought revenge, a dish best eaten cold on this world of ice and snow."

He speared me with his hard eyes.

"You see, Fedor Olrik liked to be amusing. He enjoyed showing his wit at parties and often used his little jokes to elevate himself while abasing others. You could say he was a little too enamored with himself. During a levee at the Presidential Palace a few years before his election to the Commonwealth Senate, when he was a leading Duma member, Olrik felt not just the effects of the fine champagne but of his own sense of superiority. He made a tasteless joke about my wife. Being a good sport, she took it in stride, but I swore to myself I would find a way of repaying him with usurious interest. When you arrived on Novaya Sibir to investigate a case involving Fedor Olrik, I knew the time was right. It is unfortunate he took his own life. I would have enjoyed watching him humiliated before the entire Siberiak nation."

He shrugged. "But such are the ways of the Almighty."

"How did you come across the files you gave me?"

Another shrug.

"The statements? Off-world friends of friends. The video stills? Those came from connections right here on Novaya Sibir. I was keeping both for the right moment. And that's everything I can tell you,

Commissioner." Ustinov drained his glass and stood. "I wish you a pleasant voyage home and many successes in giving corrupt officials their due."

With that, he turned on his heels and left the hotel bar. A fascinating man and obviously someone who shouldn't be crossed. I still didn't know for sure whether he was a mobster with a legitimate day job or a businessman with underworld connections. But I was convinced Novaya Sibir's next senator wouldn't pull the sort of shenanigans that supposedly gave Olrik his election win. Whether his successor would be less in the pocket of the centralists and more inclined to represent this world was a question only time could answer.

Arno showed up not long after and raised his eyes in surprise at seeing me seated well away from our usual table.

"What gives, Chief?" He asked, taking Ustinov's chair.

"I just had an enlightening conversation with the CEO of Taiga Import-Export, the gentlemen with whom I spent a few moments in the cathedral."

"And?"

I recounted what Ustinov told me.

"Fascinating," Arno said after I fell silent. "You come across the strangest allies when you stand with one foot in the murky depths of the admiral's universe. Remind me to never mock anyone publicly."

"That's not your style anyhow, so no worries."

"You think we'll ever get an explanation from anyone about what happened?" Arno took a healthy sip of his stout.

"No. But I'm pretty sure we figured it out, save for a few details here and there. This was one of those incidents which will never be mentioned again. We did our jobs. Officially, Fedor Olrik, perhaps in the grips of personal problems, committed suicide. Was it because his crusade would be revealed as a fraud once our findings become public? Who knows? He'll quickly be scrubbed from public memory, and that'll be it. The newsnets can easily turn the formerly famous into non-persons at their owners' behest."

"He's certainly no loss to Novaya Sibir." Movement at the entrance attracted his attention. "Ah, the rest of the squad assembles."

"You can mention our discussion just now to Destine in private, but it's best if we keep the sergeants out of it."

"Understood, Chief."

That evening, the five of us enjoyed a sumptuous meal in one of the hotel restaurant's private rooms — my treat. Then off to an early night. *Benton Fraser* was inbound and would land at dawn to take us home. Since I'd not received anything from ACC Sorjonen other than recall orders, I didn't know what reception awaited us.

Knowing my boss, he'd figure I was somehow involved with Olrik's death the moment news reached his ears. More worrisome perhaps, I hadn't heard from Admiral Talyn for days. No acknowledgment of my messages, and nothing passed via Commander Racitina. Maybe I was persona non grata at the moment, a troublemaker who triggered a political crisis, though we'd heard nothing from Earth so far. If that was the case, then so be it.

But I needn't have worried.

The following day, while Yekaterinburg was still half asleep, a driver and car from the 47th Constabulary Group drove us to the Joint Services Base Wolk spaceport where our ride, still wrapped in steam from landing, waited near the passenger terminal.

I'd received no explanation why the military strip rather than the commercial one, but it was just as well that we'd embark far from prying eyes. One of the first things that greeted me upon waking up was news Grand Admiral Larsson released the findings of my investigation, concluding no Armed Forces unit violated the rules of engagement on Torga and that unknown parties fabricated the purported evidence.

I could only imagine the local newsnets clamoring for a chance at me. It would be worse once word about Olrik's death by suicide was released. I couldn't see the National Police Service keeping the details embargoed for a second day. Mercifully, Elin's people didn't find out about my presence in the chalet at the time of death, and with luck, they never would.

When Captain Ryker greeted us at the main airlock, he handed me a data wafer. "Messages for you from Wyvern and Caledonia. Encrypted, of course. We received them a few hours ago."

The first missive was from my boss — a simple well done and too bad about Olrik. The other, as I expected, was from Admiral Talyn and thanked me for solving the Olrik problem on my own initiative. Her people would make sure the leading centralists understood their tame senator perished for his misdeeds and that they should remember death eventually catches up with everyone.

Yet I knew nothing would stop some people from taking the golden ticket to unearned wealth, power, and success, even with the most graphic warnings that they were selling their souls. Fortunately, there would always be people like us to take them down once they crossed the line between mere ambition and full-on corruption.

When we dropped out of FTL at Wyvern's heliopause several days later, Ryker downloaded the latest newscasts and reports from HQ. As I predicted, Olrik's accusations and his death were rapidly fading from the public's conscience, thanks to the newsnets' habitual manipulation. The Speaker of the Senate simply gave a brief eulogy and moved on to new business, the Torga affair forgotten.

What, if anything, Naval Intelligence did with the time we bought them to round up the people involved, we never found out. But a fair number of centralist politicians and senior bureaucrats along with zaibatsu executives vanished from the public sphere in the following weeks. A few retired unexpectedly to live out the rest of their lives in obscurity. Others died in accidents or from previously undetected illnesses, so something was happening. At least, I hoped so.

As for us, a new case awaited, though the target was on Wyvern for a change. And if the Fleet dumped it in ACC Sorjonen's lap, that meant he was our usual sort. Except this time, the corrupt judge in question wore a uniform.

About the Author

Eric Thomson is the pen name of a retired Canadian soldier with thirty-one years of service, both in the Regular Army and the Army Reserve. He spent his Regular Army career in the Infantry and his Reserve service in the Armoured Corps.

Eric has been a voracious reader of science fiction, military fiction, and history all his life. Several years ago, he put fingers to keyboard and started writing his own military sci-fi, with a definite space opera slant, using many of his own experiences as a soldier for inspiration.

When he's not writing fiction, Eric indulges in his other passions: photography, hiking, and scuba diving, all of which he shares with his wife.

Join Eric Thomson at
http://www.thomsonfiction.ca/
Where you'll find news about upcoming books and more information about the universe in which his heroes fight for humanity's survival.

Read his blog at https://blog.thomsonfiction.ca

If you enjoyed this book, please consider leaving a review with your favorite online retailer to help others discover it.

Also by Eric Thomson

Printed in Great Britain
by Amazon